THE LAST CELEBRITY

A Novel

MADELEINE HENRY

This is a work of fiction. Names, characters, organizations, places, events, and incidents are either products of the author's imagination or are used fictitiously. Otherwise, any resemblance to actual persons, living or dead, is purely coincidental.

Published by Little A, New York
www.apub.com

EU Product Safety Contact:
Amazon Media EU S. à r.l.
38, avenue John F. Kennedy, L-1855 Luxembourg
amazonpublishing-gpsr@amazon.com

ISBN-13: 9781662528491 (hardcover)
ISBN-13: 9781662528477 (paperback)
ISBN-13: 9781662528484 (digital)

Cover design by Faceout Studio, Addie Lutzo
Cover image: © Andriy Bezuglov / Stocksy; © New Africa / Shutterstock; © Ryan McVay, © Anshuman Tiwary, © Chadchai Ra-ngubpai, © Peter Stark, © Frank and Helena / Getty; © Annie Spratt / Unsplash

Printed in the United States of America

First edition

PRAISE FOR *THE LAST CELEBRITY*

"*The Last Celebrity* is a thought-provoking, fast-paced, and claustrophobic thriller. Madeleine Henry captures the disturbing and fantastical world of celebrity worship and turns it into an entertaining and propulsive roller coaster ride. Could. Not. Put. It. Down."

—Samantha Downing, international bestselling author of *Too Old for This*

"In *The Last Celebrity*, Madeleine Henry has created a gripping, eerie thriller set among the glitz and glamour of New York City. From the very first page, Henry jettisons the reader into a web of intrigue, lies, and murder as a vigilante group targets the rich and famous. Fast-paced and hard-edged, *The Last Celebrity* is a smart, heart-stopping thriller that will have you flying through the pages and guessing to the very end."

—Heather Gudenkauf, *New York Times* bestselling author of *The Overnight Guest* and *The Perfect Hosts*

"Twisty and action-packed, *The Last Celebrity* is a roller coaster ride through the underbelly of a celebrity-obsessed culture and its backlash."

—Tracy Sierra, author of *Nightwatching*, a Fallon Book Club pick

Anonymity advised

Myra Mane Kidnapped as Nomen Hijack Madison Square Garden Concert

BY MICHAEL GOSS
Updated 6:05 AM EST

NEW YORK (AP) — Pop star Myra Mane was kidnapped in Madison Square Garden last night while performing for her Wet Animals Tour in the first abduction claimed by the Nomen.

The Garden lost power at 10:03 p.m., when malware commanded the system to shut down. The stadium, fully booked, went dark. It lost all HVAC, sound, surveillance, and other electronic security measures. All elevators froze. All doors were left open.

Members of the Nomen, a group calling for government regulations on fame, rushed Myra offstage in blackout conditions. Witnesses report seeing white uniforms in the dark.

After power was restored at 10:21 p.m., the Nomen played a never-before-seen video on the arena's jumbotrons. This recording named their next 49 celebrity targets, including Lane Driver, Blake, Margot Kelly, Dwayne Jackson, and Carson Beck, among other actors, athletes, TV personalities, influencers, and musicians.

Their headshots were shown during a taunting voice-over. "Aren't they beautiful?" it began, then described fame as tyranny. It claimed celebrity culture has created permanent class differences that are anti-meritocratic and un-American. After the last headshot, all screens went black. The final line pronounced to a dark arena, "The only cure to seeing the same faces everywhere will be to see them nowhere."

At least 32 employees are being held for questioning.

During one interrogation, an usher refused all questions. Instead, he tried to carve the Nomen's symbol—an anonymous face—into the table with a pen. When the pen split, drowning his palm in black ink, he whispered, "I have dipped my hand in shadows."

Until last night, the Nomen had been silent for ten months, since their New Year's Eve attack. On December 31, the group hacked into ABC's livestream as the ball descended on Times Square. They used the opportunity to introduce themselves and announce their mission on national TV. They said they were "vigilantes" out for "retribution." After their message, the ball burst into confetti stamped with their symbol.

They call themselves Nomen from *nomen nescio,*
Latin for "I do not know the name."

ONE

There's one blank envelope in my mail.

I turn around in my lobby.

The front desk is deserted.

But the doorman, Alan, was just here.

He was right behind the counter, standing in a suit and tie. I asked about his weekend. Then Alan handed me my mail—three envelopes, two magazines—the way he does every morning. But now he's gone. The entrance to the building is still. The glass doors reveal a stream of New Yorkers trekking to work in dark neutrals.

The envelope is stuffed but light, as if it's packed with tissue—nothing but crepe paper, layers of empty padding. I pinch it, slow. Whatever's inside rustles in a barely audible whisper. It really does feel like there's only tissue paper inside. I turn the envelope over, slide my finger under the flap. Alan is still missing. Someone across the street raises her hand, hailing a cab. Inside the envelope, I see confetti. The triangles are all bright, sunny colors: yellow, neon pink, and saturated tangerine. They look like pieces of a shattered rainbow.

All are stamped with the same dark symbol:

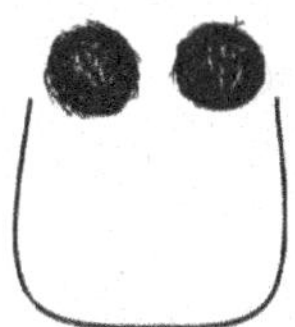

I drop the envelope.

"Fiona?" Alan crosses the threshold.

The confetti is everywhere—in my sneakers, across the floor. Alan leans closer to the bright spray of faces. The shreds are stamped on both sides, so every single piece stares back. He gives me a baritone apology that sounds sincere. But it doesn't explain how this got into the building, whether someone who lives or works here was involved.

"Do you know who did this?" I ask.

"It won't happen again."

It's not an answer.

I ask if there are cameras in the mail room—no.

I ask who sorts the mail—he does. Well, when he's here.

Alan doesn't need to say the rest out loud: The other daytime doorman, Jayden, was on duty for the past two days. He was the one who sorted this mail. But I know Jayden. After years of seeing him twice a week, I know he lives in Queens with his wife and three kids. I know he's saving for a house, and every spare dollar he earns goes toward that. Jayden has integrity. He respects this job. He'd never take an envelope from someone off the street and just slip it in my box.

Or worse, put it there himself.

Alan promises to get to the bottom of this as he kneels.

I put my coffee and mail down to join him. The triangles are the same size and shape as X-Acto blades. We push them into a jagged mound. Even after the floor is clean, Alan is still apologizing. For once, he seems nervous. I've never seen him like this. Alan is a young mid-thirties, but he usually carries himself like he's older, with a mellow professionalism. Even when I'm up early enough to catch him getting to work—in a jersey and flat-brim hat, carrying his scooter into the lobby—he moves with quiet confidence.

Now he wraps his tie around one fist.

Tugs it multiple times.

"I should've double-checked the mail," he says. "And I shouldn't have left the desk. I thought I saw something outside, but it wasn't—it was nothing." He swears twice it was nothing, still crouched low on the floor. I get the feeling that I'm not seeing the full picture, that maybe I should go upstairs and read the news. I stand and grab my things, telling Alan everything's okay, unsure if I believe it. He promises this won't happen again. He swears he's going to get a broom and wipe these off the face of the earth.

I step in the first elevator to arrive.

The door drifts shut.

Now I'm alone.

The buttons here remind me of the faces I just saw on the floor. These have fixed expressions too. I press the button for my floor. The elevator rises so smoothly I don't feel it move at all. Each floor number appears in a red flash, pulsing like a siren on mute. I shouldn't be afraid. I'm almost home. I only left a few minutes ago to pick up my morning coffee. But now I can't shake the idea that when I do get home, I might not be the only one there.

I jab the floor button under mine.

The elevator stops just in time.

I step warily into a hall of closed doors.

Each is seven feet tall, made of gleaming blond wood. I study every one on my way to the other side, hearing nothing but the pulse in my neck, the nearest intersection. At the end of the hall, I survey the empty stairwell before darting up to the next level.

My floor is bare too.

Maybe no one's waiting for me.

I creep quietly toward my apartment.

With one hand on my turned key and the door open just a foot, I scan carefully inside. My place is mostly blue, anchored around a dark-blue kitchen island, and then, a distant navy sofa. There are tributes to the ocean throughout, echoing my underwater-fantasy series, *The Redfins*. The first book came out eight years ago. Today I was planning to work on the third. I take in everything from my desk to the kitchen to the living area, where both swivel chairs are still. On my left, a photo of a great white shark extends for twenty feet. He's swimming right this way, carved with scars like extra gills down to his tail.

Everything looks as I left it.

I step forward, grabbing a pair of scissors off my desk before checking the bedroom, closet, and bathroom. Nothing has been moved. In every mirror, I'm the only one staring back. I return to my desk. It crosses my mind that I might've carried one of the faces back. I scan both sleeves, the hem of my sweats. But I don't find anything, not one smiling shard.

At my laptop, I check the news.

Myra Mane.

Myra *Mane.*

"White uniforms in the dark."

I read past the front pages in shock, so deep into one newspaper that I find myself in the obituaries. I keep reading, my browser dividing into more tabs. The Nomen came back. Forty-nine targets. And now faces for me. I picture them on the floor, like something out of a toddler's birthday party. Alan's head in a funereal bend as he took them in.

But the Nomen couldn't have named . . . me.

They're fighting real fame—mega-celebrities.

Yes, *The Redfins* became a TV show this year.

But even after it aired—and my series became a household name—my daily life didn't change. Going out in my neighborhood, I barely get any attention. Sure, people recognize *Fiona Hart*, but most couldn't pick me out of a lineup. They only rarely stop me on the street or stare in restaurants. All year, I've been a dark crack in pop culture. I've felt like a secret.

On YouTube, I search for the Nomen's video.

The first few results are dead ends. Each directs me to a page that was removed for violating a policy on harassment. One was taken down for graphic content. In each case, all that's left is a digital footprint, a trace that it was here. I try different keywords—*MSG, nomen nescio, jumbotron tape*—but every link only takes me to another error message. I stare at the cooling coffee on my desk. Almost worse than creating a video like this is making people beg to see it—crawl on our hands and knees toward it. I empty the search bar and try again, using more and more tangential phrases, digging for what might've slipped through the algorithm and landed at the back of the site.

After half an hour, I find something under the title *Nomen Grocery List*. The video has no description, no tags. The cover image is pitch black. The view count is only two thousand, but it's climbing—spiking. Now it's slipping past three.

My pulse beats in my fingertips.

My click is a muted snap.

The first few seconds are dark, dead. I turn up the volume—nothing. The whole video is ninety-seven seconds, a knife's edge of time, and still there's empty space at the beginning. I watch the red bead on the progress bar crawl across the bottom.

"Aren't they beautiful?"

The voice is artificially low.

Headshots pulse. Then mine.

I hit pause, feeling sucked into the present. As if I'd been living six inches behind my life and now I'm right here. The Nomen used my latest author photo. Usually, I'm in a hoodie, with my dark hair in a long side ponytail that twists around the drawstrings. That's how I look now, with the rope knots poking through the waves. But in this photo, I'm in a white oxford, with my hair down for once. My eyes are unusually round, and this captures them in high-definition: leaning forward on my lids, underlining themselves with tiny creases. A solid, inconspicuous brown. It's unsettling to remember getting ready for that photo—all the nano-adjustments I made, when really I was dressing up for predators.

I hit play.

More photos pulse.

Each shows someone at their best—at their shiniest, most confident. It's hard to watch them beaming as they're placed in crosshairs. *Nomen Grocery List.* The title feels sinister now. As if these people are things to rinse and arrange on a cutting board.

I pause on my friend Gwen Gordon.

At first, I don't believe it.

I know this photo—from her website.

Gwen is a shoe designer with her own brand, known for fantasy high heels. In this photo, she's mid-laugh, bleached by light. She's always loved this shot because it's an affront to the seriousness of the fashion world. I've said that it captures her manic passion. London-born and raised, Gwen grew up going to Wales every summer, where it tended to rain through August. That's where she learned to channel her energy into something imaginative. For those who know her well, her un-freckled skin still suggests those summers spent indoors.

I call her on my cell, fixated on the screen.

Gwen has ice-blond hair. Her dark brows—her natural color—are deliberate contrasts. She has strong bones in her face: square jaw, pointed chin. Wide wrists and ankles but ultrathin lips: two precise lines almost missing the Cupid's bow in the center. She's told me that she grew up not feeling particularly feminine but that heels always helped. In the right shoes, she reclaimed her femininity. Since her late teens, she's wanted to help people with the same insecurities, literally lift them up. In this photo, she stands in one of her stores—not that anyone could tell. The Nomen have cropped everything but her head. Her laugh floats in the dark.

"Hi, this is Gwen . . ."

Her voicemail greets me.

But . . . she never screens my calls.

Then again, I never call her this early. She must be busy.

Gwen's a lighthearted workaholic. She's always in the middle of a sentence, always between her last sketch and next store opening. Overbooked but at the same time, gifted with a desperation to connect, leaving her radically present with and curious about everyone she meets. It's almost nine. I picture Gwen in her SoHo office, on her second or third coffee, with a palm-size corn-muffin wrapper like a dehydrated sunflower on her desk. I see her hunching forward, tracing a steep arch for a new pair of pumps. Plunged in conversation with one of her assistants, asking about his parents, his dog, his dreams.

I stare at my phone, uneasy.

I'll call her again in ten minutes.

I finish the video, pulling my knees to my chest.

I remember when the Nomen hijacked the ball drop. Back then, they didn't seem dangerous. They were just . . . social commentators. I thought that would be it for them, one freak boon of success. Now they've taken their first target from a sold-out arena. I picture it like I was there. It's too easy to see the Garden at 10:03 p.m., how little might've changed as the roar of fandom turned to horror. I can almost hear the ecstasy shift to panic, changing key.

"To make this list, we cherry-picked from the next generation of stars." The voice is monotone. "That doesn't mean everyone is young or new. What it means is, they belong to tomorrow's Famous Elite. They're on their way to kitchen-table fame. You might not know all of them well, but you do know them. You might even love them. But they're making our country very sick, slowly giving us a terminal disease." The screen goes black. "The only cure to seeing the same faces everywhere will be to see them nowhere."

Something hits my window.

I drop to the floor, braced.

Silence grips the room.

Eventually, I get up.

I pad carefully over to the windows. The trees below are yellow, losing leaves. I scan the panes for any scratch—any smudge or stain—but they're so clean they look invisible. As if I'm one step away from falling onto Eighth Avenue. Did I imagine the noise? I look down to see a bird twitching on the sidewalk. One wing flaps, turning him in a circle.

I call Gwen even though it's only been eight minutes.

As the phone rings, I stare at a sliver of her apartment building. We live close enough that I can jog to her place in the rain without an umbrella. That she comes over when she runs out of the granola we both like, sticking her hand in the bag like they're chips.

Her voicemail answers my call.

I just want to check she's okay.

TWO

Outside, the West Village is uninterrupted by the news.

I walk on the sidewalk, head tucked, feeling alert but not unsafe.

Every now and then, I glance over my shoulder. Would Nomen stand out in a crowd? I only saw one photo of them online—on social media, reposted a hundred times. It showed a figure in all white onstage. His suit was head to toe, with white gloves and high-top sneakers. Every inch was snug, as if he'd fallen into a vat of paint. His fabric mask clung to the dips of his eyes, the bulge of his nose. The front was stitched with their dark symbol. He was running for the wings, his arms in a haze—almost like snow at night.

I slow down next to a bus stop ad for Myra Mane's latest album. Myra has electric-blue hair, even brighter eyes. In this photo, she's mid–eye roll, her arms crossed and hip cocked in the middle of Times Square. All the billboards behind her beam with the album cover for *Wet Animals*: a soaking wet and translucent blue gummy bear. On the back of the album, there's a real bear in the same position, blue fur drenched, with a cowlick.

I pick up my pace.

She's been missing all night?

It's hard to fathom how we lost track of Myra Mane. Ever since *Wet Animals*—her chart-topping breakout—came out this year, everyone knows what she looks like: wide-set, almost alienesque eyes. Sharp chin. One canine twisted forty-five degrees. Kidnapping her from *that* arena should've been impossible—unless support for the Nomen is wider than I thought. I speed across the street, slanting my face away from the row of stalled cars. The idea makes more sense than I want to believe. There must've been witnesses last night—plenty. The Nomen couldn't have filled all twenty thousand seats, plus every chair in the surveillance room, watching the ambush on CCTV. Maybe those bystanders think the Nomen have a point. And . . . don't they? We've been consumed by the same elites for too long. Maybe people who could help the case are choosing to stay silent, to give the group a little head start.

I look back at the ad, where Myra's in blue-tinted contacts and stage makeup. Her Wet Animals Tour was elaborate, with indoor rain and one hundred dancers. The photos were wild: Myra stomping puddles to froth, drenching the front row. She performed most songs with her hair pigtailed, swishing in thick, fluorescent ropes. Toward the end of the show, she ripped the elastics out and shook her head until the blue strands engulfed her face.

Gwen's building comes into view.

She lives with her husband, Logan, on the first floor of a town house that's been converted into apartments. I call her again, leaping up the front steps, tugging the iron railing like a black rope. Their curtains are drawn, windows dark. Voicemail. Is she . . . hiding? On the run? No, she would've told me. If she felt that unsafe, she wouldn't have left me behind.

I survey the rest of the block.

There's just a handful of people here. Everyone's on their own, moving at a different pace. A woman behind a stroller stares at me for a beat too long. She keeps her phone to one ear, her lips frozen. I feel hollowed out. She must know I'm on the list. Her fascination is too undressed, obvious. She disappears around the corner.

I text Gwen: Are you home?

I follow up: Are you okay?

We FaceTimed just last week. She was here, in her kitchen, finishing a sketch on the island. Her bright hair was in a splitting topknot, like egg whites whipped into peaks. What did we talk about? She said that everyone kept asking when she wants to have kids. Ever since she turned thirty, people have wanted to know nothing else. Her standard reply has been, "My shoes are my children." Did she mention any plans? She has to be busy. Her shoes *are* her children. She pours herself into them, leaving almost nothing left. Still, I check her windows for signs of forced entry. The glass is unbroken, frames uncracked. I watch the slit between her curtains, but nothing moves. The view into her place is one gray line.

I walk back to the street.

Do other targets live in the area?

I find the list again and read every name—Max Connors. He's a closer friend to Gwen, but he lives nearby. At least, he used to. I pull up an old thread between us three, coordinating a dinner. His address is here: Twelfth and West Fourth. I walk in that direction, my heart quicker than my feet, as if I'm more nervous than I believe.

A few years ago, Gwen tried to set me up with Max. I've been single since she and I met—and happy. As I still tell her, everyone is so obsessed with romance that they don't give enough credit to friends. When I'm with mine, I'm full. But Gwen had to set me up. She's an eager matchmaker, with dozens of truly heart-melting attempts and exactly zero success. I agreed to two dinners with Max and Gwen. He's a comedian and, as I found out, always seemed to be performing: Everything he said was funny or attempting to be. I did like him, but only in the sense that I was rooting for him. I saw how hard he was trying and wanted him to succeed.

Scraping sounds.

A quick, low moan.

They're coming from an alley straight ahead.

I tread toward the sounds, listening hard, worried that someone might be hurt. More squeaks, like sneakers on asphalt. Muffled collisions, like the thudding fragments of a fistfight. The alley comes into view by degrees until I see them: two men in all-white suits—long-sleeve crew necks, straight-legged pants. Two fabric masks lie crumpled on the ground by dark-green trash bins. The mouths crater, swallowing their own smiles.

One of the men pins the other to a brick wall. He does it with smooth sadism, daring to grin. It's such coordinated malice that my body knows he's one of them—not a copycat, not an admirer. He is the real thing. He pulls a fist back slowly, as if he's savoring the tight line of his knuckles, the threat of them over his shoulder.

I hear myself shout, *"Stop!"*

They turn to me.

Now the aggressor looks even more pleased. He keeps his hand raised, skirting the punch. His eyes are narrow-set, drawn together over a small, pointed nose. A scar cuts across his cheek toward an ear with a missing tip. He's broad-shouldered but thinned down to muscle, streamlined to a powerful core. In his gaze, I feel a quick swish of panic, lifting my stomach and dropping it. The other man—a teen—is still pinned, red with welts. In the pause, he wilts toward the asphalt and vomits. The aggressor slaps him back against the wall.

I can't let this fight get worse.

One more blow could do something permanent.

I grab the nearest brick and raise it, stepping toward them.

The aggressor lets go of the boy, who drops to his knees. He teeters there, precarious, before falling forward and landing on his palms. The aggressor cocks a foot. I start to run, and he wobbles, interrupted by surprise. He stands on one leg, still grinning—still enjoying the fight, and now enamored by my intervention. As if it's syrup over dessert.

Sirens approach. It sounds like a lone police car.

I keep running.

The treble rises.

I'm squeezing the brick, hoping the potential is enough to scare him. He winds up one leg with ferocious intent, then stops abruptly, only tapping the boy with his shoe. The teen lands on his side, his back to me. The aggressor retreats without looking behind him. He strides with blind confidence, step after step, and on the distant sidewalk disappears. For a second, *not* seeing him is even more unsettling. The siren changes direction.

I kneel in front of the boy.

He looks sixteen up close, a decade younger than the other man.

He's in worse shape than I thought: hollow cheeks, limbs a little starved. His chin-length hair almost wet with grease. I scan him for anything urgent—anything I should fix or stem right here. Three inches of red ooze link his bottom lip to the asphalt. The strand rocks back and forth as he breathes. His nails are packed with grime, capping his fingertips like thin brown worms. But nothing seems to need instant relief: He's not cradling any part of his body. Nothing broke through his skin. As far as I can tell, there's no spreading dark stain. Still, it's not hard to imagine the hurt that might be out of sight, the breaks that wouldn't bleed.

I tell him I'm calling 9-1-1.

His neck snaps up, and he looks—not *at* me, but close. He shakes his head slightly. His lips move around an idea he can't quite voice. But I'm already reaching for my phone. He throws a hand toward mine and misses. He tries again, landing his grip.

"Don't." His voice is breathy.

"You're hurt."

"They won't help me."

I ask him what he's talking about, but I sense that I know. Of course, any hospital would have to admit him. Any doctor would have to treat him. But it's easy to imagine how reluctant they might be. If I were in all white—after what this group has done—then the prospect might scare me too. I ask if there's anyone I can call—family, close friends. He leans forward to spit red. I have to ask twice more before he shakes his head.

He tries to sit.

I help him until he's bent over butterflied legs.

I ask where he lives, but he only pants, mouth dripping.

When he tries to stand, I lift him under the armpits—they feel scrawny, cartilaginous—and together, we get him on his feet. He's wincing as he wraps an arm around my shoulders. I'm now in the crook of his elbow, feeling it heat the back of my neck. I eye him, but he's too weak to be dangerous. He can't hurt me when he *needs* me.

I guide him to the street.

At least he can walk—no snapped bones.

But where to from here? We're on a one-way cobblestone road that empties into a busy avenue. The sun catches a glass edge of my building. A half dozen people flow past, all fixated on the Nomen with varied discretion. They must know who he is—the blood, this outfit. Maybe they think that I hurt him. They keep walking, disappearing behind street trees, one girl almost tripping. The Nomen in my arms sinks an inch. It feels like I'm going to drop him, until his knees lock and he pushes himself back up. He slides against me, pressing into my thigh, my ribs. Meanwhile, the sun hits my building in an eight-legged spot.

It shifts like a white spider on the windows.

~

Alan's alone in the lobby.

His eyes bulge when he sees us.

After a moment of shock, he reanimates. He asks if I need help—no, thank you—and then, more urgently, if I'm sure—yes, I know what I'm doing. I pass him with the Nomen still slumped against me, hanging on for support. Alan steps toward us, leaving one hand on the desk. It looks like he's about to ask one more question, or maybe even intervene, when I insist that I have it under control, sounding more convincing than I feel.

I guide the boy into the elevator.

Then over my threshold.

Maybe Alan was right to worry. Maybe it's unwise to have one of them here. But the boy needs basic attention. My apartment was so close. I couldn't leave him on the street. I'd be nothing if people hadn't shown irrational kindness to me, if they hadn't stayed when it made more sense to leave. This boy needs a place to clean up—even if it's mine. I don't see his potential right now; I just see his pain. Maybe that's my blind spot. But this is who I am.

Once he's on the sofa, I grab him towels. He stains one just touching it, leaving pink swishes. By now, his mouth has stopped bleeding, but his neck is still a slick red. It looks like his bottom lip has been pulled down to his neckline. He dabs the color.

Meanwhile, I bring him a glass of water.

He takes a precious sip, wincing.

I ask if he feels confused.

It takes him a while, but he answers—no.

I try my luck and ask if his ears are ringing—no. I keep asking questions, each time almost losing hope before he gives me a quiet syllable in response. It sounds like he doesn't have a concussion, like the blows didn't quite shake his brain. Eventually, he sets the water down and, for the first time all morning, really looks at me. Half his face has been beaten. Freckles are only visible on one side, the other under a dark-pink cloud.

His good eye narrows.

"You're on our list."

My cheeks feel cold.

I'm aware of the front door twenty steps behind me. The sharp corners of my coffee table. The thick walls muting every sound we make. The hurt side of his face looks like it's growing—flesh stretching, goo collecting. I don't think he could attack me now, not in this state. But . . . did the idea just cross his mind? Does he want to?

"I am," I admit.

"What is this?"

He looks as if he's been cornered.

He stands abruptly, then stops, swaying on his feet. After a second, he falls back onto the sofa. Sitting, he blinks rapidly. A chunk of hair falls in front of his face, the clumps coated in a dark glaze. A few are tangled in long, frayed knots. He lets them hang over his eyes, visible through the cracks.

I tell him evenly I'm just trying to help.

He fixates on me, doubtful.

"Let me get you a change of clothes—just because . . ."

I gesture to my neckline where his is red. I want to make it clear that I'm not protesting his uniform, that this has nothing to do with his mission. I retreat into my closet, facing him the whole time. He glares at me, slouching forward over his knees. His back is rounded, stomach like a hammock. His chin dips with what looks like exhaustion. The reflex is subtle and quick. Even I barely catch it, and my attention is nowhere else. He seems to be caught in a push-pull between fatigue and suspicion—not full-fledged fear, but close.

I return with a sweatshirt and drawstring pants.

He looks from the clothes to me.

"None of this makes fucking sense."

But he takes the clothes. He holds them between his legs, his hands hanging toward the floor. We stay in a stalemate, waiting for the other to move. Eventually, he leans back into the sofa, letting the cushions shape his spine. He's still glaring, but now blinking more often, more slowly. I tell him he can stay here for as long as he needs.

The offer wakes him a little.

THREE

The Nomen stirs on my sofa at noon.

His right ankle twitches first.

Then he rakes one hand down the box cushion.

I watch him from the nearest chair, where I've been sitting since he shut his eyes. I've barely looked away. For the most part, he hasn't moved, his body slack in a fetal curve. He's been facing the middle of the room—no pillow, no blanket. Just his long face on the blue twill. One elbow-shaped vein on his temple. Three moles under his jawbone, raised a few millimeters off the skin. Every once in a while he'd spasm, his legs thrashing as if he were trying to sprint out of a nightmare. Otherwise, he's been in a deep sleep—until now.

He moans as his eyes flutter open.

He scans the coffee table covered in books.

They're references on dolphin whistles, the Galapagos, and underwater tsunamis—all in slanted stacks, surrounded by too many black pens. He looks disoriented as he takes them in, still on his side, my gray sweats tucked in his arms. His gaze drifts to my bookcase, stuffed with old copies of Ursula K. Le Guin and Bram Stoker. A basilisk spreads over five covers in a series, each spine a scaly brick. He studies a photo of my parents. They're on a high shelf, watching over me; they died in a car accident when I was a teen.

And then, finally, me.

He bolts up to sit, dropping the sweats.

By now, his hurt eye has almost ballooned shut.

I tell him I'm going to get ice, standing with exceeding caution, my knees unbending by degrees. I walk to the freezer and fill a Ziploc without turning my back. Each handful bites my fingers.

I hurry back to offer him the bag.

He doesn't take it, doesn't move.

Eventually, I lower it to the coffee table. The only sounds come from shifting ice. I ask one more time if I can help get him home. But I get the feeling—from the grime, the smell of sweat gone sour—that he might not have one. He's thin enough that the shape of his skull is prominent. I ask if there's anything else I can do. He just stares at the ice, drawing my gaze. The cubes fit together in a loose mound like a dripping crystal brain.

"Why are you doing this?" he asks.

"Doing what?"

"Pretending to help me." His voice rises with alarm.

"I know what it looks like." My voice is deliberately calm. The last thing I want is for him to feel trapped, for him to snap under pressure. He stares at me, his eyes two different sizes. He cracks a middle knuckle, pressing the joint until it pops. "I know it's confusing, not just that I picked you up, but . . ." *That your own group knocked you down.*

"Why are you doing this?"

"Because—"

"Don't *fucking* lie."

"There are no sides when someone's hurt."

The words race out as if he's kneeling on my chest.

I just felt an unstoppable drive to help him. His pain was overwhelming, something I couldn't ignore. This is the kind of thing I've always done—never with so much at stake, but this is who I am. Last week, a man moved onto a bench across the street. He'd just been kicked out of a shelter for pulling a knife on someone who'd stolen his shoes. I got him two hot meals—never thought about it. Just did it. If he were hurt and refused a doctor, I might've brought him up here too. The Nomen breaks into a smirk. It looks like an amazed warp of surprise.

I ask if he needs anything else.

When he doesn't reply, I list what I can offer from my medicine cabinet—Neosporin, bandages, gauze—but the words ping off him. He eyes me with growing disbelief. I try to put myself in his shoes. Maybe he thinks that I'm naive. Dangerously sentimental. Or possibly even suicidal. I tell myself one more time that he can't hurt me; he's still too wounded, too shocked. He just keeps listening, his smirk flicking up toward his cheek. The expression gives him more wrinkles than it should. They're a web through his face, clustering in folds around his nose and giving him several dimples in a row. Eventually, I reach the end of my list. The ice melts. His smirk fades. I hear the buzz of my air conditioner, traffic.

His next words are cool and slow.

"You're not afraid enough."

"What should I be afraid of?"

He laughs without sound, just hard bursts of air.

Now that his mouth has stopped bleeding, his teeth are the color of warm white wine. His chin and neck are pink with a final, unscrubbed layer of blood. He glances abruptly around the room as if we might not be alone. I realize he's looking for something.

"Where's my mask?"

He's . . . going back to them?

I picture his mask in the alley. Its mouth had sunk into a toothless, white-gummed hole. Its round head had been crushed into a dozen folds. "You're not . . ." But I can't finish the idea. I'm too confused—not that he'd go back to hunting me. A part of me must've always known that. What's stranger is that he'd rejoin the group that hurt him.

"H-he was one of you," I fumble.

"You think I'm stupid?"

His tone is sharp.

"*No*, of course not—"

"You think I'm fucking stupid. So you sit there and tell me what I should fucking choose." Instead of becoming more agitated, now he goes still. He lowers his chin, staring at me from the tops of his eyes. "You don't know what's really happening out there. Do you? You live here. You have your pretty life. You're not close enough to the rot."

He points at the carpet.

I try not to move.

"Do you know what kind of people join a movement like this?" His tone suggests the answer is dark. "We used to be a . . ." He draws in his lips, frustrated. "Then, when you finally catch your breath, you're in a circle with everyone else, watching someone's ear dangle from their neck." He stares hard at me, as if I should know what he means. As if the memory is so vivid to him I can see it too. "I think that's why he put us in white—so we could see the blood. So we could see it for the next few days and think twice about running away.

"It didn't start out like this." He shakes his head. "He always hated fame, hated you people. I just . . . didn't know how much." He's precarious on the edge of the sofa. "Then, when he started to change . . . we didn't have a choice. He'd gotten in too deep." He points one locked finger to the center of his forehead. "When he changed, we had to keep up. And some of us . . . He'd really got to them good. He'd dug a hole straight through."

He wrings his hands.

Then stops.

"You're not afraid enough." His volume rises. "This is what we do to *ourselves*. What do you think we'll do to *you*?" Without knowing what he means, I start to sweat. I try to focus on his body, on what I saw in the alley. To stay grounded in tangible facts.

I hear myself ask what started the fight.

If that man lashed out for a reason.

"You want this to make sense?"

His eyes are haunted.

"Don't you hear what I'm *saying*? There are bad people in the Nomen. Unmothered. People who don't value life." He enunciates with clarity, his tongue flicking between his teeth. "They were kept in the House too long. Watching him over-punish, over-hurt. Grind kids until they were red in the dirt." He clenches his jaw, full of venom. "That house. That *fucking* house. It turned some of us into . . . devils. People who love pain. Not just yours—anyone's. Now it's their heroin. More than that, their . . . perfection." His right hand starts to shake. "I thought he was trying to *help* us. Now I see, he wanted *us* to help *him*." More to himself, he adds, "Sometimes, I don't know if he really hates fame or if he just needed a reason for . . ."

"For what?"

"The blood."

He holds his shivering wrist.

It looks like he's handcuffed to himself.

The room feels even cooler, my skin pricked. I can barely follow what this boy is saying. But I understand enough to feel true dread. Now the Nomen have the added terror of being indiscriminately cruel—so vicious that maybe there's no true safety from them. Even when you're in their group. Even here at home, on the sofa I've had since college—with ten years of my pen caps and hair ties in the cracks, where Gwen and I have sat a hundred times—I almost feel like I'm on their turf. As if they own the fuzzing fabric under me.

I hear myself say that if he needs support to leave the group, I could help him through the transition. I'm not thinking about what that could mean, but I have to offer. I just have to. I can't let this kid run somewhere unsafe, where he might get his skull fractured at random. Besides, he's still bleeding, battered. Still just barely lucid. "I know you don't need to hear this from me." My voice comes out stronger than I expected, almost confident he might listen. "But if the Nomen are that hellish, going back to them now would be like . . ."

"Feeding the monster."

I nod, unnerved.

Before I can say anything else, he pulls on the sweatshirt. The hood falls below his brow. His injuries sink into shadows. "And what do you think they'd do to me?" His mouth is disembodied. "Now that I know what's coming. Helped build it. Hammered in the nails. Now that I've *seen* it and *been* there—and walk around with that fucking place in my head—what do you think they'd do to me if I ran?" He shoots upright with his last few words. I'm blinking hard, eye level with his hands. His fingers look like snapped sticks.

He snatches the sweatpants.

I cup my knees, frozen.

He strides to the front door.

On his way, he swipes an arm across the entryway table, bringing everything there to the floor: both lamps, then the silver plate with my keys and matchboxes from memorable dinners. My parents had that plate at home in Pennsylvania. They kept their keys there too. Everything smacks the wood in a series of devastating collisions before he's finally gone.

I leap up before the door shuts.

Sprint over to the plate.

Pick it up.

I inspect it for scratches, but it looks okay. Even better than okay—perfect. I have my parents' things across my apartment, every one unimaginably precious. I bring the plate to my forehead, as if I'm leaning on my parents, and cry for the first time since I read the news this morning. I keep crying, loud, my chest shaking. Because maybe it's only with your parents that you can be truly weak. That you can sink to your knees and feel the pain.

~

Alone, I call Gwen—voicemail.

I check headlines. So far, the only target in the news is Myra.

A few papers share the same photo from last night, capturing an empty Garden stage. It must've been taken right before the Nomen rolled their tape. The jumbotrons are a bright, blank gray, as if power had just been restored. Two dozen spotlights cross on no one—ice blue on top, diffusing to royal blue by the ends. In the shadows around them: chaos. Figures bear-crawl over rows. Only a handful stay in their seats, apparently stunned in place. The paralysis makes them look eerily rapt, as if this is the show they intended to see.

I scroll past with a quick thumb.

Gwen has to be safe.

If she wasn't, it would be in the headlines.

Then again, I'm still not sure how fringe the Nomen are. No one knows how many are secretly rooting for them and chipping in where they can. I can see the dark itch creeping into newsrooms as reporters mull over the Nomen's promise: a shift to talent over fame. Breaking a cultural obsession. A Renaissance for lesser-known creatives. Would that be so bad? Maybe a few journalists are holding on to news—just for an hour, to do another round of fact-checking, so the Nomen might get farther away. Because maybe the group is onto something. Maybe all they need is a little help to change the world . . . just this once.

I open Gwen's Instagram.

Her last post was two weeks ago.

In that shot, she sticks her tongue out at the British Fashion Awards, giraffe-like in her own shoes. She never designs a heel under four inches. Her profile photo is dim. No story halo—not unexpected, given what's happened. In normal circumstances, she always has something to share: manic mid-haircut selfies, a passion fruit margarita on an airplane tray table, or snapshots from a flea market in DUMBO, where she's hunting for inspiration. Her following has grown steadily with time, the smooth gains tracking her tireless work.

I open Messages.

Gwen uses read receipts, which she claims were invented for failed people-pleasers like herself: people who are overbooked but desperate to keep you from feeling ignored. I always found that harsh. Gwen was never too busy for me. She responded to my texts on airplanes, in Asian time zones. She answered my FaceTimes at the dentist, on set for product shoots. I never caught her with nothing else going on, but I always caught her. At least, I used to.

She hasn't even seen my texts from this morning.

I ask again: Are you okay?

~

By the afternoon, still no sign of Myra.

The banner headlines from this morning haven't changed.

Once I've read everything in the news, I search for more on the Nomen. Their Wikipedia teems with silent activity: over four hundred citations. It makes the white space around the text look like picked-over bones. I read that, on New Year's Day this year, the group sent their Declaration of Grievances and Manifesto to all major news outlets. Their Declaration catalogs the damage caused by the status quo. Their Manifesto proposes fundamental change. Its appendix goes so far as to suggest a series of laws that would dismantle fame.

I end up on Reddit, reading rumors.

Some say the Nomen's control center is hidden on the dark web. Apparently, that's where they keep their messaging boards, the uncensored step-by-step of their most gruesome plans. Otherwise, they never could've coordinated an attack this logistically complex, this Machiavellian. And this collective, with maybe hundreds involved. It's the only way they could continue to avoid detection, with their internet traffic scrambled, their devices off the grid.

I read another thread analyzing the list.

Someone asks why the Nomen are targeting tomorrow's A-list instead of today's. The most popular reply is that maybe they will. Maybe this is just the tip of the iceberg and there's plenty still to come. Someone else points out that the easiest time to uproot something is always in the beginning. When it comes to weeds, molds, infestations—bad habits, rot, disease—it's always easiest to stop something when it's just getting started. I stop scrolling when I read that comment. It makes a chilling amount of sense. Maybe the "next generation of stars" is really the most accessible one. We are the ones without extensive security. The ones who aren't used to mortal threats. We are the low-hanging fruit.

My phone glows next to my elbow.

I jolt until I see it's a FaceTime request from my friends Marlowe, Caroline, and Emma, who I've known since middle school. They've been texting me all day in our group chat. I've done my best to respond—I've told them that I love them, that I'm safe—but I've struggled to keep up with their concern. I'm sure they want to see that I'm truly all right.

I answer.

We slide into a grid.

Marlowe's on the upper left, watery-eyed. She's always been a deep feeler, with intense and precise reactions to things as seemingly ordinary as commercials, the overheard problems of strangers, and the moods of animals. She checks our horoscopes daily and sends highlights to the group chat. Now she's at her kitchen table in San Francisco, the spikes of her aloe plant behind her. Her round cheeks are teary, her lips pale and tight.

On the upper right, Caroline's in a conference room. She's a lawyer in Philadelphia, the reliable organizer of our group. She's the one who always makes sure we actually get together for weekend trips—most of the time, to my place here in New York, where we sleep, the four of us, in one bed. She's in a dark crew neck, with her blond hair in a neat bun, leaning forward over glossy mahogany. Next to me on the bottom is Emma. She's on her living room floor in suburban Pennsylvania, with her nine-month-old on her lap. Emma is a stay-at-home mom of three. She's practical and wry, claiming that the ultimate motherhood hack is finding humor in your kids' tantrums. Now, though, she's concerned, squinting into early crow's-feet.

It's so good to see them, even like this.

Marlowe cries into her hand.

I promise her it's okay.

"Are you safe?" she asks.

Her doubt unnerves me.

I'm hyperaware of the locks on my door.

The triple-paned windows across the room.

I tell them I'm safe—perfectly safe—even though I'm not sure if I believe it. Marlowe nods, raking three fingers down her neck. I tell them everything from today. They go rigid with shock as I describe letting a Nomen rest in my apartment. I plow ahead, telling them I've been trying to get in touch with Gwen all day and haven't gotten her on the phone. They digest this last part in tense silence. They've all met Gwen plenty of times. They know she's my bedrock in this city, that I've grown as close to her in five years as I am to the three of them. They know if they can't reach me at the end of the day, I'm probably at Gwen and Logan's, sprawled on their sofa, feeling fully at home.

"You went to Gwen's?" Caroline asks.

"She wasn't there."

Emma's baby shrieks, startling everyone.

"Actually, she might've been," I realize.

I never knocked on her door, never rang her bell.

I just assumed she was out since her place was dark.

I reassure my friends that Gwen and I are fine. I remind them that I live in a mid-rise with a doorman. There are cameras in the building, every access point surveilled. My friends don't seem any more relieved. I go on, stating that I'm in one of the busiest cities in the world, where there are a hundred eyes at every curb. Where no one can get away with anything—not really. The reassurance comes out sounding hollow. After all, there's still no sign of Myra. I carry on, telling them that I'm going to check on Gwen again, and this time I'll do the obvious: knock, ring. What I should've done already, if I was thinking straight.

They're quiet.

As if the idea makes them nervous.

Caroline asks if I want them to visit. Before I can answer, she changes tack, asking if I want to visit her in Philadelphia. "I could pick you up and drive you here." She leans forward, energized by the idea. "Or we could go somewhere—anywhere—the four of us." Marlowe nods, Emma too. Something about the offer reminds me of being in high school. In the months after I lost my parents, I rarely slept at home. One of them would host me almost every night, folding me into their family dinners, their TV hours. Their everyday routines.

"That might be the safest thing to do," Marlowe adds.

"Get you out of there," Emma agrees.

But the thought of leaving Gwen feels not just wrong—physically painful.

I tell them we should wait. "Things are still too . . ." I don't want to say *dangerous and unknown,* so I end up saying nothing at all. I picture Gwen's building—the door, the bell—and feel an urge to go. I tell all three that I love them, that they're the sisters I never had. Today the words come out with a sense of foreboding, solemn and final. Caroline insists their offer stands. I thank them one more time—really thank them, looking each of them in the eye. But the truth is, I can't leave this city until I figure out what's happened to Gwen.

FOUR

After we hang up, I leave again for Gwen's apartment.

I never checked on Max.

I stop at the ad for Myra, where dead leaves cluster at the bottom.

Should I visit him first? I barely know him, but I have the feeling that if I don't run to his place just to make sure he's okay, then maybe no one else will. From what I remember, his schedule had turned him into something of a lone wolf. Most days, he slept until three p.m. He was at a new comedy club almost every night, testing new material, sometimes staying up until dawn for just five minutes with a live crowd. It wouldn't take long to check—ten minutes. Before I realize what I'm doing, I pull up his number on my phone.

I ask if he's home.

I'm on my way there by the time I press send.

I turn left, past a row of designer boutiques: Ted Baker. Rebecca Taylor. Diane von Furstenberg. All famous name-brand stores. Aren't these what Nomen want to replace? Inside, just a handful of people scan the racks. Are these places less crowded than usual? I don't know; I don't shop. Most of the time, I'm at home with my laptop, thinking about deep-sea vents, inventing eyeless shrimp. So what if the stores are empty?

That's probably normal for a Monday.

Max's place comes into view. He lives on the top floor of a nineteenth-century walk-up. The ground floor is an Italian restaurant known for hard-to-get reservations and house-made ricotta. Today a police car is parked at the entrance. What's that doing here? A small group has formed around the restaurant. I start to run, trying not to read into it.

I slip through the crowd, drawing eyes and flickers of recognition—this usually distant mob, for once, zeroing in on me. Some people still struggle to place me, squinting as if I'm buried in smoke. Two police officers leave Max's building.

I stop at their feet.

"What happened to him?" I ask.

Behind them, someone emerges with a roll of caution tape.

I dart inside before the door shuts, jump up two steps at a time.

I brace myself for shouts from the sidewalk—"Hold it!", "Hands!"—but nothing comes. Maybe the officers have bigger problems. Maybe they think I live here too. After two flights, I'm sweating into my hoodie. I pass people standing motionless around the stairwell: a young professional working from home, then an older bohemian woman. She leans over the railing, her red caftan fluttering between the bars, looking hesitantly up.

On the top floor, three lines of yellow tape cross what must be Max's doorway. A man in khakis is thumbing something into his phone. He has the professional air of someone involved, maybe an investigator. I ask what happened to Max.

"Fiona."

He says it like he knows me.

"I'm so sorry about what's happened," he adds.

Of course he saw the video. I feel more vulnerable than I expected.

For as long as I've been on my own, it's been natural to treat most strangers like friends. I've felt like we're all responsible for each other: We can't let each other slip through the cracks. But when people do the same for me—when they see where it hurts and reach out, when they show unexpected generosity—I can be thrown off-balance.

Gwen and I have psychoanalyzed it to death.

She says I'm more comfortable giving.

She says it's why I hide from the world when I'm sick—disappearing in bed and telling no one, not even her or Marlowe, Caroline, and Emma. She says it's why I never accept a third date: I won't look someone in the eye and be the weak one. Late one night, picking apart the emotional scar tissue, she said quietly that maybe being too vulnerable takes me back to when I lost Mom and Dad. To being seventeen years old on May 16 and seeing a police car pull into the driveway. Maybe she's right. Because the only times I truly break down anymore are when I'm thinking about them. And standing here now, with the investigator showing more sympathy than I want, I stiffen. I cross my arms, break his stare.

"I'm a friend of Max's," I add.

Returning to my question.

He nods, then glances at the bright tape, the shut door.

I sense his internal debate of whether or not to tell me the truth. Maybe he's considering the fact that I'm on the list too. That whatever took place here has relevance to me. I press my luck and ask one more time—politely but directly—what happened to Max.

"We don't know," he says.

"You don't know?"

He shakes his head, grim. "A neighbor reported loud noises, maybe a fight, a few hours ago."

And now Max is gone. I remember the Nomen who backed up in the alley, then turned out of sight. Did he run straight here? I picture a half dozen of them trotting up the stairs, their mood deliberately casual, pace intentionally slow. All hiding in plain clothes, only revealed by their white gloves. Loud noises . . . a few hours ago. Then they were just right here. I picture a shoulder-to-shoulder group where I stand, their sleeves dragging against the walls.

"Was he expecting you?"

"No." I sound distant.

I look closer at the door.

The frame splinters at hip height. The lock itself is warped, hanging on to screws at diagonals. Max wouldn't have been able to do much against them. He was thin with weak posture, his back caving in around a neglected core. I haven't seen him since he finally taped his Netflix special earlier this year. Still, I doubt he stopped seeing himself as the underdog, saying yes to every gig, asking strangers to follow him on YouTube. I picture him the last night I saw him. He was fidgety and relentless, entertaining the waiters. With a theatrical laugh.

I thank the investigator, rush downstairs.

There are more people now on every floor, by the railing, peeking up. The investigator calls my name, but I've already spent too much time here. I should be at Gwen's.

~

Outside, I get a FaceTime request from Gwen.

"Hi, Fay." Her nickname for me. She's in bed, with her black leather headboard behind her. Her hair is a wild mess of dive loops, pinned by a DELTA mask on her forehead. I stop short, my hand on my heart, leaning forward over the sidewalk.

"I was worried sick about you!"

"Sorry, I just woke up maybe twenty minutes ago." But she doesn't sound like herself. Her words come out one at a time, not in her usual rushed smear. She's barely moving too. Her chin is tucked, shoulders immobile. It's unnerving to see her this slowed down. She says she got back from Korea this morning, that she's been asleep since the taxi home. "I should've called right away. I'm sorry—" I tell her not to be. "I just couldn't stop reading about . . ."

I picture the empty stage.

I have to tell her about Max, but I want to do it in person.

I ask if I can come over, and she tells me of course. She says Logan's there, too, that he took the day off. Her eyes narrow abruptly. She pulls her phone closer, focusing on something over my shoulder. I glance back, braced for reaching hands, white fingers coming for me. But there's nothing—only street trees and the crowd by Max's place, too far away for Gwen to see. I return to my phone, confused and with a simmering panic, as if she found something I missed. Gwen lowers her voice to ask, in disbelief, "What are you doing outside?"

I pick up my pace.

I tell her it's okay, that I'm close.

She nods, but it's subtle, as if she doesn't quite believe me.

"You know," she adds, glancing sideways, "this sounds crazy, but . . . my blinds have been shut all day, and I still feel like I'm being watched."

~

Logan answers their door, solemn.

His powder-blue oxford is too wide, as usual. Most clothes for his height—six five, he'll shyly admit when pressed—aren't narrow enough, and he's too unconcerned with looks to get them tailored. We hug, shutting the door behind us.

He waves me gravely ahead.

He and Gwen were married when we met. He's a corporate lawyer, a perfect rational balance to her right-brained life. At a glance, he's a knockout: tall with sensitive eyes, a neat beard, and strong neck. Up close, though, he's endearingly awkward—sparing with eye contact and stiff with his hands, as if he thinks you're eager to leave. What he lacks in charm, he makes up for in earnestness. Almost every time I've seen him, he's asked me such an emotionally precise question it's almost taken my breath away. And he's always been kind, never failing to cover a table corner with his hand when Gwen leaned over to pick up her napkin, her phone—she's always dropping things, trying to hold too much at once.

That's the Logan I know.

In five years, I've never seen him this . . . shipwrecked.

He walks heavily through the living room. All the lights so far have been switched off. Are he and Gwen hiding? Trying to make it look like they're not home? Even in the dark, I know this place like my own: the high ceiling, fireplace, and stony neutrals. The only pop of color comes from the photo over the mantel. It captures the two-story pub in London where Logan and Gwen met eight years ago—a place covered in bright, ballooning graffiti. Back then, he was a shy law student, following his mates out of his comfort zone. Meanwhile, Gwen was going out for her third night in a row. She was hoping to thread the needle of having men buy her endless drinks while she spent the whole time with her friends. They've been together ever since.

We find Gwen in bed.

She's on her phone with the shades drawn, shadows filling the room like smoke. I knock, and her neck snaps up. Once she sees me, she spreads her arms into a T.

I speed over to her, and we hug, falling sideways. She still won't let go when we land on her sheets. She's a furnace, as usual. She's always had an almost feverish core, wearing tank tops in air-conditioned rooms, letting me have the full blanket when we watch TV. I smile into her shoulder and tell her I'm so happy she's okay. She says everything's going to be fine, repeating the line twice in a grim chant. She sounds even more subdued than she did on the phone. It's unsettling, as if the Nomen have already gotten to her, hurt her from a distance. It makes sense that she's rattled. I'm rattled too. But I didn't expect her to . . . sink this soon.

I squeeze her tighter, hanging on to the fact that she still *feels* like Gwen. She's still "unbelievably hot," as she humorously describes it, melting my chest and the insides of my arms. Eventually, I lean back and look at her from a couple of feet away. She's limp on the sheets, clutching her phone. Her neck's at an unnatural angle, bent over the bulge of her shoulder. She asks if I saw anything outside.

I sit up. She follows.

I break the news about Max.

She bobs her chin less and less until it flatlines.

I remember our last dinner with him. We ate at a tapas place that Gwen chose with persuasive enthusiasm. The restaurant looked like a wine cellar, with bottles lining every wall and fewer than twenty seats. Coming from a quiet slice of Pennsylvania—where my parents didn't value adventure with our food—I'd never had anything on the menu. I remember glaring at Gwen for choosing a place where the only entrées were organ meats. When she gets uncomfortable, she laughs, and she spent the entire meal howling. It encouraged Max to monologue for most of the evening, interpreting her reaction as a sign to keep going.

Gwen looks at Logan over my shoulder.

I turn to see him in the doorway.

There's a haunted pinch between his eyes. He palms the back of his neck, as if he's patching his spine. They're making me feel weirdly . . . missed, like whatever's dragging them down by the ankle hasn't quite grabbed me. Of course I'm scared. If the shades were open, I'd scan for anyone looking back. But I'm not as . . . deathly submerged. They look too blindsided to think straight, to come up with the plan they need. I face Gwen, her sheets like white fire around her, and say what they must be thinking—what they would if they weren't in shock.

"Maybe you shouldn't be at home."

FIVE

I call the Hyatt in Midtown. The hotel doesn't have any connecting suites available for tonight on such short notice, but they offer two rooms across the hall. I book them under fake names and pay with Logan's credit card. His last name is Bell.

No one should be looking for him.

Once my call's over, I walk back to Gwen and Logan's room. They've been packing suitcases on their bed, but now they stop short, hands full. The sleeve of one sweater hangs down Gwen's leg, looking like a lifeless blue arm. They start up again as I download the call. I only booked us rooms for three nights, but it looks like Gwen and Logan are packing for a longer stay. She drops another armful into her bag, letting the clothes go in a landslide.

Logan carries their bags to the door.

In the entryway, Gwen puts on a newsboy hat and wide scarf. She wraps it three times around her neck, then fluffs the layers up over her mouth. I'm behind her, a head taller in the mirror. At five three, Gwen's always said that she "leaves room for shoes." Her heels usually disguise her height, but in old sneakers tonight, she looks uncharacteristically small. Logan hands me a baseball cap. I'm about to refuse when I remember that I'm on the list too. Gwen notices me pause and goes still. I don't remind her that I've been outside all day with nothing, no one. That *this* is the most unsafe I've felt—now, as we're starting to hide.

Their fear feels like a mandate.

I put on the cap, tightening the back strap.

At the same time, I watch Gwen in the mirror. Her eyes are still empty, the bright and gooey part of her gone. It hurts to see her like this, nervously adjusting her scarf.

Once she's ready, she hugs me hard, fast. There's a buried seed of her old energy in it. She holds my hand as we step outside. It's getting dark, the city fading to a deep gray. It looks like there's a thin layer of ash over New York—on the iron fence around a private garden, on the cobblestone road. Logan carries their bags down the steps. I keep Gwen's hand, scanning left to right. There's no one else on the block, no one staring through the grid of orange windows. Gwen wraps her free arm around mine. Their Uber arrives at the curb.

Logan loads the trunk.

Gwen gives me one last hug goodbye.

I'm just going to pack, then will meet them uptown. Still, she seems uneasy to be letting me out of her sight. I kiss her hair and smell her green tea–scented shampoo, some Purell. She usually hugs so many people that she always has a small bottle with her, sometimes two on flights. Logan asks one more time if I want to come with them. I tell him what I have already: I need my laptop, clothes that fit. It's all four minutes away.

"I love you, Fay."

Gwen says it like a warning, like she doesn't want me to stop between here and my apartment. She gets in the back seat. I tell her I love her, too, suddenly misty-eyed, choked up. Logan asks if he can at least walk me to my building—if he can please just see me to the front door. I insist that I'm fine, but really I'm just eager to see them on their way. Gwen's fingers slip out of mine as Logan finally gets in beside her. I shut the door and step back toward my place. I tell them to leave something for me in the minibar, trying to smile so they feel lighter for just one second. But Logan stays solemn. Gwen looks even more nervous.

They wave from the Uber.

I watch their car until it's gone.

Alone again, I head home, leaving their quiet side street.

The next road is packed with an after-work crowd. I weave through the onslaught, scanning everyone from the neck down. At one point, I glance over my shoulder, but there's nothing out of place behind me—no white flash in the group.

In the distance, six people stand outside my building. My heart rate spikes. They're in pairs, glancing up at my windows. But my apartment's dark, just like I left it. There's nothing visible from here—no one opening my fridge and pouring milk on the floor. No one crouched and waiting for me. One woman snaps a photo of the glass. They must be . . . tourists, people who've been wrapped up in the news and stopped by to see my place for themselves. Gwen was probably able to sneak away because their place is in Logan's name. She'd started her brand by the time they bought it, so they kept her off the deed. But this one is mine, searchable. Anyone can ask their browser where I live and scroll right down to find it.

I keep my pace steady, quick.

The front door opens when I get close, triggered by the key fob in my wallet.

I keep my eyes low, hoping no one sees my face. If anyone's whispering about me now, I can't hear them over traffic, a motorized bike. In the lobby, Pavel's replaced Alan. Pavel's in his early thirties, with a wide face and dark buzz cut matching the length of his beard. He has a habit of watching sports on mute behind the desk—not tonight. He's alert as I walk in, doing nothing but watching the door. It stirs my unease, but I know him, the same way I know Alan. Pavel's told me that he and his wife have been trying for a year to have kids. They're Catholic, living in South Brooklyn. For as long as I've lived here, we've had mutual respect.

"Fiona, the police were here for you."

"For me?"

"Yes," Pavel says. "I called you. A couple of times."

I say that I haven't been prompt today with my phone.

"They just wanted to make sure you're safe. They had to leave . . ."

I thank him, saying I'll get back to them, though I'm not sure that I will. I'm not sure I should trust the police after what happened to Myra last night on their watch. Besides, for all I know, it could've been two Nomen who stopped by—dressed in blue, swearing they wanted to help. They took Max, just minutes away, while he was still at home.

In the elevator, I check my phone.

The story about Max is starting to hit major outlets.

I skim headlines—no news beyond the fact that he's missing.

The door opens before I read more. I approach my apartment, unlock it. Peering inside, everything seems to be where I left it. I cross the threshold, picking up speed the deeper I go, the more confident I am I'm alone. I grab a tote and load it with three days' worth of my things—and my passport, just in case. Last, I walk to my desk and pick up my favorite photo of my parents. They were high school teachers: Dad, Natural Science; Mom, English. In this photo, the three of us are in the ocean in Weekapaug, Rhode Island. We used to spend two weeks there every summer. They're lifting me up by my hands, my feet hovering over the water.

"I love you," I whisper.

The frame glints.

"Please, I need you. Please, help us." I'm not very religious, but I do pray to my parents. I talk to them as if they can hear me, because a piece of me believes that they can. That, in a way I don't understand, the permanent parts of them never left and they are close when I need them. "Help Gwen, Logan, Max. Help all of us. Please, make sure we're okay."

I rub my thumb across the frame.

This was in their house too.

I clean it every month so the silver never loses its shine—like the sun on water, something transcendentally perfect. I don't need to clean it as often, but the act is a sacred ritual of mine. I like polishing the metal, the glass. Holding this thing that connects us.

"Talk to you soon."

I wipe my eyes.

Wrap the frame in my clothes.

After zipping my bag shut, I check again for news. An interview from this afternoon is trending. In the thumbnail, a woman stands by Max's building. A line of yellow tape runs behind her, twisted into a razor-thin edge. Apparently, she lives below Max.

"The first thing I heard was the door—" I stop the clip, disturbed. Her tone's too haunted, body possessed by fear. I scroll down to the auto-generated transcript instead. "But I didn't know what it was . . . if something—furniture—fell over. If it was just the TV . . . A man started to shout, but he was muffled. Then everything went still." She tells the reporter that she wishes she'd called the police sooner, but she kept listening, waiting for something concrete—a real scream, a shout for help. A clear sign to get involved.

Marlowe, Caroline, and Emma are texting me. They saw the story about Max and are asking if I should get security. I've never had security—never needed it. Since my first book, I've had one stalker. He set up camp last fall on a bench across the street. For the next week, he stared at my window, reading a copy of *The Redfins*. He'd lift the paperback over his head, replacing his face with the cover; it shows a gorge through underwater mountains. The heroine's in the center, under tail-length red hair. She's an all-red S shape, hovering in blue. That week, I came and went through the side door. Then, as quietly as he arrived, he was gone.

Security? Maybe.

But now I need to get uptown.

I text my friends I'm okay, that I love them.

Someone knocks twice on my door. I freeze before turning at my desk, my body a degree cooler. Both front locks are secure. I watch them closely, as if one might drop to the floor. As if a crowbar might slip through the hole. *"The first thing I heard was the door."* Did the Nomen knock on Max's before they broke it down? I creep toward mine, staying off to one side. The silence deepens. It's the reason why I chose this apartment; I need peace to think. But right now, I want to hear everything in the hallway: every breath, every heartbeat.

I lower my gaze to the seam between the door and carpet.

The strip of light doesn't shift.

"Fiona?"

Pavel?

I check the peephole—it's him—and open the door. He's standing next to someone I've never met. The man wears a green hoodie with an airplane logo over the promise SAME-DAY DELIVERY. He digs into a messenger bag, his arm disappearing up to his elbow.

"Delivery for Fiona Hart."

"He showed it to me," Pavel interjects. "Just now, in the lobby. It's safe, perfectly safe . . ." He's palpably nervous as the courier removes a dark envelope. *Fiona* is printed in black, the font barely visible. No return address. Pavel says that he called me twice, but I didn't answer. I must've been packing. "And I should say I know Tim—" He gestures to the man beside him. He has long, pin-straight brown hair. "He's been coming to the building ten years. These guys are the real deal." Pavel wipes his brow. "Sorry, there's no protocol for this."

Tim extends the envelope.

I ask who it's from.

"I'm under orders to give this to you."

It's not an answer, but I get the sense that he doesn't know more. His tone is polite but pressed for time, as if he's at the start of a busy shift. I lean in and take a closer look. The envelope is the size of a greeting card. From here, it looks thin, almost empty.

I decide I'm not going to be afraid of mail. I'm going to make all the choices the Nomen think I won't. I'm going to be so *un*afraid that it's going to confuse them. Because they don't have me—not even close. I take the envelope. Tim removes a handheld device, asking for my signature. As soon as I sign, he steps back and tells me to take care. Pavel asks if I want him to stay. He's fidgeting, his voice invested. I tell him no thanks, I'll be okay.

He says he should get back to the desk.

In my apartment, I study the envelope. I pinch it a dozen times, seeing inside with my fingertips. It feels like a heavyweight card. I twist the envelope, watching it bend into S curves. Searching for a reason *not* to open it, but nothing comes.

Fiona

the PLEASURE of YOUR COMPANY
is REQUESTED

the THIRD of NOVEMBER
at eight in the evening

THE OAKWOOD
Manhattan, New York

dinner and conversation
black tie, please

I turn it over: blank.

I root around in the envelope: empty.

I study the front again. *Fiona.* If this were from the Nomen, I don't think they would've used my name. Even in their video, they never said any names out loud. As if some have spent too much time in the sun and now should be buried in the ground.

Also, the Nomen wouldn't do anything this . . . glamorous. They'd never flatter me with a personal invite—send me formal cardstock, refer to the "pleasure" of my company. They'd never ask me to step into black tie. That dress code is too elite, hand in hand with the galas and red carpet events that their group resents. Besides, if the Nomen wanted me somewhere, they'd take me by force—the same way they did with Myra, then Max. There's too much vengeance in their group for anything this polite. But if the card isn't from them . . .

Then who?

~

I bring the letter to Gwen and Logan's hotel room.

It took longer than I expected to get here. With traffic, it was a forty-minute drive. I spent it on my phone, combing through my four hundred unread texts, responding to everyone who'd reached out. I've spent most of my life talking to the same four friends, but this felt like everyone I'd ever met. A woman from high school thanked me for standing up for her after her ex had shared private photos. A woman from college said she always admired me for being resilient and inclusive. The messages helped, but a few felt a little close to eulogies. They smelled uncomfortably like death. At one point, I answered a call from Emma and asked if we could please talk about something normal.

Gwen shuts the door behind me and hugs me tight around the neck. Logan looks over from his seat by the window, his fingers between the slats in the blinds. Their rolling suitcases are still fully zipped. One's erect, the other sideways, handle extended.

Gwen returns to the bed, holding my hand.

"Did you get it?" she asks.

"Get what?"

"The invite."

I almost feel like there's someone else here. As if the Nomen I saw this morning is right behind the closet door, my gray hood over his eyes. I know that's not true, but my body seems to believe it, with tense hairs up my neck, a stiffness in my spine.

"Fay?" she asks.

I pull out my invite. "How did you know?"

Gwen drags one finger down her throat. She tells me that two others—Ella Kline, the designer, and Darren Star, the makeup influencer—texted her about it. They got the same dark envelopes with the same black text. "Then, right before you got here, our super called me. He said there was a courier outside with something just for me. I said I wouldn't be home for . . . a while. But the point is—whatever this is, it sounds like it's for everyone on the list."

"Maybe," I admit.

"You think it's from . . . ?"

She glances at Logan.

He's still perched by the window, twisted toward the blinds.

"The Nomen can take someone out of Madison Square Garden," he says. "They can break into an apartment and take a grown man, in the middle of New York." I remember Max's door, the splinters around his lock. "So I don't think they're the kind of group to send a letter. Why would they, when they can do so much worse?" His question is met with silence. "In my view, whoever sent these isn't involved with the Nomen. From the lack of return address—no signature of any kind—it looks like they're trying to hide too."

He asks if he can see the note.

I walk it over to him.

"Ella's and Darren's were like this." He examines the envelope. "No last names." He lifts it for Gwen to see. She barely nods, her chin floating up and down. "So I could be wrong, but it looks like whoever sent these wasn't just thinking of themselves. They were sensitive to your identities too." He removes the card and runs a thumb across it. He appears to read every word before handing it back to me. "Again, I could be wrong, but I think it's from someone else on the list." Gwen asks why they'd do this. "I don't know. But assuming this person is rational, acting in their best interest . . . maybe the dinner's a way for you to put your heads together, figure out how to respond."

I drop the envelope onto the sheets.

All three of us stare at the letter.

November third—the end of this week.

And the Oakwood—I've heard of it. From what I know, it's an old-time, and exclusive, Upper East Side club. I picture tufted leather sofas, grandfather clocks, and cigar smoke slipping under closed doors. I pull up its website on my phone. The home page requests a member log-on. Underneath, it lists the club dress code and house rules. I find a phone number for the club and call, telling Gwen and Logan what I'm doing as it rings.

No one answers. It's after six.

Maybe the front desk is managing the dinner rush.

Gwen leans back on the headboard. I sit next to her while Logan stays at the window. She rejects an incoming call. "Reporter," she explains. "Now that I'm a target, they want to know my hot take. You know, what's my sound bite now that we're on this list, being hunted one by one?" Her tone is grim. "Another one called before you got here. He asked what I thought about their 'mission,' if they had any 'good points.'" Gwen adds that she barely knew this man, that she only met him once at an opening-night party for one of her stores. "I know some people are rooting for the Nomen—they must be. But on that call, I felt like I was talking to one. I don't think he wants anyone to get hurt. But if we're roughed around a little, threatened . . . the reversal of fortune would be more than fair, given everything that we've had."

I hold her in a side hug.

Her heart beats into my forearm.

"How big do you think the group is?" she asks me.

"I don't know, but they must be getting help from the police." Logan nods in agreement. "There's no way they could've taken Myra without some of them involved—or at least, looking the other way." Last night, the arena would've had boosted security—police dogs, barricades, vehicle checks. The Nomen must have known what they were up against. Leading up to the concert, they must have worked with people who let them in on the security plan, emergency protocols, and evacuation routes. I ask Gwen if she's thought about security for herself. Until now, for big events, she's relied on the venue to safeguard the area. She looks at Logan as if security might be wise, and says she'll text around for a reference.

~

That night, Gwen pores over the news on her phone.

She's stayed put since I got here, scrolling with a nervous thumb. It's midnight already, but we're wide awake, making it feel like a dark noon. Logan's joined us in bed, sitting against the headboard on the other side of Gwen. But every so often, he'll drift over to the window, lift the blinds a narrow inch, and take a hard look through the gap.

I'm on my phone, digging for the Nomen's hub.

Gwen hasn't asked what I'm doing. I'm not sure what I'd say if she did. I know law enforcement must be looking for it too—vets with special intelligence and professional tools. Sophisticated teams, pooling every lead. But this feels like the most useful thing I can do. I can't just sit in this triple-locked room, feeling Gwen stiffen every time the elevators ding, every time a conversation gets louder in the hall. If this website exists, it could have the address of every safe house in the group—the full details of what's to come.

So I downloaded the Tor browser on my phone. Since then, I've been wading deeper into something known as the "Reddit of the Dark Web." This is where people share how to phish and make ketamine. Where they traffic stolen data. I just scrolled past someone known as the King of the Damned, selling Social Security numbers in bulk. I've found two chats so far about the Nomen. In the first, hackers analyzed their malware. In the second, fans praised the group for "fucking doing it, doing it for real." Every now and then, I have to give myself a break. Back on social media, I search for buzzwords: *Nomen, Myra, Max.*

Logan heads again for the window.

Gwen grabs my arm and tilts her screen toward me, the way she's been doing on and off all night. The video on her screen now is called

The Silenced Speak. The cover image shows three masked Nomen in a semicircle. From here, it looks like they're surrounding us. They're all sitting on stools, their six legs bent and dangling in predatorial arachnid shapes. Their shadows color the wall behind them—all slanted, distorted impressions.

"What is it?" Logan asks warily.

He strides back to us.

Major news outlets would never interview Nomen. They'd never give the group that kind of platform. If they did, it could be seen as obstruction of justice, or even support for terrorism. But this freelancer seems to think differently. Gwen clicks the link slowly—so slowly she still hasn't lifted her finger by the time the video begins.

It starts with silence.

The Nomen move just enough to distinguish themselves from a photograph—pumping chests, twitching fingers. I hear their white sneakers scrape against the rungs of their stools, a few muted swipes of friction. Logan gets back on the bed.

REPORTER: How did you get involved with the Nomen?

NOMEN-RIGHT: That's not the right question.

[Others nod.]

REPORTER: What's the right question?

NOMEN-RIGHT: What happened in the House?

[Others nod.]

REPORTER: What . . . happened in the House?

NOMEN-LEFT: We got ready.

NOMEN-CENTER: Sixteen concrete blocks.

NOMEN-RIGHT: Twenty bags of concrete mix.

NOMEN-CENTER: A shovel until you were numb.

REPORTER: Ready for what? What do you hope to achieve?

NOMEN-LEFT: We have a problem in this country. [Others nod.] The Famous Elite have become a ruling class. They have more control than they should—what we see, what we don't. What we think about. With power they pass on to their kids.

NOMEN-RIGHT: Fame is royalty.

NOMEN-LEFT: But this country wasn't built for monarchs. We fought the American Revolution against them. We fought taxation without representation—the same problem we have now. Because these elites are taxing our time. The American Revolution really is a perfect analogy. [Others nod.] Because the elites are taking over our lives. They're staging a mass invasion—on every channel, every screen. They're in our grocery stores, in the labels on our food. This has become an imminent danger. They are an immediate threat. The colonists were forced to take military action. This isn't what we wanted to do.

But people will have to get hurt.

REPORTER: The question was, what do you hope to achieve?

NOMEN-LEFT: A revolution.

[Others nod.]

REPORTER: What would you say to those who disagree with you?

NOMEN-LEFT: That you haven't seen the vision.

NOMEN-RIGHT: Haven't read it for yourself.

NOMEN-LEFT: It explains everything you need to know. When you read it, you understand that all the problems in your life can be traced back to fame. You have to read it. Have to see the white on black firsthand. Stare until you're . . . one of us.

The interview rolls on.

Every time a Nomen starts to speak, it takes me a second to trace the voice. With their mouths hidden and lips painted, the words could be coming from any of them. Gwen keeps hold of my hand. The Nomen's cohesion is palpable. They keep nodding, affirming each other, sitting the same way on their stools. At one point, they say a few words in unison: "*The famous are modern monarchs.*" This group didn't come together overnight. They didn't even come together in January.

Whatever they're doing—and whatever they have coming, if it involves concrete and a shovel or not—they've been at it for a long time.

Gwen replays the video before I can stop her.

We watch the Nomen again.

"What happened in the House?"

Did they live together? While they were . . . getting ready?

Maybe that brought them even closer. From how unified they seem in this video, I wouldn't be surprised if their routines have converged—if they get up within an hour of each other, if they're all eating the same food. Didn't the other Nomen say something about that? *"That house. That* fucking *house."* I picture an old warehouse or abandoned building, hollowed down to its bones—a row of buckets in the cellar, with cement crusting the rims. *"That* fucking *house."* He said some Nomen had been there too long. Now I see what he means.

I remember that Nomen on my sofa: his hand wringing, shifting weight. His visible fear of what he'd joined. I can only imagine what it would be like inside this group, hiding a secret urge to leave. After the replay, Gwen lets her phone slide out of her hand. I hug her with one arm as Logan gets under the sheets beside her. The three of us stare at the ceiling in funereal silence. I'm not sure which of us eventually turned out the lights.

But when I wake up a few hours later, it's dark.

SIX

The next morning, I call the Oakwood at nine.

This time, I get through to Events Director Margaret Clark.

She assures me that security will be their top priority this weekend.

She says that the club has hosted plenty of high-profile individuals and more than a few world leaders. Her team is well equipped to handle those with special protection needs. She promises there will be security guards at every entrance, plus discreet surveillance. Yes, the club will do bag checks. Yes, everyone on-site will be vetted.

I remind her that Nomen kidnapped Myra Mane during a live event in the Garden. They've proved they can breach top-tier defenses. She says that she understands my concern—and it sounds like she does, breaking from her formal tone with unexpected humanity. She says the club only agreed to host because they can guarantee safety. She points out that Myra's concert was publicized for a year in advance, while this dinner's been kept private—happening within a week of being booked. And unlike the Garden, the club is only truly known to a handful of staff and members. No, she can't share the name of the organizer; they've asked to remain anonymous. No, she doesn't know how many will attend, but the club's planning for about fifty.

After forty minutes on the phone, I relay everything to Gwen and Logan in their room. She's sitting balled up in the corner armchair, with yesterday's sweats tucked into yesterday's socks. Logan's standing next to the desk, with his shoulders raised, arms crossed. I tell them that the club took the threat seriously. They have good infrastructure in place to keep people safe. Then again, nowhere is perfectly secure—not even this hotel.

"Do you want to go?" Gwen asks.

"I don't know."

She nods. "We read more about the Oakwood while you were on the phone." She keeps one hand on her stomach, as if she might be sick. "At least, we did what we could. They're more private than we thought." Logan glances at the blinds, looking tempted to check outside. "Apparently, it's been a 'gentleman's club' since 1915. And from what we could tell, it still caters to the same dynasties it did back then. It only has a few hundred members, all old money. So Logan and I thought . . ." He soberly nods his agreement. "Believe it or not, we thought that might be a reason to trust them. This is a place that thrives on exclusivity. Sure, it wasn't built for artists, entertainers. This isn't a Hollywood hub. But for all they know, they're next."

"Maybe," I hedge.

Gwen rubs her stomach.

"What's the alternative?" I ask.

I look back and forth between them.

"If we skip it, then what should we do?"

I didn't mean it to be rhetorical, but no one answers.

I remember the Nomen, again, on my sofa—his eyes spooked, throat suctioned around his Adam's apple. He told me that I wasn't afraid enough. I'm not sure I like the idea of staying here, with no end in sight, just waiting to see what he meant.

~

The next day, Nomen kidnap Lane Driver.

I'm by the ice machine on our floor, refreshing the news on my phone, when the headline stuns me in place. I read the story—"Nomen kidnapped the actress Lane Driver at 12:34 p.m. today at Mirabel's Café in Brooklyn. She is the group's third hostage in two days . . ."—until I hear the rustle of falling ice. My knees are still locked. Saliva pools on my tongue. Of course I've heard of Lane. I picture her in detail: long chin, magnetic Southern charm, and a smiley way of being assertive. She's best known for playing strong heroines. Like everyone else on the list, she's popular, at the start of what looked like a meteoric rise.

I run back to Gwen and Logan's room.

They're mid-lunch when I swipe myself in.

Gwen is stirring crackers into tomato soup, sitting over a room service cart. Her appetite's been shot since we got here, and she's survived mostly off saltines. I step on a wrapper by accident, like a plastic mine. Logan puts his fork down next to a half-eaten Cobb salad. He's always been a health nut, often having big salads for dinner and avoiding almost all dessert except for anniversary crème brûlée. They watch me, waiting for bad news.

"Lane Driver," I announce.

We read the article separately, together.

Apparently, Lane was eating smoked salmon when five Nomen lifted her out of her chair and into a van. She was with her husband, one block from their apartment. We read every story we can find—then every social media post, sharing what we learn in snippets out loud. Lane is thirty-two, no kids. She was in a knee-length trench coat. She and her husband were on Mirabel's covered terrace, one of their regular spots, where they were seen holding hands.

Just yesterday, Lane was speaking out against the Nomen. She was posting on all her socials, saying she wasn't going to change her life: *Terrorists only win when you're terrified*, and *The Nomen prey on fear. I won't feed them.* She got #DontFeedtheNomen trending for a few hours, showcasing her defiance. Lane even went so far as to provoke the group: *They want to fight fame, so . . . they make everyone on their list more famous? They don't sound too smart to me*. People reacted to her with amazement and respect. No one else had dared to tease the Nomen. In the times that the subject has come up on late-night shows, it's been in earnest—mourning Myra and Max. Praying for everyone else on the list, as if we're already dead.

I put my phone down, digesting the news.

Gwen asks if we should stay here through the week.

Logan nods, and I see no reason to disagree. I make the call from their landline and book five more nights in our rooms. Once it's done, I face them, and the reality of the decision sets in. Logan bows his head. Gwen drowns red crackers in soup. Broth seeps into the hard edges, softening them with a barely audible fizz. She and Logan must be thinking it too: Hiding won't change anything. I don't feel any safer now that we've committed to stay. If anything, I feel more powerless, more trapped here. But maybe there is a way out, something we could do.

"How do you feel about the invite now?" I ask.

SEVEN

Fifteen hours until the dinner.

I'm scanning news in my hotel room, on the edge between night and morning.

I've been getting up early all week—half the time in Gwen and Logan's bed, where I always stay until she falls asleep. Otherwise, right here, where I keep the blinds open. It's helped me ward off claustrophobia, along with walking a daily mile in the hall—smelling the lemon-scented disinfectant, the ethanol deep in the rug. On my walks, I only stop to check the exits: peer up and down the stairwells, looking for white blurs.

I skim my phone.

No one's been taken since Lane.

But Gwen's been getting worse. She says that nothing's physically wrong—it's just the threat, the list. She promises that she's fine, then asks how I'm doing, if there's anything she can do for me. But she isn't the person I knew last week. Whenever she moves, it's with uncharacteristic slowness, as if her bones are heavier. She tucks herself into bed by the afternoon, falling asleep by eight. And no matter how rested she is, she seems distracted.

I scroll, looking for signs that the Nomen are growing, that the group isn't as niche as people say. The news still describes them as an "extremist subculture." But I want proof. I want to know the limits of their silent support. Last night, Gwen asked for a second time how big the group might get. I only shrugged, because the truth is alarming. They could recruit everyone who wants to reevaluate celebrities in society. Everyone with a frustrated passion, who might finally break out if Nomen move some people out of the way.

I check the ten biggest accounts on every social media, the way I have every morning this week. Their followings are unchanged. Then again, the numbers are so large—450 million, for one—that maybe it's impossible to see a tiny ebb. I find an announcement that an unknown actor just landed a major role in an upcoming series—but that's not unusual, is it? I keep reading, lingering over photos in other news: a well-attended NFL game, a selection of the best new restaurants. I search every pixel for a smile spray-painted in the background, for any white fabric flickering over the edge of a purse. Eventually, I drop my phone onto the sheets. Even without Nomen in the news, I sense them in the white space behind the text.

Present but unseen.

~

I find Gwen that night dressed and ready in their room.

She's in a coat and dark jeans. Her newsboy hat rides low, clipping her ears. Her lobes are bare for once, nothing but pinprick holes. I almost never see her without her usual row of studs, huggies, and crawlers—her signature inch of silver balls, X's, stars, and short feather climbers. Logan is next to her with one hand over his mouth. His watchband is missing its loop, the strap sticking toward me. I'm in a similar outfit to Gwen, with the cap from their place.

"Do they really expect black tie?"

Her tone is wary.

As if there might be consequences.

I shrug, more sympathetic to our limitations. We've done our best with what we packed in a rush last week. I tell Gwen that if our host turns us away for the wrong clothes, then they're not the ally we need.

Meanwhile, Logan watches her as if she's about to leave for much longer than a few hours. He looks neat despite the circumstances: miraculously clean shaven, his shirt tucked. But his eyes are caving in, bending under something heavy.

It's hard to believe, but just minutes ago, I was laughing. On FaceTime with Marlowe, Caroline, and Emma, Emma was in a nursing top, and the slit across her chest was so loose it revealed a full inch of her bra. She's still nursing her youngest, and until last week, she'd send us a steady stream of amusingly uncomfortable pumping selfies: during a rock concert, on an airplane. Tonight, her shirt just put us in a mood. I told them I'd call or text as soon as I got back. And walking here across the hall, I felt . . . not safe, but not doomed. Maybe it was because of my friends. Or maybe because the Nomen haven't been seen in five days.

Logan reaches for Gwen's hand.

It's the first time all week I feel like I'm intruding.

I say I'll give them a moment, but Gwen interrupts, pulling me into a three-person hug. Her forehead warms my shoulder, his chest. I've never known another couple more inclusive, letting other people stay so long in the safe place they create.

Gwen backs away first, shaking her head.

"We're coming right back!" she insists.

He brings her in again for a kiss.

They stay like that for a moment, his body curled around her, one palm eclipsing her cheek. She's standing on her tiptoes, fully at peace, as if he's the only place she's truly relaxed. When she pulls away, she's shaking her head. She repeats with more conviction that we're coming right back. She threads her arm through mine, and we head for the door. She's facing straight ahead, body stiff. She seems determined to go now, to stop drawing out the pain.

I take one last look behind us. Logan stands in place, his eyes pink, shirt slack. The door shuts, sealing off the wall between us. Gwen and I keep moving toward the elevator bank. I'm steady while she cries into my arm, suddenly thinking of Dad.

He had a hundred thousand strengths, and among them, he could stay calm in a crisis. When I was twelve, a kitchen fire ruined part of our house. Mom had been at the stove and left the room for just a second. By the time the fire department got there, smoke was pouring out of the open front door. I remember when Mom, Dad, and I were finally let back inside. Mom cried when she saw what was left, the counter that had turned to dark sand. But Dad was . . . steady. Stronger than the ovens that had started to melt, the bulging dishwasher warped by heat. Confronting the damage, smelling burnt grease, he was preternaturally serene.

We reach the elevators.

It will be good to get out of this hotel.

The eleventh floor has been physically safe but emotionally deadening—the blank walls, repeating identical doors. Besides, with the Nomen attacking our identities, staying in a place so deeply standardized was beginning to feel like we were losing the war. I've been wanting to get outside—hear something other than vented air and the regular whoosh of housekeeping carts—but I didn't like the idea of leaving Gwen for long. This morning, I caught her staring at the faded-brown rug, looking like the color was dripping out of her eyes.

We sink toward the lobby.

Gwen was hoping for security by now.

After a friend recommended Pinnacle Protection, Gwen contacted the agency at once. But it took them a few hours to respond. Then a half day to schedule an introductory call. Then a full day to send us profiles for seven potential bodyguards. Gwen chose thirty-eight-year-old Russell Jones with seven years of experience. Their interview is scheduled as a video call for tomorrow morning. If all goes well, there will be a contract to look through, followed by a week-long trial period. I'm in a similar situation, with an interview tomorrow afternoon.

The doors open to a full lobby.

A middle-aged crowd mills in business casual, as if they're here for a networking event. I take a split second to scan for white suits—for anyone with a suspect bulge under their jacket, anyone off by themselves. But no one seems to stand out.

Gwen and I head for the exit.

Our heels click against tile.

I try to vet everyone as we move, without being vetted in return.

Stepping onto the sidewalk, I feel the cold like an invisible wall. It's bright, even without the sun, thanks to the overwhelming number of windows—sky-high lines of deep honey and dark yellow. I hail a cab, hurry Gwen into the back, and climb in behind her. The driver watches us in the rearview mirror. His gaze is overtired, as if this isn't his first shift today.

Five feet apart, I feel unseen.

I give him an address on the Upper East Side—two blocks from the Oakwood, keeping that place to ourselves. I lean back as he accelerates. Gwen finds my hand on the seat and pumps it. Neither of us knows what to expect. We've talked about this dinner dozens of times, but never with much to add. We just rehashed the same logistics, our intention to go. She leans her head on my shoulder and double-crosses her legs.

I watch the city through her window.

Manhattan looks unchanged as we head up Madison Avenue, as office space gives way to designer flagships. The names are still in proud neon type or petite elegant script on awnings: Saint Laurent, Jimmy Choo, and Calvin Klein—all unmarred, just like they were last week. People are still shopping at a Marc Jacobs pop-up, walking out with bone-colored totes. Security guards doubling as doormen part the amber-tinted glass.

Gwen lifts her head and looks right at me. There's something on her mind. We stop at a red light, float forward and back. She keeps staring, her cheeks with an oily sheen after a week without washing her face. Light slips down her nose.

"We're pregnant," she admits.

I squeal, pulling her in for a hug.

She's laughing now, crying and laughing. She brings her knees to her chest. I hold her all balled up. When we pull apart, I look her up and down for anything new. But she looks like herself, maybe a little thinner after a week at the hotel. Every night, I've watched her stir a bowl of soup for dinner, then leave it unfinished, content to watch the broth spin.

"We just found out."

I ask her when, exactly when.

"I started to feel different in Korea, but I thought it was something I ate. Or maybe I was sick. I kept writing it off, until I realized I was late." She touches her stomach. "I tested in the airplane bathroom on my way back." I have to laugh. Only Gwen would test there. "The second one was positive too. I have no idea how far along we are. Six? Seven weeks?"

I tell her congratulations, ecstatic, shocked.

I knew Gwen wanted a family eventually. But when she talked about their future kids, they sounded far away. As if they were playing on the distant horizon. Is this why she's been so drained? Now that I think about it, she stopped drinking coffee too. All week, not one cup. And this afternoon, next to each other in bed, she fell asleep on my chest. Her ear was folded in half, hand pinned under her shoulder. She'd never taken a nap, not in her adult life.

"We just started trying. I thought it was supposed to take longer, be harder . . . Everyone I know has done IVF. Otherwise, it's taken months—years." She shakes her head, stunned. "I figured I'd tell you when something happened, but then . . ." Myra. Max. Lane. I glance at her stomach, her secret. "I don't know. Can you believe it?"

She gives me a devastated partial smile.

"When I told Logan, he was happy, of course. But there was this . . . veil over everything. Our baby's on their list." I picture the Nomen on my sofa, half his face looking waterlogged. His gaze cycloptic, fingers interlaced like pale spider legs. Describing how twisted his group really is. "I thought about telling you all week. I can't explain it. I've just been . . . terrified." She hugs her legs even tighter, her chin wedged between her knees.

"You're going to be a great mom."

Her lip shakes.

"I mean it, and I know everything about you, so I'm confident here." She swats the air as if I'm indulging her. "It's the truth. I *do* know everything about you." With everything that's at stake, I suddenly want to prove it. "I know you still have dreams of falling because of your years of gymnastics in middle school." She looks briefly amused. "You can't taste anything sour. You wear your wedding ring on your right hand because you're embarrassed by the birthmark on your left—even though you shouldn't be, because it's beautiful and interesting." She has a port-wine stain over the back of her left hand, a plum-colored archipelago.

And I know that while she can seem recklessly spontaneous—freewheeling from one project to the next—there's a hard thread of diligence running through everything she does. I know she can be too hard on herself, neglecting sleep, subsisting off airport yogurt parfaits. I'm one of very few people who knows that it comes from growing up in a house where her parents stopped loving each other, where there was always insidious tension. Gwen told me that when your childhood home is always on the verge of collapse, you don't learn how to relax.

"And no matter what's going on in your life, you always make space for other people. You show up for your friends, even people you don't like that much."

She dares to smirk. "I like everyone," she says before her eyes darken again. She leans into my chest, crying, "I just want to meet my baby."

"I will make sure you do."

~

I step out of the taxi onto Madison Avenue.

The closest streetlamp vibrates like a strobe.

I'm uneasy to see it blink, in case it's drawing attention.

"A great real estate agent is the bitchy friend you *love*," a passing woman says on a call. "They'll have the best, completely factual insult for every house you see. You know, *Needs a lot of work.* Or *It photographs better than it looks.*" She disappears into the crowd. The next few to pass are consumed by their phones or a one-handed search through their bag. As far as I can tell, there are no signs that we're unsafe. The sidewalk is full, streaming. No one is waiting here, backed up to a shop window, oddly quiet and still.

I help Gwen out of the taxi.

She lowers the brim of her hat.

Traffic continues to move. Across the street, a UPS truck is parked in front of a van that lists AIR CONDITIONING·HEAT·REFRIGERATION in a wraparound banner. A third van is parked behind that one, the name of a contractor across the door—three trucks in a row. That's not unusual, is it? All three are empty, a little unclean. I stare, alert for something truly strange—but there's nothing on the roof racks. No one in the dark windows. The strangest thing here might be me, frozen in place, while a current of people flows around us.

Gwen and I walk uptown. The Oakwood should be one block north, then one block to the right, tucked into a strip of brownstones. On our way, we pass stilettos behind yellow glass. Then a seminude ad for over-the-knee boots. Eventually, we leave Madison Avenue, passing a Michael Kors. It's open late for a special event—the ground floor packed, music faint. A young woman inside sees us from steps away. Her brow furrows as we slip out of sight.

The Oakwood is a few brownstones ahead.

The club has a dignified brick facade. Two flags flap overhead, tracing the shape of the wind. It looks like a diplomat's home or a small private school, somewhere the upper crust learns Latin and Greek. I check the windows for any hints of what's inside. All I see are parted curtains, dim lights. The only other person on this cross street is a man in uniform. He's pushing boxes on a hand truck, most of them stamped with Amazon's melting arrow.

Gwen and I pause outside the club.

I'm looking for a sign to leave.

Ivy grows out of the window boxes, lush but neat. The sedans parked out front are in good condition. Someone emerges from behind us, ambling toward Park Avenue. He's in workout sweats and sneakers, his ears plugged with AirPods. I face the entrance again: one door in a limestone mantel. Wrought ironwork on top, a lantern nestled in the spiraling arms. There's nothing that draws the eye, no reason to turn around.

I cross the threshold.

Gwen's right behind, holding my hand.

Inside, the first thing that I feel is a rise in temperature. A chandelier hangs from the low ceiling, its soft light on dark walls. Street noise is replaced by piano music. And just like that, we're transported. The foyer is dim and cloistered, making it feel like we're underground. As if there's nothing but packed dirt past the rich wood paneling.

A middle-aged woman greets us at the front desk.

"Good evening." She carries herself with sophisticated caution, tone hushed, gestures subtle. Her pearl studs look like halved white grapes. The security guard beside her asks if we've brought any bags with us tonight. Gwen and I shake our heads. We've only brought our phones—for the moment, in our pockets. I glance at Gwen. She looks tired, hesitant, and all I want right now is for her to be back in her apartment with Logan, choosing a name they love. They should be talking about the parents they want to be. The best place for the crib.

"This way, please."

Our host leads us forward.

Gwen and I follow her up a spiral staircase. The banister is satiny black and noticeably warm. I check the carpet for stains, anything fresh or suggestive. All I see is a line of nails securing it in place, their heads nearly buried. On the second floor, our host guides us into a sitting room. She knocks on a far corner, where one panel opens like a door.

Gwen and I move toward it.

Our host waits patiently.

We're on the edge of a banquet hall, where two long tables are set for dozens each. Centerpiece bouquets are dense with black roses, dark ivy, and something like purple lettuce. Tall candles fill the space between them, each a crimson foot of wax. Gwen and I step inside, eye level with a row of old portraits in golden frames. Toward the back of the room, a small group stands in black tie, talking quietly. Shadows pool under their eyes. I hear the door shut behind us, and our host disappears. The room is even dimmer now, a dusty yellow.

Gwen and I move forward. I can't hear a word that the group ahead of us is saying, just the low buzz of their voices. Their gowns are dark—plum, black, and navy blue, the colors of a bruise. Their clothes add to the Gothic feel of the room.

The door opens again.

It's Blake, thinner than usual.

Blake got his start in the singing and dance group BRT, which rose to fame on social media. The group was bright-eyed and precisely coordinated—except for Blake, who grew more withdrawn. He became a wounded rebel, radiating sadness and *fuck you* at once. He left BRT last year to release his first solo album, which catapulted him to the mainstream. Tonight, his black hair is bob length with an unwashed sheen. Tattoos color his neck, a pair of wings over his Adam's apple.

It's strange to see him in the dress code—a tux and formal loafers—even though he went to the Grammy's this year in skinny jeans, then showed up to the Met Gala in the exact same outfit. Dressing down already showed some indifference. Repeating the outfit took it to another level. Now here he is, on time, following the rules.

The actress Molly Newcastle follows in a red gown. She walks with Blake to the end of the room, nervously meeting our eyes. She's a few years older than I am, petite with muscular arms. I've never met her, either, but in the interview clips I've seen, she was infectiously upbeat. Now she's somber, spooked. Her hair's tamed in a low bun, but the swirl's off-center, a few strands already loose. She must've done that herself, unwilling to trust anyone else's pins. She's followed by a broad man in a black oxford, dark pants. He's bald, with a thick neck and wide nose bridge—private security. He stays within arm's reach, surveying the room.

The stream of people gets thicker.

Tay Riley, the edgy personality behind the new podcast *Bad Friend*, enters paler than I've ever seen her. She's deep in conversation with Margot Kelly, the regal Bond girl in a new release. Ryan Marks follows next. I haven't seen him since ThrillerFest a few years ago. Back then, he was promoting *The Void*, his sci-fi novel about an astronaut who falls into a black hole. It only just aired on Netflix this year, for the first time, thrusting his work into the spotlight. He looks the same: square-frame glasses, round face. Tonight, he's in a silver vest and bolo tie. I remember he lives in rural Colorado, in a sagebrush desert.

That's a long trip just for dinner.

People keep coming. I recognize almost everyone, even if I can't summon their name: That painter. Broadway star. NFL player. Plus, two more who must be bodyguards. Both men are physically imposing, alert without being tense. Gwen stays at my side. On the surface, she must seem calm to everyone else. But I know that she's only this quiet when she's fighting something. She leans harder into me, her hand firm on my arm. I wish that I had more to give her, that there was some way I could make all this easier for her.

"You're doing great," I say.

"I'm just standing here."

"You have a gift for it."

She laughs, her first all week. I hug her with my free arm.

Three notes chime. They sound like taps on a xylophone, rallying an audience after intermission. The noise unifies attention. Small groups turn inside out, as if they're looking for the one holding the mallet. Some people start to move toward the tables. More and more join until footsteps are louder than conversations. The notes chime again. People are circling both tables now, like a shifting figure eight, checking place cards.

Gwen and I enter the fray, shuffling with everyone else. People take their seats. Gwen finds her card first, next to Blake, but part of me doesn't want to leave. I know she can take care of herself. Still, my instinct is to stay—even though it's unreasonable, overbearing. In two or three hours, we'll be back in her and Logan's room, rehashing every detail. Then I'll ask her when she's going to see a doctor—because she is going to see one, isn't she? I don't know how this works, but isn't there a blood test she could take? Advice a doctor could give?

"Love you, Winnie."

"You, too, Fay."

We hug, and I step back.

I'm not leaving her for long.

I drift around the table, reading place cards.

When I glance back at Gwen, she's in her chair, her chin propped on one hand. Her wedding band is a continuous curve. She's reserved as she introduces herself to Blake, then reaches across the table to meet someone else. More and more people sit down. There's a growing pressure to find my place, to avoid distinguishing myself as the last one on their feet. I creep faster, no longer reading the cards, now just looking for an open chair until I spot two.

Cole. Fiona.

I stop in front of them.

The director Sean Ridley sits across the table. He has unkempt, wispy black hair. It softens his receding hairline and continues around his jaw, one dark, circuitous inch. He nods serenely at me, his eyelids drooping with middle age. With his reputation, I would've expected him to carry himself with more tension, intensity. Sean is famously severe, known for imposing method acting on set. He once locked his lead in her trailer for hours just to make her terror real. But here he is now, one elbow crooked on the back of his chair.

I am the last one standing.

Cole's nowhere in sight.

I sit, checking briefly on Gwen. She's listening to Blake, nodding. He reaches forward to grab something small—and for the first time, I see trays between the centerpieces. Each is filled with rolls, gougères in paper cones like bready scoops of ice cream, and tiny pancakes finished with sour cream. They'd all but disappeared into the dark.

"You wrote *The Redfins*," Sean says.

He points a butter knife at me.

"Guilty," I confirm.

I glance at Cole's chair.

"You really expect him?" Sean asks.

Cole Harper, who writes mind-bending horror, is reclusive.

Sean has adapted a few of his novels. But apparently, they've never met, and there have been simmering disagreements. Things escalated this year when Sean released *Controlled Burn* with a different ending than the book's. Cole broke his silence on social media to condemn it. He wrote that, ending aside, the actors looked like they'd been coerced. Then he deleted the message. The spat went viral, drawing major attention to the release—and book.

Almost overnight, they were mainstream.

I read *Controlled Burn* before it was a hit. It follows ecology professor Sly Jones, who's so frustrated by the tedium of his life that he wants to recast it. Finally, he decides to do it: kill everyone one by one. The book opens with his lecture on controlled burning, a way to revitalize forests. He gives this talk in a pilling sweater and comb-over. A few students talk over him, laughing. The story then follows his transformation. Sly's targets become more shocking until his final conquest: you. He becomes aware he's being watched—being *read*—and aims outward. He draws up a master plan to cross into the real world and hunt you down.

Sitting near Sean and Cole makes the room feel even darker. I generally like what they do, but tonight, I'd prefer a lighter side of the table. I glance at Gwen, who's facing Tay Riley, known for her no-holds-barred way of talking about sex, dating. Tay captivates a small group, gesticulating with energy. Gwen's just touching her stomach.

A door opens at the back of the room.

Waiters enter in a line with two plates each.

They're in black dinner jackets and white gloves.

Conversations lull as the waiters serve duck over melting purple onions. Black pepper darkens a swoop of mashed potatoes. Meanwhile, the three bodyguards stay put, spread out along the wall—right in front of the paintings, hands quiet, eyes sharp. Conversations return only once the waiters step back, once they start to file out through the back door.

People dig in, separating meat from bone.

Margot Kelly asks Sean about *Controlled Burn.* I miss his answer, the noise picking up. Sean asks about Margot's latest project. No, the production schedule hasn't changed, and she's flying back to Chicago first thing tomorrow. She must know someone with a plane. I doubt anyone here would walk through an airport right now, with the risk, the confinement. I take my first bite, one slick onion. Who's going to bring up the Nomen? *"It turned some of us into . . . devils."* Maybe I should do it. Maybe I have a duty to tell people how twisted the group really is. Like a demon that gnaws its own fingers, chews its own tail.

Behind me, there's a polite chime.

People twist in their chairs.

I turn to see Cole by the far wall, tapping a fork against a wineglass. Cole Harper, for once, in the flesh. For someone with a public career, he's kept a low profile—refusing most interviews, even around new releases. His fans have mythologized his absence, fallen for the allure of the unknown. Then again, he's in his late thirties and has ten books out, all of them five-hundred-page juggernauts. I figured he just worked all the time.

Cole's on the edge of the candlelight.

I adjust in my seat for a better look.

From here, he's the striking image of his author photo. A side part cuts through his short curls. A few dark spirals fall on his forehead—thick, cottony. He's taller than I thought, over six feet, with broad shoulders, long hands. He has an athletic build and stands with a physical sense of readiness—surprising for someone with such a mental job. Narrow-set eyes, a strong nose. Handsome, with enough imperfections to be relatable. But having read his work and seen the infernal loops in his mind, something about him isn't attractive.

He lowers his glass, holding the stem.

"Thank you for making the trip," he says, "and for everything you risked to be here. The fact that everyone came tells you how limited our choices are." He projects to the corners of the room. A few people continue to eat—I hear the forks tap, knives slide—but most give Cole undivided attention. "This isn't just about our safety. I don't think it's an overstatement to say this is about the future of our country—if we erase the people who stand out. So I brought us together because we're all facing the same question. Instead of thinking about it separately, maybe we can think about it together. The question is: What should we do?"

I picture the Nomen from my living room. I can see him with perfect clarity, as if he's at the next table, sitting in his red-splattered crew neck between two people in black tie. Long-limbed and insectoid, elbows on the table. Staring with one squeezed eye.

"Hi." I get on my feet in the middle of the room. Every face turns toward me. I thank Cole for putting this together. "Before we answer your question, though, there's something everyone should know." I admit I saw two Nomen fighting in the street the day after they took Myra. People stare at me, blinking, radiating collective tension. I don't mention I took one of the Nomen home. I don't feel like the room would be sympathetic to his injuries, to how close my apartment was. "One of them told me there's a vicious culture in the group. They present themselves as . . . moral criminals. But really, these people are brutal, and some of them just want blood. It sounded like being part of the Nomen changed them, and now fame is an excuse for what's next."

"What *is* next?" someone shouts.

"I don't know. But he said they built something. Apparently, he helped 'hammer the nails.'" A few people sit too perfectly still. Their shadows are long and fixed, like fence posts across the wall. "I'm not trying to scare anyone. I just wanted to warn people that the Nomen won't be open to reason. And whatever's coming, they've been planning it for a long time." I find Gwen's eyes as I sit. She nods, assuring me I did the right thing.

A chair shuffles.

At the end of her table, Ryan Marks makes an effort to stand. He pushes his chair back another inch, making room for his girth. He turns this way, adjusting his glasses. "Thanks, Fiona. I'm sorry you came so close to them." He sounds haunted on my behalf. "But your story's only strengthened my belief. To me, the answer is simple: We need to disappear. I'm not saying we should stop working, but we should step back, give people what they're asking for—"

"Not *everyone* wants us gone!" someone shouts.

"Well, who has the momentum?" Ryan asks. "Sure, there's been outrage, mourning . . ." I nod, having seen the photos: fans across the country have been holding vigils for the taken. In those shots, they stand with their arms linked, candles lit. Other fans have been sharing online tributes. Others have rallied outside news organizations, ensuring this remains the highest-profile case. "Sure, some people are moved. But the truth is, most aren't involved.

"The vast majority have read the news and haven't done a thing. They haven't stepped out of their routines. Which makes it look like the Nomen are tapping into something. Doesn't it? They've struck a chord. So no matter how many put on a mask"—he dots two eyes in the air, draws a smile—"who knows how many are rooting for them?"

Dust motes shift in the candlelight.

It's devastating but true.

"If we disappear by *choice*, people will understand what they're allowing." He coughs through a sudden rasp. He reaches for water and takes a medicinal gulp. "Sorry," he adds, flummoxed. "But some time in the dark isn't the worst thing. For me, it's always been part of making something new. If the Nomen want us gone—and if most people are letting them wage this . . . war—then this is an opportunity. Eventually, people will realize that they *do* want professional creatives. They *do* want powerful artists." A few people lower their gaze—a news anchor, a reality TV star—and I sense their dissent. Their careers rely on being seen.

"I disagree," Margot says, rising. She stands with a poise that only comes from acting school or a lifetime of performing. "I'm sorry, but the *buzz* is part of what we make. People don't just want to read *The Void*"—Ryan sits—"they want to be part of a cultural moment: read reviews, discuss the ending. There's no art without some kind of fame, some buzz. We can't hide from the world and make things, because without an audience, there's nothing."

Someone claps twice.

"I agree," Sean says, standing as Margot sits. On his other side, the painter Devon Ferrell stirs her mashed potatoes with a fork. Earlier this year, I read about her new show at the Museum of Modern Art. She seemed fearless, visionary, obsessed. Now she lets her wrist droop as she stirs, looking mildly ill. "Stepping back would be giving up. If we only make what's popular when it's easy, we're not making anything worthwhile." A few slap the table in accord. "This was never about giving people what they asked for."

"What *was* it about?" someone shouts.

"Personally? It was about making what *I* believed in. And getting to this point . . . It's worth defending. Because it's cost almost all that I have." He picks up his wine and takes a long sip of red. "It's always been hard to make something great, not just because of what you put *in*, but because of what comes *back*." His mustache is a black scowl that supersedes his upper lip. "There have always been critics, censors, fascists. The Nomen are new, but to me, nothing's changed. And if you quit now, you never had what it takes."

Sean takes his seat.

"I agree with you, Sean." I trace the voice to the other table, where the rising country music star Jo Belle stands. "Besides, if you're like me, you never chose what you do anyway. You were always just *doing* it—" I have a flashback to being nine years old, sketching flowers that don't grow, mapping cities that don't exist, complete with contour lines. "No matter the costs and no matter the risks. I don't think we can change."

I sense a fervor building, a single mind with one conclusion.

The designer Ella Kline stands with grace, as if she's aware of every link in her spine. She says that obeying the Nomen would be "weak." The actor Tony Graham climbs next on his chair—hair floppy, shirt unbuttoned—to echo Sean. He says his business has always been a "fight," repeating the word several times. "I wrestled for everything I got, and I'm not the only one. Every one of you paid a price for your intensely personal career. You had to. Because you can't make your name your business—your taste your business—unless you fight for it."

Applause breaks out in pockets.

Almost everyone now is digging into their food.

I slide my knife across the duck. The meat gives way like murky water. I start to eat, enjoying the gamy salt and the syrupy purple reduction that covers the meat, the onions—everything. Speeches get louder, competing with the sounds of clinking metal. Devon's red lipstick looks slick with the glaze, as if she just stood up from licking a bowl of berries.

"I agree with you in *spirit*," Ryan says, his voice squeaking as he stands again. "But if we disappear, people will see that's not what they want. They don't actually want to erase us. My point is—" The conversation splinters, no longer centralized.

The spreading noise drowns him out.

Ryan shakes his head and sits back down.

Cole leaves the wall, headed this way. He takes his seat quietly. Up close, he smells like leather. Without a word, he cuts a thick cube of duck. Juices drip down the meat as if the animal continues to bleed.

I catch moments in a few different conversations. Someone says that the problem isn't celebrities; it's the media that fuels the obsession. The Nomen should go after tabloids, gossip accounts—the decision-makers there. The system, itself. Someone farther down the line looks uneasy. He says this was his first day all week outside.

Sean greets Cole. "It's nice to meet you."

"Is it?" Cole asks.

"I couldn't help but notice you didn't answer your own question." Sean studies Cole, darkly amused. I sense their shared work building up to this first encounter. "Care to join the discussion? You might enjoy being part of something you started, for once."

"I'm eating." Cole cuts another bite.

"Convenient."

Cole stays steady, calm.

Gloss collects on the blade of his knife.

"Shouldn't you be butchering one of my books?" Cole asks.

"If you don't like what I do, why do you keep licensing them to me?"

"Because you overpay."

"Stop it," I cut in. "Both of you."

Cole turns to me.

"What about you, Fiona?" he asks. "What do you think we should do?"

Across the table, Sean waves Margot closer and whispers something, gesturing with a limp wrist. Everyone else has been drawn into another conversation, leaving Cole and me in a private moment. He waits for my answer, finger on the neck of his fork.

Cole has a square face, full lips. This close, I notice uneven peaks in his Cupid's bow, making the pink look smeared. He cuts another bite of duck, and a dark tattoo peeks out from under his sleeve. He's still looking straight at me, his eyebrows thick with plenty of hair under the brow line. They're patient, awaiting my response.

"Honestly, I think all of this"—I gesture down the table—"could've happened over doughnuts and a box of coffee."

"You don't like duck?"

"Not tonight."

He lifts another bite.

"We're up against a group we don't understand," I say. "They've built something . . . Something that took gallons of white paint and ten boxes of roofing nails." I recall the chilling detail from the interview I saw with Gwen. "And the way they speak . . . They'll suddenly interject with something cryptic and wild, like, 'Do you really want your life to be a TV dinner?' Or 'It will make you seasick. It will make you mutiny.' It's like they have their own language—like they've been living together for years and have their own . . . logic. And so far, they've been able to defy the odds, make good on their word to hunt us down.

"Doesn't that deserve more . . . sobriety?"

I gesture to the wineglasses.

"Of course it does. But if we're going to be targets, I figured we might as well have a decent meal." He swallows a large bite, visibly hungry. I can sense his body craving the meat. "These days, we never know which one is going to be our last, right?"

I put my silverware down.

"Sorry, it's hard to joke about . . ."

"You're right," he admits, more solemn. "But clearly, I take this seriously. I brought everyone together. Forgive me if I didn't want to serve cat food from inside a bunker. I didn't think that would fill seats." The dark humor feels inappropriate. "Not to mention, I wanted the invite to look purely social—to hide what we're doing in case it fell into the wrong hands." He whittles duck off the bone, the meat splintering. "The theater, if you will"—he waves his knife around the room—"doesn't change the question at hand. Which remains: What should we do?"

I'm glad that Cole asked the question, but maybe he isn't the best person to answer it. I understand he wants tonight to look more like a party than a meeting. That might be shrewd counterintelligence. Still, recommending black tie suggests a lack of reverence for the attacks. Maybe his job has made him too familiar with the malign.

I remember discovering his books in college.

In a bookstore downtown, one was on a high shelf, almost out of reach: *The Unfinished Ritual.* It follows a grudge between two families, passed down for centuries. The story unfolds in the present, but the medieval origins of their dispute seep into the atmosphere of the novel. In the end, as one character tries to escape a maze, the text changes. The sentences no longer read left to right. They become a maze themselves. Some of his fans claim they're still stuck in that book, unable to finish. They're still submerged in Dark Age details, unable to find their way out.

"You don't strike me as someone who scares easily." Cole leans back, his shirt buttons a dark dotted line down his torso. "Maybe you think we should counterattack, that we should write books and make movies about the Nomen. If they realized they were famous, too, that might short-circuit their system." He shrugs. "Personally, I don't need to fight back. I wouldn't mind disappearing for a while, stacking pages in a closet. It sounds nice."

"It's easy for a recluse to disappear."

"I hope not." He takes a sip of wine. "That will be the last thing a Nomen says to me."

"Would you mind not joking about . . . ?"

"Right."

He holds up his palms in surrender.

"How *do* you stay out of the public eye?"

Even since he broke out more broadly this year, he's shunned nearly all media. People know everything about Cole, the author, and almost nothing about Cole, the man—only that he's from Chicago. He's made offhand remarks about the winters there in interviews published at the end of his books. Snowdrifts used to barricade his front door, burying him inside. Otherwise, his private life is a mystery, a murky shadow around his work. The lack of detail had all but turned him into an idea, but here he is in the flesh—long eyelashes, strong chin.

"I get my groceries delivered." His tone is dry. "But you must be something of a recluse yourself, judging by your books." He looks at me, his dark eyes flecked with candlelight. "I believe *The Redfins* is seven-hundred pages? The sequel too?"

"I still go on morning shows."

"Yes, but I've read your books. A series like that only comes from a spectacular amount of time alone." I don't like the idea that we have much in common. He's too morbid, unsettling, and . . . wrong. Cole is only seen in his backflap photo. That is, unless you count the symbol some of his mega-fans use. They brand themselves with a red handprint, slid down to leave a fading trail. I've seen the sign cropping up on social media ever since Cole was put on the list—presumably, from those same fans, posting their unshaken support.

I look down our table.

Someone frowns.

"Do you really think we're all going to agree on something?" I ask.

"Not at all," Cole says. "But this is better than the alternative."

"What's the alternative?"

"Exactly." He takes another bite.

"Sorry about that," Sean intervenes.

He and Margot face us again, offering their full attention.

He reminds me that they missed my answer. I'm about to repeat it when the back door swings open. Waiters return in a crisp line to clear plates. I turn to check on Gwen. One of her sleeves has fallen sideways, in a shallow hammock across her arm. A man steps between us, lifting my dish. I smile at him, but he avoids my eyes.

Was that . . . on purpose?

I glance around the room.

None of the waiters are looking at any of us.

They watch the dishes and each other, their expressions wooden. I can't tell if this is professional distance or something else. Are they . . . going to an extreme to give us privacy? Or is this how the Oakwood expects them to behave? I don't know. I never eat in places like this. Gwen and I prefer street-cart chicken and rice, noodle houses, and taco bars—cheap, casual sodium bombs near our apartments. But if any of the waiters were Nomen, they would've done something to us by now. We've been sitting here distracted for over an hour.

"Are you with us?" Sean asks.

"Of course. Sorry, I just . . ."

Waiters file out the back.

"Yes?" Sean asks, vexed.

"I don't think we should negotiate with terrorists."

"Do *nothing*?" Margot gawks.

No, I meant that we should find Myra, Max, and Lane ourselves. We have the freedom and platform to make a difference. Instead of getting grandiose—thinking about social change—we should help the ones who need us now. I've spent much of this week combing through the dark web, looking for their site. Trying against the odds to find it before things get even worse. I should explain, but now I'm focused on the back of the room, on the black hole filling the open door. Waiters disappear one by one, straight into the ink.

"If we were meeting in January, after their New Year's surprise, I might've agreed with you," Cole says. "But now, they're coming to get us. We're on a modern 'Wanted' poster. That deserves a response—a public one—doesn't it? I'm just not sure what it should be. Should we release a statement? Should we start a countermovement?"

"*Start* a movement," Sean scoffs.

"You mean propaganda?" Margot asks.

"I mean what we've always done. We're all here tonight because we've stumbled on the formula for a contagious idea. For what kick-starts word of mouth. If anyone's going to write an anti-Manifesto—one that will catch—it's someone in this room."

Waiters reappear, carrying slices of devil's food cake. Dozens of twentysomethings walk in a line. They look a little thin, now that I'm paying attention. A little wide-eyed, wired.

Do these people work for the club?

A man with a buzz cut presents my plate. He smells like nervous sweat, a trace of fruit-flavored gum. We're inches apart, but he won't meet my gaze. He removes his arm and strides out of the room, scratching the back of his neck. He's raking one hand over his spine, attacking the spot with short strokes. I turn to my dessert. The dark wedge is under a decadent slash of white chocolate sauce. Everyone else is picking up spoons, severing soft corners.

"Unimpressed?" Cole asks.

I lean toward him.

"Have you noticed—"

The back door swings open.

Waiters return—this time in bone-white masks. They mummify every head, the fabric tracing their skulls. A thin black smile haunts every chin, the ends curling up to their ears. Across the chest, every Nomen carries a semiautomatic rifle. It's hard to see the guns against their jackets in the wavering candlelight. I can just make out silencers on the ends of the barrels.

My cheeks run cold.

Screams break out, shrill, quick.

A few Nomen race to the bodyguards, guns drawn.

The bodyguards are outnumbered, surrounded. Two raise their hands. The third backs up even closer to the wall. The rest of the Nomen walk to the front door, then turn to us. The person in the middle steps forward, facing both tables, with a casual grip on his gun.

EIGHT

"Good evening." The Nomen's voice is morbidly amused, every word spiked with a wicked sense of fun. He taps his gun's silencer on his palm, waltzing in one direction, while the line of men behind him is still. "We regret to inform you dinner has been cut short."

Tony Graham stands at the end of the room and bolts toward the sealed entrance. He's a blur until one Nomen opens fire on him. Tony twitches in place, reacting to the bullets so many times that it looks like he's being electrocuted. People bend over their knees in the fetal position. A few crawl under the tables, tipping chairs. Screams break out on all sides—non-reverberating sounds, as if the walls are wrapped in acoustic foam.

Tony hits the floor.

The shots stop.

"Would anyone else like some individual attention?" the ringleader taunts. He looks from one side of the room to the other with devastating slowness. I can almost feel his stare dragging across us. "That's something you like, isn't it?"

I'm barely breathing.

I look for Gwen, but she's gone. Blake is still in his chair, doubled over at the waist. His back is rounded so severely he looks headless. Tay is hunching, too, her fingers clawed on the back of her neck. It takes a moment to spot Gwen's hand on the table between them. She's gripping the edge, only visible up to her knuckles. I see her fear in that tight inch.

I watch her as if I could hold her with enough attention, tell her that it's going to be okay. I picture her on the balls of her feet, with her chin on her knees—and one hand on her stomach.

Nearby, a woman starts to cry. The Nomen aren't going to like that. *Wonderful, a new request for attention.* It's too easy to picture how he might respond. Still, she continues to sob. The sound is high pitched, ragged. I'm one of the few still sitting up. I bow my head to blend in, watching the Nomen. Some of their suits don't fit quite right: pants grazing the floor, sleeves bunched at the wrists. It makes them seem even younger, like preteens who don't grasp the power of what's in their hands, the carnage they could start with a flinch. A few of them bounce their knees, the fabric rippling in the shadows, as if they're getting excited.

The ringleader nears our group.

Another Nomen closes in, faster. He reaches the first table and picks something up. Then again. One more time—phones. He's collecting any left in the open. I sense mine in my pocket. The idea to make an emergency call crosses my mind, but it feels worse than risky—suicidal. They would see me move. The collector reaches inside one man's jacket, slapping his cheeks before plumbing the inner pockets. He removes a slim phone, then slips between tables, his stash growing. A second Nomen on the same mission approaches from the other direction.

Whoever's crying must've just closed her mouth. Her noises are muted, disappearing. I imagine her biting her cheeks, sucking her own wet flesh to save her life. The two collectors are crossing in front of me when one of them stops short. My pulse floods my ears. From just a foot away, he stares at my pants. He must see the bulge. There's no choice. He reaches for the phone as I pull it out, hand it over. My fingers brush his glove.

"No one wants to speak up?" the ringleader asks.

He turns between the tables.

Getting close.

"But you love to talk." He has a wider neck and shoulders than the other Nomen, a T shape thickened by muscle. He's smoother on his feet, too, moving with sinister patience. I wonder if I've seen him before—in the alley. He has the same frame, the same sadistic flair. "You have so many opinions, don't you? So many *valuable* opinions. You've been sharing them for as long as I can remember. Isn't it impressive how smart you are? You see everything so clearly. It's a good thing you've been talking over us. You saved us from our ignorance."

He's so close now I hear him breathe. I see Gwen's fingers in my periphery, the pale mound on her table, and all I can think is she needs to survive. She needs to meet her baby—hold them, tell them their name. Does she know how much I love her? We've told each other a thousand times, but does she know how deep it goes? She is family I found.

As he passes, I blink nonstop.

When my eyes close, I see my parents.

It's just for a moment, like a masterpiece on a grain of sand.

Mom and Dad are waist-deep in the ocean in Rhode Island. They're ten steps ahead, with their chests toward me, hands reaching this way. Waves hiss as they recede. Kids scream-laugh, splashing toward whitecaps. Memory or not, I don't know. I've pored over photos from our summer trips so many times I can't tell the memories from the dreams. Right now, I move toward my parents, smelling seaweed on the jetty, sunscreen.

The ringleader passes me.

His steps come to a stop. I dare to look over, and see him next to Tay, picking up her spoon with a playful wrist. Gwen is frozen. Tay stares straight ahead, eyes wide with terror. Tiny spasms undo her lips. The Nomen wiggles the spoon over her plate. I picture him gouging her eyes out, and feel an overwhelming urge to stand. My knees twitch. My chair creaks. But he only lifts a bite of cake to her mouth. The chocolate mass jiggles on the utensil.

I watch as if I can protect her from here.

The Nomen puts the food on her tongue.

Her teeth chatter on the pewter, canines rattling the neck of the spoon. Tay swallows the whole bite in one gulp, as if she's desperate to clear her airway. The Nomen drops the spoon, letting it clatter. A white bead of sauce drips down her chin.

"If you don't want to get hurt, then obey me." The ringleader returns to his group, in a line behind him. The collectors hunch on one end, dumping phones into a bag. "I understand this may be your first time following orders. But think of it this way: After dragging us through *your* imaginations, it's time you walked through ours. That's fair, isn't it? And if you disagree, well . . . Tony could use some company. He looks lonesome on the floor."

He waves the Nomen ahead.

They surround us in a giant oval.

I imagine the teen I saved in every suit—ungroomed, amped. The one who warned me that this group corrupted and deranged. Some break off to snake between tables, passing just an arm's length away. I feel the air moving behind them, until everyone comes to a stop. The nearest is so close I see the three buttons on his cuff. Each stares back at me with two dead eyes. The ringleader lets us know they came bearing gifts, his courtesy filled with venom. As the Nomen reach into their pockets, I glance at Gwen. She's still gripping the table, on the floor.

The Nomen remove white masks.

The man in front of me shoves two forward. Each is folded in half, teasing part of the smile. I take one. The fabric feels like a blend of canvas and elastic, almost coarse but easily stretched. People are sitting up, putting theirs on. I open mine. A stiff crease divides the face in two. The wrinkle is hard as bone, as if these masks have been folded for months, lying in wait for their debut. Cole slips into his, pulling it all the way down to his collar. When he turns to face me, I don't recognize him. Black sockets replace his eyes.

I don't want to stall. The Nomen might see any pause as a rebellion, proof of my inability to listen. I duck under mine. The eyes are mesh, stiffer than the rest of the mask. But I see more than I expected. The Nomen in front of me tosses more masks to those who are still bare-faced. As he flings them across the table, a couple unfold and flutter like doves. He takes another step forward. His cummerbund is uncomfortably close.

His gun is within reach.

Could I grab it?

It's the same color as his suit, but I make out the edges. I picture myself reaching out, grasping the handle. His grip is probably loose, his focus somewhere else. The Nomen steps back too soon. I wonder if that was my last chance to save our lives.

"Stand up," their leader commands.

Chairs screech.

I stand with everyone else.

Gwen's mask rises above the table. She's facing the nearest Nomen, with her back to me. I want to sprint, wedge myself between her and them. I feel my whole body lean that way—one protective inch—but I need a better plan if I'm going to help.

"In one straight line, walk to the back."

We obey.

"Good, very good." His tone becomes lighthearted. "I see that we're off to a wonderful start. Left, right. Left, right." He mocks our pace with exaggerated steps. "But I'm afraid it won't be this easy for long. *Does that scare you?*" The question rushes out of him with a vengeance before he breaks into a laugh. "When the night starts to get unpleasant, I have a tip: Remember that you don't matter. How freeing is that? You *don't* matter." Anger tears through the middle of his sentence, disappearing by the final word. "Your experience isn't special. You, ladies and gentlemen, are bug food. Terminal pieces of cosmic trash."

One by one, we step forward.

I've never tried harder to walk, to land each foot heel-toe without stepping out of line. The leader continues to taunt us, his tone taking drastic turns. He's mild, then giddy, then spitting in a rage. Each time, he recovers quickly, reverting back to a state of smooth authority. I can't tell if he's in control or the most unsound of them all.

"Would you look at these exquisite pieces of art?" I force myself to glance left and right. In this mask, the paintings look muddy. "Starting now, you're no longer the artists. You're *inside* the frames. We're here to arrange you—every part, down to your teeth."

The overhead lights go off.

Behind us, Nomen blow out candles.

When the line stops, I realize it a second too late and find myself an inch from Cole's back. The ringleader orders everyone to put their hands on the person in front of them. I grab Cole, eye level with his shoulders. Someone touches my own, their fingers grazing my neck. I stiffen but don't turn to see whose. The march resumes. We're coming to the limit of what we can see, the ragged boundary where candlelight ends and pitch black begins.

People disappear over it one by one.

"I have news," the ringleader says, near the front of the line. "You just left your names in that room. Margot Kelly, Jack Payne. Sleep well in eternal peace. May you only know quiet now." Someone trips, then regains their footing. "I know you might think your name is part of who you are. But you were born without one. Don't you remember?" He lets out a maniacal laugh. "Do you know what that means? You're *nameless*." Again, anger flares. He seethes for one quick word. "You're no one and nobody, just like the rest of us. Well, that's not entirely true," he interrupts himself. "Starting now, you're who we tell you to be.

"I know you've been lied to. Your whole lives, you've been told that you're rare. You've been told that you're the voice of a generation, that you speak for millions who can't speak for themselves." I picture the eighteen-year-old Layla Wainwright, who's here tonight. That's what people have called her. She broke out last year when one of her videos went viral on social media. In it, she sat alone at a piano, belting her heart out. People said she didn't sing, she *channeled*. Hers was *the collective voice* with *the weight of shared experiences*. She went on to sing at the presidential inauguration. "I'm sorry to say none of that was true. You don't speak for us, not anymore. Now you can't even speak for yourselves."

I step through a door.

The way forward is dark.

But ten feet ahead, blue light streams in through an arched window. It brightens a slant on the floor. Everyone stays in the shadows, trudging invisibly past it. I sense the fear keeping them in line, stiff as guardrails. But . . . isn't that our best chance? The window frames an alley, sheer brick on the other side. Traffic is audible from here, the friction of multiple cars in a row. I could make a run for it, launch myself through the glass. We're on the second floor. It wouldn't be far to fall. If I sprint with everything I have, I could be on the curb before Nomen react.

But then . . .

What about Gwen?

She's already passed the window.

I'm torn, running out of time. My nerves drip down my palm. I just don't know if I'd be more useful *here* or out in the world, where I could do something. Maybe that's the answer I don't want to hear: Out there, I could do something. The light shifts toward me. My eyes feel like they're steaming, as if I've already made the decision. Of course I don't want to leave Gwen. I don't want her to face this alone. But I can't help if I'm a prisoner too.

Three feet away now.

I'm tempted to say *goodbye* out loud.

I want to tell her *I'm coming back* so she doesn't think I abandoned her—but of course, she'd never think that. Cole turns to the window—he's going for it too. I bolt on reflex, and now the two of us are sprinting between scattered Nomen. I barely see Cole, just hear him grunting, his shoes slapping the floor. My forearms fly up to protect my face. I throw my body sideways against the glass, holding my breath as if it's my last taste of air.

The crack is earsplitting. I'm passing through the frame with my chin low, eyes closed. For a moment, I'm suspended, my knees tucked into my chest. Then the air starts to rush. I feel it race up my bare arms, over the back of my neck. Gunshots break out above.

I land on something soft—trash bags.

They look oily under the moon.

Next to me, Cole makes an effort to get on his hands and knees. I watch him teeter on all fours, then grope his way forward. He makes crucial progress over the sinking, uneven bags. But I'm still in shock. It takes me a second to realize I can move. I can breathe. Finally, I roll onto my stomach, and we scramble out of the dumpster. I'm pushing as fast as I can, but it feels like a sprint underwater, like there's too much weight on every bone.

We fall onto the pavement.

I get up and stagger forward, swaying left and right.

I yank my mask off and drop it in the alley. My ears are still ringing with breaking glass, the spray of bullets. Cole drops his mask, too, and I pass over it. The mouth ripples like a scar that's been stapled too close together, bunching up in folds.

We round a corner onto Madison Avenue.

Cole's a couple of steps ahead, raising his hand. I stumble toward him as the yellow blur of a taxi pulls up to us. He puts me in first, then sits. I'm just coherent enough to distrust the driver. Anyone could be a Nomen, even if they're not in a mask. He turns to face us, looking stunned. His mouth opens in the shape of an ink splotch, one dark irregular splat.

"Dountowun," I say.

"Fife . . . Tudor . . . Place," Cole says at the same time.

My lips feel numb.

Cole repeats the address.

The driver whips around and accelerates.

I don't recognize the destination, but we can't waste time arguing. The traffic signals are all on our side, lighting a green path straight ahead. I ask Cole for his phone. Did he bring one? If he did, I didn't see the Nomen take it. Cole pats the front of his jacket. He slaps the lapel twice—fumbling, slow—before finally, the collision is firm.

He removes his phone and hands it to me, rubbing his eyes. Something's wrong—his face. It's starting to . . . smear. I blink. He resets. Then comes the creep. His eyes drift over his shoulder. His mouth gets wider than a dinner plate. And it's not just him—everywhere, colors ooze. The green slips out of an awning, spilling over the next few stores we pass. A streetlamp becomes a long, twinkling line. When I blink, the world becomes crisp again.

Then it starts to bleed.

There must've been something in the food.

I squeeze Cole's phone until it offers to make an emergency call. After a couple of tries, I manage to slide *yes*. The driver keeps checking his rearview mirror, maybe in case we're being followed, in case whoever did this to us isn't done.

"What's your emergency?"

"Ki-napd . . . Nomer . . ."

My words are indistinct.

"Where?" the responder asks.

"Oakwood . . . Clum," Cole tries.

His words are just as muddy.

"Who was kidnapped at the Oakwood?" the responder asks.

"Gwen . . . Scordon."

"Who?"

"Gwen . . . Scordon."

Cole and I list everyone we can remember. The names sound splattered and shaky, but the responder stays on the line. Finally, she informs us that she's dispatched a team to the Oakwood. When she asks who she's speaking with, the phone slips out of my hand.

All stores on this block are dark except for a furniture shop, where hundreds of light fixtures beam. It's a glut of chandeliers, floor lamps. It's the one dazzling thing in sight, and it's dead empty, bedrooms abandoned in perfect condition. We head farther east, watching the city drip. Skyscrapers give way to shorter buildings. There are more residential spaces here, built up over dry cleaners and grocery stores, the retail engine driving the city below.

Cole leans against me.

The next turn pushes me into him.

I look down to see he has three hands. Fifteen fingers spread over his thighs. When I blink, five disappear. They return slowly, growing like roots out of his wrist, across his pants. I keep blinking, snipping them back, until we come to a stop.

NINE

The blue awning beside us reads *Five Tudor Place*. I keep blinking to keep everything solid, the colors in their lines. I shake Cole awake.

He looks around, confused.

"Heanow," I say.

Cole reaches for his pocket, misses.

I do it for him and find his wallet. It's filled with cash, but no cards, nothing with his name. He must be more afraid than I thought. I remove two bills, unable to read them. The driver raises his hands in protest, as if he doesn't want our money, as if our doom might be contagious. Still, I slide the bills under the partition, and we scramble outside.

The driver speeds off, wheels screaming.

Cole stands in place, hinging forward at the waist. The East River runs beside him, deep and silent, as if it's absorbing sound. I loop one of his arms around my shoulders and help him shuffle into the glow of Five Tudor Place. Now I see what was hidden in the dark: The window carved him down the middle. His left side is a slick red. His curls are in tacky clumps, one eye painted shut. Half his suit has been scissored, shredded, the cuts razing all the way through his skin. Some are inches long, others the length of a fingernail.

A doorman hurries toward us under the awning. He's a pale smudge under a green cap, reaching for Cole. After two slanted steps together, he insists on carrying Cole alone. I feel myself nod and let go. He offers me an arm, but I refuse. He's already straining under Cole—I won't be why he buckles. We cross into a Gothic lobby, where a bouquet with black ivy colors the center of the room. I veer over to the wall and press it for support. The doorman tells Cole he's going to get us upstairs, then call Cole's doctor. Cole grunts with approval.

They turn a corner.

I follow, my palm bobbing along the wall.

Electric lanterns beam at eye level. One starts to melt, the glass and iron dripping to the floor. The bulb leaves a molten trail. I rub my eyes and stagger past a leather bench. I find my face in the mirror above it and see a version of Cole's: half wounded, half clean. But my cuts are shallower, grazing. He must've hit the glass first.

The doorman guides Cole into the elevator, then presses the PH button. I slur that I'll take it from here. When the doorman looks at me, his eyes roll down his cheeks. He stays put, apparently torn. I beg him to please, *please* call the doctor. Cole needs help now. The doorman backtracks, frantic. He swears he'll get the doctor on the line.

Doors seal us inside.

Cole leans against the wall, with his red side to me. I can't tell whether the blood is running—if the seep is real or only exists in my mind. Once the doors open, I offer him my arm. He grabs me on his second try. Together, we step into a foyer. On the wall in front of us, there's a painting even taller than he is. It dissolves into rain, soaking the wall, dripping onto the floor. I blink, but blinking doesn't help anymore. My world is colorful slush.

Cole's knees give out, and he's too heavy.

I lower him to the rug, going with him.

My eyes shut on their own. I remember our masks in the alley, fingerprints in the taxi. Blood dotted across the lobby, leading all the way here. Are we safe? I'm fading—losing touch with where we are, mind sinking into the dark—until a mechanical ding. I manage to flutter my eyes. It almost looks like the elevator's opened and someone else has arrived.

TEN

I wake up in an unfamiliar bed, dazed. The bedposts are tall and dark, with Gothic finials. I keep staring, woozily fascinated, every muscle limp. There's a painting on the wall straight ahead. It's the brightest thing in this room, shades of gold in a beige frame.

I blink, mouth dry.

Sit up against the headboard.

A stinging pain emanates down the right side of my body. There's a deeper throb on my right hip, a burn across one knee. I need to figure out where I am and what is going on. The painting looks like a rendition of Rumpelstiltskin, now that I think about it, a small boy almost entombed in hay. There are curtains to my right, heavy, drawn. Candelabras line the walls, giving the room a dim glow. I listen hard, hearing nothing but my pulse.

"You don't like duck?"

Now I remember sitting next to Cole. He was pinching the stem of his wineglass, waiting for my answer. His shirt and jacket were the same shade of black. Was that last night? It comes back in flashes. One Nomen stood two feet away, gun level with my nose. He handed me a mask and flung more across the table. Other Nomen joined him, scattering masks like bird food. *"Left, right."* My world became that voice—that chameleon voice, changing keys and personalities. When Cole and I finally jumped in a taxi, the world was dripping.

Two sharp knocks on the door.

A clean-cut man enters the room, with a stethoscope around the collar of his shirt. He introduces himself as Dr. Mason and asks how I'm feeling.

"Where's Cole?" My voice is small.

"Down the hall, but let's talk about you." He looks late thirties but has the energy of a younger man, as if he's between classes in medical school. He says he gave me four stitches for an inch-long laceration in my right shoulder, then four more on my right knee. There are minor cuts and bruises up the right side of my body. They should heal on their own. Meanwhile, I touch my shoulder and feel the row of tiny knots. He adds that I ingested a powerful sedative. At the dosage he found in my blood, he wouldn't be surprised if it caused hallucinations.

"How's Cole?" I interrupt.

"You're not that concerned with yourself, are you?"

He looks intrigued, and without warning, I remember being in high school. The small duffel that I carried for weeks after my parents passed: taxicab yellow with a black shoulder strap. Back then, the bag was always packed with clothes and toiletries, so I was ready to stay at a different friend's house that night. I still have it in my closet, the inside colored with swishes of toothpaste. Dr. Mason watches me, his question in the air. I don't know anything about this man. But if he's ever lost home in a similar way, maybe he understands: Sometimes all you have are the people around you. When you lose it all, you take care of who's left.

I ignore his question about me.

And prompt him about Cole.

"I found him with a two-inch piece of glass in his chest," Dr. Mason relents, with a professional efficiency. "He could've bled out, but it was lodged in tight. I gave him nine stitches." He draws a line under his collarbone. "Like you, he slept through the whole thing—not peacefully, though. I think he was dreaming of being in pain. He kept talking about 'rotator,' his 'rotator' . . . Probably his bruised rotator cuff. He woke up twenty minutes ago."

"What time is it?"

"Noon. Do you have other pain I should know about?"

I shake my head without thinking. I don't want to get stuck in an endless loop of pain management—not while I still haven't seen Cole. Not while there's still so much to remember. Then figure out what I'm going to do. I keep all the pins and needles, all the aching throbs, to myself. Dr. Mason nods and tells me in that case, he'll be on his way.

He shuts the door on his way out.

I step slowly out of bed. Dr. Mason never said where we are, but this must be Cole's home. It just . . . feels like him. His ideas are on the wall—he wrote *They Come at Night* a few years ago, starring a cast of fairy-tale villains. Rumpelstiltskin was among them, along with the Mad Hatter and the wolf from "Little Red Riding Hood." I remember the all-black cover, the title only on the spine. The image of the Mad Hatter throughout the story, with leaves in his hair and dirt on his suit. Mushrooms in his pockets and a coy half smile.

I should get out of here, find Cole.

The bedroom opens to a dim sitting area with shadowy furniture. I call Cole's name, weaving through chairs, passing bookshelves along the wall. I try to ignore my sore ankles, the twinge under one arch. I find a hallway and call his name one more time.

"Here." His voice is distant, from the left.

I follow the sound, past another painting. It looks like a scrap out of "Little Red Riding Hood." Cole must live in his ideas—Gwen. I stop short, remembering her in a mask. Under the fabric, her high ponytail warped the shape of her head, elongating her crown. She might be waking up now, too, her fuzziness metabolized, the world in crisp detail. Six or seven weeks pregnant. Surrounded by armed men. *"After dragging us through your imaginations, it's time you walked through ours."* The prospect had their leader gleeful, practically spitting into his mask.

Gwen. *Gwen.* What would a sedative that strong do to an embryo the size of a seed? And what have the Nomen done since then? Who knows what torture they might be drawn to, what pent-up urges they might have? The thought of someone hurting her sends a defensive pulse through my body. I pick up my pace, eyes starting to sting.

I push the door open.

Cole's in bed with one black eye almost ballooned shut. A bruise colors his jaw. This room has the same cloistered feel as the rest of his apartment, with books stuffing every wall. He looks at me without getting up, leaning against stacked pillows.

"I need to go," I think out loud.

He asks me what's going on.

"I'm sorry—I have to find them."

"Alone?"

I hold my ground.

"Mason did say you'd make a quick recovery."

I'd already forgotten about the doctor, feeling pulled in ten directions—remembering the back of Gwen's covered head. People screaming when the shots broke out. Terror turned them into skulls, the skin tight over their bones, teeth exposed.

I thank Cole for the doctor's help—being quick but authentic—and pivot in the doorway. But as much as I want to go *do* something, it feels wrong to strand him here, with his eyelids squeezed together, the ink across his jaw. I turn back and ask if he needs anything. Cole flips his phone over beside him, where it disappears into black sheets.

"First, before you run off in a blind sprint, you might be interested to know that there's no sign of them. The story's on every front page, but so far we only know they were taken. At this point, I think the best-case scenario is that they're being held as bargaining chips. Otherwise, the Nomen don't have a reason to treat them well."

Every second feels important.

But I can't leave him here.

"Would you help me?" I ask.

He doesn't react.

"Help me find them?"

"Even if I *did* agree to that, it would start with a few mundane tasks, including coffee." Cole presses up on his palms, grimacing. "And I know this won't make me the most popular person in the room, but let me remind you: There are professionals out there, with every known tool, whose sole focus is to find that group. You and I are not among them." He slides his legs off the bed and stands in a black robe cinched at the waist. I follow him into the hall.

"You don't want to *try* and help them?" I ask.

No answer.

"But you *invited* them."

"Yes, and before you demonize me, let me remind you that you and I are only really good at one strange, specific thing, and it's not rescuing people from violent fanatics." He glances back at me, fully present in his unharmed eye. "I understand where you're coming from, Fiona. I really do. This is pure evil. But I am curious: Why do you want *us* to find them, instead of, say, talking to the police and letting them do their jobs?"

"The police are *involved*."

He's skeptical.

I walk after him, padding over hardwood floors.

"I mean, not *all*. But the Nomen couldn't have taken Myra without *some*." I remind him that in the Garden, the Nomen were up against perimeter control, encrypted radios. Special units in the stands, trained in counterterrorism. Then the Nomen went after Max and Lane in the middle of the day. Then forty-seven of us at once. "You don't take those odds unless you have help. If we reach out to the police, we risk talking to the same people who let this happen. I don't know if they were bribed or if they're . . . believers. But I don't want to find out." I follow Cole into a kitchen with black marble counters. "This isn't a conspiracy theory."

"It's not." He's unconvinced.

"Of course most of the police are fair. They wouldn't go near this group. But it's the few who've been . . . turned. *They* are the ones who worry me. Besides"—I try a new angle—"even if we got through to the good ones—if we only worked with them—they'd still be looking for some of the most privileged people on earth. If you don't *know* them, maybe the crime won't dig at your soul, make you want to work late and miss time with your family."

"You might have a point."

"Which is why I—*we* have to do something."

Cole opens a cabinet. He's reaching for a mug when he stops midair and drops his arm. He presses one fist into the marble, lips in a tight line, sucked in as if pain is a flavor. I grab the mug for him and leave it on the counter. Without a word, Cole moves it under a coffee machine and presses a button. As the brew drips, he keeps his gaze low.

"My best friend was in that room," I say.

"I'm sorry."

"I won't leave Gwen alone with them."

"Let me see if I understand this," he enunciates. "You've spent your career on *The Redfins*, about a band of Natare—your version of mermaids—who set out against the one trying to enslave them. The consensus is that not since Tolkien's Middle-earth has anyone crafted a more intricate world, so complete it feels discovered, not invented." He reminds me there are multiple invented languages in the series. Two are logographic, with a unique character for every word. One has its own alphabet, almost nothing in common with the Latin. I wait impatiently for his point. "All I mean is that we each have our expertise. I'm not saying you couldn't track everyone down or contribute to the effort in a meaningful way. But this conversation deserves more humility. People's lives are at stake, including yours." He offers the coffee to me. When I reject the mug, he takes it back for himself. "It's not often I'm the more realistic one in any situation."

I turn around.

"Fiona—" he says.

I don't stop.

"Fiona, please."

He manages to get in front of me.

"I'm sorry." His tone is fully sincere, face grave. It's a sharp break from the irony that was just spiking his words. He saw everything that I did last night, and right now it's in his eyes—unblinking, solemn. I set my jaw, once again unable to leave.

He walks back to the refrigerator.

I turn and watch him open the door.

"I would like to help, Fiona, but I won't throw myself at a problem before I know what I'm dealing with." He removes a papaya and places it on a cutting board. "That includes them, and, candidly, you. I've read your books, but I need to know you better than that if I'm really going to trust you. Especially if we're going to talk seriously about . . . outmatching the Nomen. Regardless of what you might think, I only like to hurt imaginary people."

"You have no choice but to trust me: We're the only two targets left. And the group we're up against?" My eyebrows soar. "The only thing that unites them is a belief, which means anyone could support the Nomen—even your doorman, even Dr. Mason. Anyone except *me*, because my life's on the line too." I take an overdue breath. "Not to mention, I'm already inside your apartment. We made the choice to trust each other when we jumped in the same taxi."

He pulls a chef's knife out of the block.

Rests it on the fruit.

"You trust me with your life?" he asks. I watch the blade on the papaya, gliding past the skin. The edge is so sharp it cuts with gravity alone. "Exactly. Just because we're both targets doesn't mean you trust me, and it doesn't mean I trust you. If anything, it means we should probably spend some time apart. You know, make it more difficult for them to whack us both at once." The knife hits the cutting board. "Now I'm going to make breakfast. Please don't hate me for it. If you'd like, I can show you to a computer, and you can read everything the world knows about where they are. Then we can figure out if there's something we can do."

I give him a terse nod.

He leaves the knife, and I follow him into the hall. The doors on either side of us are shut. I ask Cole if anyone could find us here. He says that he keeps all his property under an LLC. Nothing's in his name. Soon, he gestures into a dim library.

I step inside to find the room lined floor to ceiling with books. They're all shades of gray, purple. But there's something about them—on them. Cole flicks on the lights. The books are carved with . . . words. Someone's knifed the covers, hacked across them without curves, just angles. I'm stunned in place, momentarily rigid, before this starts to look familiar. It's the way the pages peek through the carvings, the letters warp on the spines.

Now I remember his book.

Amazer follows Aaron Roth and his growing obsession with crosswords. Eventually, the physical book reflects his mental breakdown. Pages devolve into typos, white space. Aaron ends up locking himself in a library just like this, surrounded by books he scribbled to shreds, solving puzzles no one else saw. In the final pages, Cole's novel is splintering too—the paper fringed, as if Aaron had reached through and butchered it himself. That story haunted me for a while. I'd never seen one just fray in my hands, cross into my physical world.

I move toward the desk in the corner. Most of the words around me are only visible in fragments, but every now and then, I see one in full. *Acidic. Attic.* Did Cole carve these himself? I stand by the desk, fingers on the laptop. *Ultra. Exquisite.* The cuts go deep. I imagine the force it would take to knife through all that plastic, cardboard. And now I don't feel fully at ease, standing here inside a horror novel. I turn to Cole to see if he's going to explain the room. He only tells me the password is "Aaron," eyeing the computer on his way out.

Mass Kidnapping by Nomen: At Least 40 Confirmed Missing

BY ALEX TEAL AND MICHAEL GOSS
Updated 12:03 PM EST

NEW YORK (AP) — At least 40 of the Nomen's targets were kidnapped last night out of the Oakwood, an Upper East Side social club, in an attack claimed by the Nomen.

Authorities were alerted to the incident by a 9-1-1 call at 10:04 p.m. Almost unintelligible, the call begged for immediate assistance to the Oakwood.

First responders were dispatched at once but delayed by a crash involving two utility vans and a truck. The pileup blocked all traffic at 62nd and Madison Avenue, where the team had planned to access the club. The drivers involved fled the scene. Others abandoned their vehicles in the gridlock for up to an hour until the wreckage was cleared.

First responders arrived to find the targets already gone.

Three of the targets' bodyguards were recovered on-site, bound with white zip ties.

Nomen took responsibility for the attack with hundreds of loose flyers found this morning on the Upper East Side, most between Park and Fifth Avenue.

“Something hit my leg as I walked into our store,” manager Rachel Kempner of the 61st Street Hermès said today. “I was there early and looked up to see the whole block covered in white papers. In the wind, they looked like ghosts.”

“People kept walking through the flyers—sure, it’s New York,” Loews Regency employee Carl Lancaster said. “But to be honest, I thought more people would’ve stopped. We all knew what the flyers were. But people just kept passing them, stepping on them. It was cold. Man, it was cold. I saw a thousand people like that all in a row. Maybe I’m no better. I just watched. But . . . it was something.”

The flyers read:

THIS IS THE BEGINNING OF TRUE DEMOCRACY.

*NO ONE CLASS SHOULD HAVE A MONOPOLY ON **MUSIC**.*
*NO ONE CLASS SHOULD HAVE A MONOPOLY ON **TV**.*
*NO ONE CLASS SHOULD HAVE A MONOPOLY ON **FILM**.*
*NO ONE CLASS SHOULD HAVE A MONOPOLY ON **FASHION**.*
*NO ONE CLASS SHOULD HAVE A MONOPOLY ON **SPORTS**.*
*NO ONE CLASS SHOULD HAVE A MONOPOLY ON **ANY AND ALL ENTERTAINMENT**.*
THE FAMOUS ARE MISSING.

An investigation is underway by the New York Police Department, led by Chief of Police Randall Hersh. On his way to the scene this morning, Hersh was asked if any sympathies for the Nomen might affect the department's work.

"Of course not," Hersh said.

62nd Street between Park and Madison Avenue has been cordoned off as part of the crime scene. There is increased police presence in the area.

1,023 Comments *add comment*

Pam Roberts
God bless the taken and their families.

Harry Kipster
Lifelong cop here. No mention of the FBI above, but trust me, the Bureau is involved too. This case is too high-profile. Too many victims, too many jurisdictions.
The powers that be probably want to protect the search. The FBI has their own units, their own tech. Never smart to tip off the ones who did this with what we're doing in response. But take my word for it, this isn't just the NYPD.
Everyone's on this. Everyone.

ANONYMUST
THE FAMOUS ARE MISSING. THIS IS JUSTICE.

Cat Bird
This has gone too far.
God bring them home safe

ANONYMUST
GOD IS NEXT. #NOMORESTARS

GradZillaaa
The Nomen have never targeted God or any spiritual leader. They want to democratize arts & entertainment, mainly, to break up the entertainment monarchy

ANONYMUST
WRONG. THEY CALL FOR AN END TO ***ALL*** FAME, A SHIFT TO LOCAL ART, SPORTS, ***EVERYTHING*** AND IT'S TIME.
IT'S TIME WE ALL STOPPED WORSHIPPING.

Ry Anderson
So what happens when the Nomen become famous?
Are we supposed to kill them off too?

ShelbyGDesign
That's what I've been saying. They're doing what they claim to be fighting.
They're in the spotlight, making their mark.
Taking over everyone's feed.

TXYallStar
No, the Nomen don't have names. They are anti name power.
So, they can't become famous.

Jake Thomas
Don't be naive. It's only a matter of time before they show their faces. They're not creating a new world. They're just promoting themselves.

Paul McBride
List of missing people includes Cole Harper.
Who's going to scare us now?

Narci
You'd king him just for a book?

Paul McBride
Ever heard of the Bible? The Bhagavad Gita?
We've been doing this forever

AJorgensen
Millions of self-published books come out every year. Chances are there's something better than Harper in there. That's the whole point of the Nomen. Yes, they're sick. They're going about this in the worst possible way. But they do have a point: no one person is talented enough to dominate an industry.

Irene Kelly
Looks like you've never read Cole Harper
And clearly, you haven't thought this through. Some people are more talented than others. That's

life. I'm okay rewarding people who make things I love. I'm NOT okay with art terrorism.

Kipper007
Cole's been missing for years

Clay Langdon
I want art without idolatry

ItsMargie
When you love, you have no choice.

PraiseHimDaily
It is a dangerous fetishism to think something other than God can bring us peace.

Sara Knight
Artistic apocalypse

ELEVEN

"I thought you might want some water," Cole says, walking into the library. He sets the glass down by the laptop, where the comments are bright.

"Anything?"

He leans toward the screen.

I show him the answer, scrolling through reactions. There's horror. Shock. Grief for the missing. Some debate theories for how the Nomen pulled it off—whether another cyberattack was involved, whether the Oakwood has subterranean routes. And then a few posts are . . . jubilant. They could've been written by Nomen themselves, with typos, over-punctuation. As if the commenters were typing with gloves on, straining to see through their masks. Eventually, I flick the trackpad up with my fingers. It sends the window into free fall.

"No answers," I say, frustrated.

"None?"

"Then again, those wouldn't be here."

Cole puzzles. His lashes are intact around his wounded eye—long, almost feminine. I explain the rumor I read on Reddit, about the Nomen keeping a central hub on the dark web. Cole leans back from the screen. The V-neck of his robe has widened, revealing a swath of his chest tattoo. It looks like an overgrown forest: vines on knotted branches, murk. I find the tattoo again on his wrist and see it now as the leafy edge. Eventually, Cole invites me to join him for breakfast. He says he knows that food isn't my chief concern, but eating something might help. He suggests we could finish the conversation we started in the kitchen.

Reluctant, I follow him across the hall.

We cross into a dining room, where dark chairs circle a black table. Cole sits before a bowl of cubed papaya, with an identical bowl beside it. I take my seat, and this close to fresh food, I wonder if Gwen's eaten since last night. She never ate breakfast, but she ate breakfast *foods* all day—ripping the ends off croissants that went stiff with neglect on her desk. Biting into muffins with the paper lining still on the bottom. And when she was on a health kick, opting for smoothies she'd stir more than she'd drink. She'd just swish the straw around the bottom, swirling the pink. Staring at my bowl, I have the impossible urge to give it to her.

Cole takes a bite.

"So, I was thinking about this issue of trust." *Just because we're both targets doesn't mean you trust me, and it doesn't mean I trust you.* "Obviously, most people have more time, where they can let trust evolve on its own—or not. But time is one thing we don't have if we really do . . . try to find them." He sounds cautiously open to the idea. He's looking straight at me now, his right eye a clear deep brown. "If you're right that we can't depend on the police—if there are one or two Nomen where it counts—then really, we *have* to do something ourselves. It's not just about who's missing. It's about . . . self-preservation."

I don't deny it.

"Which brings me back to my initial idea." Cole digs for another bite, wedging his spoon into a glossy seam. "I think we should make an effort to trust each other—before we talk about anything else. Because if we work together and run into something like last night, we'll need to have faith in each other's support. It will have to be instant, unquestioned. Hesitations could be nails in the coffin." Meanwhile, I stir my papaya like solidified soup. The idea of *trying* to trust each other—when people need us now—sounds like a waste of time.

"How do you know I don't trust you?" I ask.

"You look at me like I'm the devil."

"I don't think you're the devil."

"That's promising."

I put my spoon down. "If you think we should . . . nurture a connection . . ." He doesn't offer a better phrase. "Fine. If that's what it takes to make a plan."

Cole doesn't fill the pause that follows.

He eats toward the bottom of his bowl, blinking often. This close, his finer injuries creep forward. A red spiderweb crawls up one side, from his collarbone to his hairline. A honeycomb patch carves up his temple. The cuts are subtle, sweeping. That many looks as gruesome as a deeper gash. He really did take the brunt of the fall for the both of us.

"Tell me about Gwen," he says.

"She's my . . ."

My voice cracks.

"How did you meet?" he asks.

"She opened a store near me downtown." I hug myself. "I just happened to walk inside. Gwen was there in a pair of her shoes. The first thing she said was, 'My feet are killing me.'" I smile, even though it hurts to remember. "She started talking about how much she wanted to get home. She'd had a crazy week and told me all about it." Back then, she was planning her first international store in London. She'd just come back from scouting locations. On her way, she stopped in Italy to check on a factory, taking all twenty people who worked there out to dinner until three in the morning. When she got back to New York, she'd invited her design team over for Thanksgiving, so she spent a full day cooking their vegetarian entrées. As a Brit, she doesn't even celebrate, but for some reason, she felt compelled to host, make it a party.

"I couldn't stop laughing. She was nonstop. Unselfconscious. One hundred percent relatable without being relatable at all. When she asked about me, she'd just been so open that I found myself completely uncensored. I talked to her like I'd always known her. She invited me to her housewarming party the next week. I was so carried away, I said yes.

"More?" I ask.

Cole nods. "If you wouldn't mind."

"So, I went to the party," I go on, fidgeting. "When I showed up, it was packed. I didn't think I'd stay long. Then I ran into her, eating takeout sushi she'd brought to her own party. She waved me over with chopsticks. It was just so . . . warm. She made other people look like they were holding back, if that makes sense. She was what happened when you let yourself spill out. So we stuck together the whole night." We played a game where we each gave the other a ridiculous phrase to work into our next conversation. She gave me *wakey wakey*. I gave her *quesadilla day*.

"I ended up staying longer than I should've. It was almost rude how long I stayed. I helped her clean. But we weren't just having fun. It was more than that. She had depth. We started talking about . . . Never mind." I feel some resistance to sharing our private conversation. Cole looks even more intrigued at the hint that I'm holding back.

Now I don't have a choice.

"We started talking about this weird idea—that art is bad for you," I admit. "We talked about how when you make something original, and you try to perfect it, it costs a bit of your soul. We thought the phrase *pouring yourself into* something wasn't a figure of speech. We really do *pour ourselves into* what we make. It's counterintuitive, because people think of artists as a little more alive than everyone else, but what if the opposite is true?" I shrug. "That's what we thought. Because when you *pour yourself into* something, you lose that chunk of yourself forever—whether it's vitality, health, or a whole relationship. A sacrifice must be made."

I look at my hands.

Gwen and I have talked about everything since.

She's the only one who knows my biggest regret: not hugging my parents goodbye. I remember watching them get in the car for a weekend trip together. I just stood there in our kitchen, rinsing a cereal bowl, my feet on the uneven floor—it never was level again after the fire. I waved until their car disappeared, but I didn't *hug* them. I didn't go outside while they were loading their bags. I can still see my mom on that day: wild dark hair, expressive hands. If Dad kept our house steady, she kept it warm. She was its beating heart, with a passion for photography, antiques, indie films—and the list kept getting longer because she never stopped falling in love. I remember her philosophical questions at the dinner table. Her contagious love for books.

Gwen's told me her secrets too. She doesn't have *secrets* the same way, open as she is. But she does have stories that she's told only once, because only one person has asked. Sometimes she'll let me know when it's happened. She'll smile like she'd almost forgotten the story herself, like we'd just saved a part of her from oblivion.

"I think you're right," Cole says. He takes another bite, holding his spoon like a pen. "I think artists tend to be obsessive, invested, like you said." He chews more slowly. "Does our art really kill us over time?" He swallows, considering the question with care. "Well, the Nomen are coming to get us. So maybe the answer is yes."

I stir my papaya.

"Does our art *kill* us?" Cole repeats, still thoughtful. "It makes books and paintings sound carnivorous, doesn't it? Maybe that's what it takes. You don't get *The Redfins* if you're clocking in and out of that universe. To build an ocean from the ground up . . . you have to commit. You have to dig in your heels, stay until you taste salt in your sleep. So whether it's the Nomen, mental illness, or the ideas itself, maybe the process just eats you alive.

"That's why it's mad this group wants to erase us. They have no idea the dark nights of the soul that it takes to make anything worthwhile. No one wants the second draft. They want the fiftieth draft, revised over ten years. They want the labor of love, something unreasonably and self-destructively important to whoever put in the time." A beat. "If the Nomen get what they want, that will be the end of great work. We'll have to empty all the museums, grind the statues down to sand. And the rooms will be filled by hobbyists—people who care a little, but never so much that it hurts." He puts his spoon down and leans back.

"Tell me about you," I ask.

"What would you like to know?"

There's plenty to choose from.

I remember sitting in his library—*umbilical, unblind*—and a creep of nerves comes back. After all, Cole's spent the past decade hatching sadists. He nurtured them inside these walls. I almost want to leave, but I can't abandon him here, with his body shredded, people hunting him. I have to stay, find Gwen *with* him. And before we go, try to trust him.

"What happened to your library?"

"I know this apartment is strange." His left eye is thin between swollen lids. The brown scraps focus with intention. "If you weren't a writer, too, this would probably sound disturbed. But . . . I always wanted my stories to feel real. So parts of them had to be true—not the illegal parts," he adds. "I just wanted to know where the shadows fell in my characters' rooms. I know we could talk about writing for days. For now, I'll just say: I think great writing is true. Something in there has to be sincere and exact. And maybe I took it too far."

"Are you as reclusive as people say?"

"What do people say?"

But he shrugs, as if the question is fair.

"For a while," he admits. "For the sake of time, I'll just say that my work used to be my life. I probably had some demons driving me. I'm not sure if I escaped or if they finally gave up. But a few years ago, I started to get interested in a fuller life. There was no breakthrough moment, no tipping point event. Maybe it was just getting older. Still, I didn't change in any public way. My readers seemed to like me unknown. It gave me an edge."

I ask more basic questions. I ask where he was born—Chicago—and when—December 5, at night. He says he was born with an unusually high number of birthmarks, including a salmon-colored patch between his eyes. They've all disappeared, but every now and then, he'll spot pink on his leg and be convinced he's found one again. He doesn't have siblings. When I ask about his parents, there's a shift in his tone, becoming clinical. Neil and Anne Harper are physics professors at the University of Chicago, where they met getting their doctorates.

"They must be very proud of you."

"Not particularly." His spoon scrapes the bottom of his bowl. "I grew up in a house where science was king. The closest my parents got to the humanities was philosophy, and they hated every second of it. At the same time, I was always writing fiction. They must've done something vicious to deserve me." Leaning forward, he winces. He peeks under one cuff, where his tattoo sleeve is heavily nicked. The short cuts are slanted, like red rain.

"We haven't talked in six years," he admits. "The last time we spoke, they had some choice words for me. They didn't just say my work is useless, but that it's destructive, distracting people from what matters. That I'm wasting my life on fiction, while the world needs real help." I tell him I'm sorry to hear that, knowing how much that relationship can shape you—even when so little of it remains. He nods, appreciative. If I knew Cole better, though, I might ask if there's any way the relationship could be saved. The thought of distance from your parents while they're still alive feels . . . deeper than any of our gashes, like spiritual pain.

"Is there anything else you want to ask me?"

"What does 'rotator' mean?"

Cole looks spooked.

For the first time since we sat down, I wonder if I went too far. I explain that Dr. Mason told me Cole was muttering the word in his sleep. "He thought you meant your rotator cuff, but . . . that didn't sound like something you'd say in a nightmare."

"*Rotator* was my first book." By now, Cole seems to have moved past the shock that I know what he said in a dream. "Before the ones you know. Before anyone called me a writer. It's something I wrote that I wish I didn't." I believe him, the way I've believed him all morning. Maybe it's his body language—shoulders open, hands quiet. His left eye is blinking more than his right, clearing a film that collects at the corner.

"Is that all?" he asks.

"For now."

"Then I have one more. Will you really work *with* me?" Before I can answer, he adds, "I know you can work alone, build ecosystems alone. But this is different. If we want to have a fighting chance—and get out alive—we'll have to work together."

"Of course."

He studies me. "Because if you can't—"

I tell him that I can, my tone impatient. I don't sound like the partner I'm swearing to be. But what does he expect? My family—one of the precious few who are closest to family—has been taken. I'm not going to lose her too. I can't live with the idea that she's in the back of someone's car, speeding toward the last hours of her life. I'm going to save her from that car—or wherever she happens to be. The clock to find everyone is running down.

I don't want to talk about us anymore.

I want to talk about them.

~

I suggest we search the Oakwood. Cole hesitates, calling it one of the riskiest places to go next. Of course, that's probably true. The club will be overrun with police all day—along with reporters, activists. And maybe any Nomen who stayed behind, too unsound to follow the instructions that led the rest of them away. Stragglers who couldn't make it onto the bus—or truck, van, whatever they used to bolt. I picture at least one of them still on the curb, mask in hand, cup out for change. Invisible to everyone who came for the Georgian brick facade.

Still, that doesn't make me wrong.

We have to check the last place Gwen was seen. The Nomen might've left something behind. I know the police must be combing through it now, but we can't leave this to them. We have to do all we can. I talk with my hands, casting shadows over the table. Cole warms up to the idea when he realizes how limited our options are, how few leads we have.

I suggest we leave tonight, bringing the conversation to a halt. Cole faces me, his body frozen, blinking. Maybe it's the pressing reality of it—*tonight*—when the rest had been theory. He agrees that *might* let us slip in and out unnoticed, but he sounds unsure. He's holding the edge of the table, as if it might keep him here, out of the place we just escaped. I tell him grimly there's no safe choice left. Even here, there's a risk that Nomen figure out the name of his LLC, then find their way into this room. Going back could be our best chance.

"Tonight . . ."

He sounds almost convinced.

"But not just any time," he adds, his tone thoughtful, tempted. "We'd need to pick the darkest hour, with the fewest possible people. Seeing as how we'd be breaking and entering . . ." He leaves a gap between his thoughts, maybe to emphasize the crime or give me one last chance to change my mind. " . . . and we're no use to anyone from jail."

I ask him how four a.m. sounds.

"As empty as it's going to get."

~

That night, I zip Cole's backpack shut.

We decided our best chance back into the Oakwood would be through the window that we broke. It's probably still open, lined with glass teeth. So we managed to pack an extendable ladder. We just had it delivered from the closest Home Depot. Along with the ladder, we stashed two flashlights, one box cutter. I saw it on Cole's entryway table—for packages, I assumed—and grabbed it just in case. I picture the cutter now, its yellow handle in the dark, retractable razor asleep. Next to Cole's phone at the bottom of the bag.

And that's all we'll have.

It's ready to go, in my room.

We did consider bringing masks. After all, it's unclear where the Oakwood has cameras installed. But since the Nomen escaped, there must not be any in the second-floor dining room, or on the window where we jumped. I get into bed, facing the bag, the ladder shaping it like a rib cage. It's the last thing that I see before turning out the light.

TWELVE

I wake up with my alarm and forget where I am. It's almost too dark to see, just gray enough for one lamp, the corner of a nightstand.

I'm in Cole's guest room.

Reality sets in like slipping into a cold pool.

I get up and change into the outfit we chose yesterday: a black oxford and slacks from Cole. He patted them down before handing them over, removing a ballpoint pen. It was clear except for the ink, like a loaded syringe. He waited while I tried the clothes on in his bathroom. When I was finally done, the pen had bled out in his hand.

I bring the backpack into the living room. Cole's waiting, his black eye with a yellow rim. I wonder one last time if he's fit for this. But last night, he swore he was—he said it multiple times over dinner, when we finalized our plan. We aren't going to stay long, just walk through and look for what might've been left behind. Anything that stands out.

We take the elevator down.

A black Mercedes SUV is parked outside, running.

Cole already vouched for his driver, Nick. Apparently, they've talked about so much on long drives, they barely have secrets left. Cole told me Nick grew up in the Bronx. He and his wife have been together since they were fifteen, and now, they have three adult kids, who still come over for Sunday dinner every week. He has one tattoo for everyone in his family. *"I swear on my life that Nick isn't going to pick us up, then drive straight to the Nomen."*

Cole and I slip outside.

It's cool, dark around the awning.

He reaches abruptly for my hand, holding me back.

Was I getting ahead of him? He keeps my hand, making me nervous. Here, we're flooded with light. I glance around the block, but there's no one else in sight—just vacant intersections through parked cars. An orange steam stack pumping out endless mist.

"I should've brought this up sooner," Cole says, "but please, if it becomes clear that we should leave, then let's leave." I ask what he means. "Just that we can't afford any debate. Five seconds could end up costing our lives. If one of us wants to take off, then let's run—no questions asked." He looks for my consent, and I nod. He seems committed to make us work as a team, but still unsure I'd listen in a crisis. I think he trusts me—enough, but not fully.

Now we're out of time.

We climb into the car.

Nick is stocky in the driver's seat. He greets us without smiling, just tensing his mouth. Cole thanks him for being here, squeezing his shoulder. Nick says *of course*, refusing the praise. I feel the trust between them, built over years. Wasting no time, we move.

The stars are out, and I wonder if Gwen can see them—Logan too. I haven't thought about him enough and feel the sudden urge to call. But what would I say? I don't have good news. I don't have any news at all. I wonder what he did Saturday at midnight, twelve thirty, and then one a.m., when he realized she wasn't coming home. He must've spent all of yesterday with the police, listing her height, weight, and eye color. No tattoos. A one-inch scar on her knee from a fall in middle-grade gymnastics. Reducing Gwen to a fact sheet.

Soon, we're crossing Sixty-Fourth, getting close. A few people are sleeping on benches. One of them sits up and takes a swig out of a shampoo bottle. Nick slows down on Fifth, then slides into a parking spot. We're two blocks from the club, on a residential stretch.

I step cautiously outside.

Cole stays put, murmuring with Nick.

It's quiet except for a man wrestling with a trash can. Three blocks behind us, he hangs on to the steel rim, wrenching it back and forth. When the can flips over, plastic trash pours out in a dry waterfall. He disappears inside Central Park.

Cole shuts the door behind him and lets me know Nick will wait here. We walk side by side down Fifth—faster by a doormanned building, with our faces to the street. Neither of us checks to see who's on duty, if they're sleeping in a chair or upright at attention. We cross over to Madison, keeping pace. I side-eye Cole. He seems focused, alert.

We slow down near the club.

Crowd control gates seal off the entrance. Neon tape runs over the bars: **POLICE LINE DO NOT CROSS. DANGER**. The tape loops several times around the blockade, with one line backward. There's something about a scrambled warning that feels even more cautionary. **REGNAD.** As if the warning itself has been compromised.

A lone police car is parked outside, but I can't tell if anyone's inside. The headlights are off, windows black. Cole and I keep walking. I imagine two officers in the vehicle, a few coffees into their shift, tracking everything that moves. We'd expected police, but seeing their car—with the heavy-duty wheels, the push bumper—comes with a prickle of nerves. Cole and I say nothing, just listen. The only sounds are occasional cars up Madison.

At the next curb, I glance toward the back of the club. There it is: the iron gate across the alley we jumped into. We found it last night on Google Street View and thought it was our best shot. There's no police tape here, no one on patrol.

We move toward it.

It has the wrought iron arch we expected. Through the bars, I see the dumpster that broke our fall, and on the other side, hints of the blockade. The second-floor window is still broken, gaping. Cole and I stop at the gate. I'm already taking off my backpack and reaching inside for the ladder. I scan the building straight ahead, backing up to the

Oakwood. It looks like an upscale cocktail bar with tall double doors, plum velvet ropes tucked to one side.

We freeze as an empty cab passes behind us.

It turns onto Madison, no signal.

I extend the ladder, moving fast.

Cole climbs first, in case he needs an assist.

I watch him with an eye to the street. One awning ripples, with an inky smudge along the edge. Cole pauses on top of the ladder, staring down from twelve feet. My heart beats in my throat. Maybe this *was* too much for him. But slowly, he lifts one leg over the arch. Then the other. He proceeds to lower himself, wedging his sneakers into footholds. He's almost down now, two feet from the pavement. He lets go and grunts when he lands.

We listen hard, but that's it.

No siren, no rush this way.

I collapse the ladder, pack it, and scramble after him. Rust scrapes against my palm as I climb. My backpack's off-center, slanting me to the left. I pull myself over the gate, straining, and make my way down in Cole's steps. Quietly, I arrive.

We hustle to the window.

Another car passes behind us.

It doesn't slow down, doesn't stop.

I unpack the ladder again, this time to its full height. We slant it against the brick, leading up to the ledge. Cole goes first, favoring his right side. I'm holding the base, smelling the trash that's behind us—vinegar, coffee grounds, cigarettes. Cole reaches the top and stares into the dark center of the window. It's like a vat of oil, unreadable.

Does he see something?

But he hoists himself over the ledge.

I climb after him, feeling like we can't have much time. If we can find our way into this club, then other people certainly can. At the top, Cole offers me a hand. I take it, so alert that I feel everything—the lines in his knuckles, dip in his palm. I step into the hall where we jumped, my heel splitting broken glass. Cole stays next to me, his features muddy. I have to remember his long eyelashes, his full lips, and project them into the murk.

We lift the ladder together, pack it.

We start for the dining room as planned.

I feel in sync with him as we move, in the same clothes, on the same beat. I'm sore, but it's nothing compared to what Gwen must be facing. A familiar door waits ahead of us. It's open, the color of smoke. What's on the other side is even darker. I cut through the gap, and for a second, I can't see. But I don't want our flashlights yet. I still don't trust the shadows, don't want to reveal where we are. Maybe it's the memory of being here, drifting in that slow line—the mesh on my eyebrows, the taste of canvas. Terrified of one missed step.

The longer I wait, the more edges appear.

The dining room emerges, one gray line at a time. It's exactly as we left it—but even more desolate now: deserted, with the flowers starting to wilt. I walk down a ragged line of chairs. A few are turned over, legs up. Every candlestick looks like a melted black crayon. I keep walking to my seat and find it angled toward Cole's, his toward mine. My slice of cake is untouched. It looks like a chunk taken out of a grave, dirt brown, crumbling.

The Nomen stood right here.

I kneel, my hands on the floor.

I crawl under the table, around one support. I'm patting the ground, feeling the seams between boards, small divots in the wood. Cole passes me—I see him, knees-down—heading for the front of the room. When he's gone, there's something else. There's something ahead of me, two of them against the far wall. Oblong, bean-shaped.

I crawl toward them, squinting. But it's dark, everything deep in grayscale. I emerge from under the table, palming across the floor. I'm teasing them out—feet. I freeze, two paces away. My blood feels cold, heavy. I'm staring at someone's rubber soles. His legs—I see them now, going backward. His upper half is rag-dolled against the wall, chin dipping into his neck. Every part of him a victim to drift, and right now, dead still.

"Cole," I whisper.

Nothing.

There's something on the wall around the figure. It's thin and clumping—Silly String. Dense, white helical globs of it. The figure still hasn't moved—not his eyes, not his chest. The string arches around him, extending all the way onto the floor. It's chilling to find something playful where someone's soul was taken. How long can Silly String stay up? How fresh does this have to be? I reach out and touch one strand. It collapses to foam in my hand.

More of his details creep toward me. He's in a white long-sleeve and pants—no mask, but here, the outfit only means one thing. He has slick black hair and a long forehead. His nose dominates his narrow face. But I don't see where he was hurt.

"Cole," I say, louder.

I hear him coming.

And now I see the dark pool, a few inches on either side of the Nomen's seat. I crawl toward him, looking for the wound, until I'm right over his shoes. Cole says my name—sharp, maybe even scared. The man in front of me opens his eyes. I launch back onto my heels. He straightens himself up to sit, moving slowly, as if he's underwater. I hear Cole stop beside me, but I'm watching the Nomen. His gaze isn't fully here.

"He needs help," I say.

"Not from us."

But I'm already taking off the backpack. I tell Cole I'm going to call an ambulance, digging inside for his phone. Before he can say another word, I make the emergency call. The Nomen pushes himself up another inch, his hands pressing into the ink. His mouth looks like it's coming to life. I stare at the shifting black hole.

"9-1-1, what's your emergency?"

"Send help." I'm quiet.

The Nomen leans forward without muscle, just slanting over his legs. I crouch, telling the dispatcher that we found someone in critical condition, then sharing our address. The Nomen's gaze hangs on to mine. I feel the urge to hold his hand, but he has something there already. I can just barely see the edges: short, thin—a knife.

"They're coming," he whispers.

"Who's coming?" Cole demands.

Cole rips his phone out of my hand.

The Nomen's knife looks compact, its blade just two inches long. But his arm is slack, the knife neglected. He's still trying to speak, all his concentration in his face. The black scruff around his jaw makes his mouth look like part of the night.

"*Now*, Fiona—" Cole starts.

Laughs in the hallway. I can't tell how many voices—two, three, more. They're a united wave of sound, now sinking into murmurs. I hear them right before I see them—no time to run, move. Three rangy men in white cross the threshold, backlit by deep blue.

They stop short, soles squeaking.

One of them turns on a flashlight.

The glare shines on Cole, then me, and then around the room—maybe in case we aren't alone. It zigzags over abandoned chairs and stale cake, fast and chaotic, the batteries rattling. I'm standing one step closer than Cole, silently raging with alarm. The Nomen let out noises of discovery. Cole and I stiffen during their shrill laughs of disbelief, drawn-out *ohh*s, and thumps on the back. They're visibly wowed by their good luck, shaking each other's shoulders—and now walking toward us. Two look a little broader than the other, with scruff in the hollows of their cheeks. They must be a few years older. But the younger one grabs my attention.

He has a long face and teeth the color of warm white wine. Bruises circle one eye—he's the one I helped at my apartment. Does he remember? He has to. I haven't forgotten a second, down to the musk in his sweat, the shape of him asleep. The watered-down red stain he left on my shoulder. But when his eyes meet mine, there's something missing. There's no shred of connection, nothing but a demented joy to have found us. Is he . . . pretending to feel nothing? A terrifying clarity sets in: It doesn't matter. Either way, he's acting like we've never met. He closes in with the others, celebrating as if I never helped him at all.

"It's *them*!" they say over each other.

"We're going straight to the top."

"Straight to the *fucking* top."

They circle us, pushing Cole and me together. He and I jostle against each other, stiff. I watch the doorway, but this time, I doubt we could outrun them. They're blocking the way to the exit. And their attention isn't scattered; it's fixed right on us.

"I see you found what we did to Drew," one says.

"Little fucker."

"*You* did that," Cole realizes.

"He was making too much noise."

"We had Mack do the honors."

They point at the one I met.

My fingertips feel cold.

"Bad people . . . Unmothered . . . Who don't value life." So there's been pressure to conform.

One Nomen hands the flashlight to Mack, who rests it under his chin. His nose glows orange, nostrils white, while the rest of his face dissolves. Someone orders Mack to "call him." The command sends a jolt through the boy, prompting Mack to pull out a phone. He dials on speaker, and the ringing brings a hush. The Nomen fall silent, almost grave, as if they respect the call. The voice that answers is slow and smooth.

"Rex, we found them," Mack says.

"The last two."

"Cole and Fiona."

"We found them."

"Right on the scene—"

"—going *nowhere.*"

They spit over each other.

As they inch closer, a gap widens between them. The blank space opens to the front of the room—Cole and I could run for it. But then we'd have to find the door in the dark. I picture running my hands over the wall while the Nomen closed in behind us.

Mack neglects the flashlight, letting it dip. It spotlights my shoulder, drifting like a speck of dust in a glass of water. How long until the ambulance gets here? Eight minutes? I scan the Nomen without moving my chin, skimming from the bottom of my eyes. I don't see any guns. Then again, the Nomen might have them tucked out of sight. I didn't see what they did to Drew—not exactly. But they couldn't have done that with bare hands. Maybe our best chance is to stall. Any sudden move might tempt the Nomen to use . . . whatever it is they have.

"They just walked right over to you?"

Rex's voice is familiar—the ringleader.

The three Nomen tell him *yes*, patting each other on the back. One snorts without making a sound—his eyes shut, sunk into wrinkles. One grins with an open mouth, slim gaps between short teeth. Mack joins in a half beat behind them. These Nomen make Rex seem unnervingly composed. He tells them to bring us where they're keeping our "friends."

"Don't touch them." My tone is sharp.

The Nomen blink at me.

Briefly stunned.

"Fiona," Rex says, "how are you?"

The question seems to bring him pleasure.

"I think I know why you came back," he goes on. My heart pushes blood into my arms. Every hair is pricked at attention. "You wanted to get caught, didn't you? You know you have more than you should. You know it's wrong, and you can't enjoy it. So you went looking for a trap. And now you want to hurt. Don't you?" The Nomen restrain their vicious glee, sucking in their lips. They're barely making noise except for their clogged snorts, strangled laughs.

"Don't touch them," I repeat.

"You know, not everyone scares the same way. Sometimes all it takes is suggestion: just showing someone a gun. Other people need to be threatened directly. Which type, Fiona, are you? Do you want me to tell you what we're going to do?"

"You don't scare me," I lie, tone steady.

"You must think you have nothing to lose. You don't have a family, do you?" I feel gut-punched. "Your parents died on Interstate 95. Correct me if I'm wrong, but it was a beautiful day. I've seen photos of that blue, blue sky . . . It started when a pickup truck stopped with a flat tire. From what I've read, it was a red GMC Sierra." A pause dares me to disagree. I'm too shocked to do anything but listen. "Right, a red Sierra. It's really an attractive car, isn't it?" The Nomen nod, even Mack. "Unfortunately, a second car stopped behind it. When your parents tried to avoid them, they spun out in the center lane. The next Freightliner just could not stop. I believe it was carrying pharmaceuticals. Ironic, isn't it? A truck full of medicine."

I feel psychologically invaded.

"If you're wondering how I know that, Fiona, it's because we've been planning this for a long time. Enough to learn all about you—" Mack howls. The sound is booming, tormented. He falls forward, reaching for the back of one shin. The flashlight rolls toward the nearest table. I just barely see Mack land on his knees, then onto one side. The Nomen from the wall—Drew—crouches beside him. He holds his knife in one fist, blade dark.

The other Nomen scatter.

I grab the flashlight—warm—and pull Cole's arm.

We sprint for the back of the room, hearing sirens out front. I picture an ambulance turning off Madison, and push forward as fast as I can. Past the window, at the end of the hall, there's an EXIT door. The flashlight reveals it in manic swipes.

Footsteps slap after us.

I turn to see one Nomen rushing this way.

I whip back around, trying to run even faster. The ambulance sounds like it's arrived, the sirens just rooms away. Police might be lining up out front. I glance back again to see the Nomen jump onto the windowsill. He looks spooked, gripping the ledge. He's just staring at the jump, his feet shifting, his palm crushing shards of glass. But he stays put, clearly stunned with fear. Cole and I sprint downstairs, passing a ground-level door. It appears to be one-way: no handle, no way to open from here. But there's no time for more than a glimpse.

Finally, we lunge for the exit.

THIRTEEN

Cole and I make it across Madison alone. We left the ladder, threw the flashlight in the dumpster. Now we hurry up Fifth, ignoring the itch to run, panting with closed mouths.

Nick is parked where he left us. His car's polished to a mirror shine reflecting sleepy apartment buildings. My heart's a constant blare. I'm still picturing the Nomen—the one laughing on mute, his eyes squeezed shut. It looked like they'd sunk to the bottom of his face, leaving nothing but ripples. Then Mack, with that flashlight under his chin, the glow seeping up from his mouth. And then the one frozen on the window, staring down the jump.

One block from Nick.

I can't hear sirens anymore.

I check over my shoulder, but there's no one who shouldn't be there. A young woman in spandex jogs past us, her hair in a samurai bun. A construction worker walks on the other side of the street with a fifty-foot hose looped under his arm. Meanwhile, the city keeps flowing in two lanes. The cars sound like waves—deep-toned, powerful. A biker pedals next to the traffic without any lights at all, just a smear of motion into the night.

Cole knocks twice on Nick's trunk.

The doors unlock with a muted click.

We jump in, and Nick speeds ahead. My body still won't slow down. There's too much energy in my arms and legs. They feel light, uncontrollable. Cole puts his hands on his knees, looking drunk on an emotional cocktail. We cross Sixty-Fifth Street, all the way to York, then move downtown. I keep reliving the night, smelling the dumpster, hearing Rex describe the red car on Interstate 95. We're almost at Cole's before anyone makes a sound—and it's Cole, adjusting in his seat. He's reaching into his pocket, removing something in a fist. His hand drifts toward me. The longer he hides what's inside, the less I want to see it.

Nick makes a sharp turn.

Cole and I swing left.

Once we're steady, he opens his fist to reveal two . . . I'm not sure what they are. They're shaped like bullets—a stubby two inches each—but each has a round, white plastic tip. Cole pinches one, and the tip gives way under his thumb—as if it's designed to break on impact. He says there was no blood on the floor.

"No blood?" I repeat.

"Pristine."

I'm not sure what he means until I remember Tony: His heart-shaped face. The volume in his dark hair, lifting over a side part. I barely saw him move for the door before the Nomen stopped him. No blood where he was shot? There should've been plenty. Nothing else had been moved, let alone cleaned. There was still cake in the bowls of spoons.

"Which means . . ." Cole starts.

There never was.

"What did you see when they shot him?" Cole is barely louder than the engine. "I saw the *impact* of the bullets, the *pressure* on him, but I didn't see him . . ."

"Bleed."

Now that I think about it, Tony's death wasn't in the news. All the stories I found were about the kidnappings, the flyers on the Upper East Side.

"Blank rounds," I think out loud.

"Which means . . ."

Tony worked with the Nomen.

Maybe he struck a deal as soon as he got the invite.

I picture him on one side of a table, facing his own predators in masks. Maybe he gave us away to save himself. The stunt did scare the room into submission. After he hit the floor, not a soul dared rebel. I remember Tony's speech. He kept using the word *fight*. His whole life had been a *fight* for every next rung—through dead-end assistant jobs, failed pilots, and unreliable cowriters. The Nomen were new, but the *fight* was the same. His tone was just a bit desperate, squeaking once or twice in the back of his throat. I wonder if that was regret.

~

In Cole's guest room, I drop to my knees.

With my forehead on the carpet, safe, I cry.

For the first time all night, I shake with fear, rage, helplessness—the whole time, careful to stay quiet. Cole's not far, walking back to his room. I don't want him to hear. Don't want him to ask what's wrong, to think this is too much for me.

"I've seen photos of that blue, blue sky . . ."

It was blue. Mom was wearing sunglasses in the driveway. Dad had one hand on her shoulder as they waved goodbye. I cry harder, holding the back of my neck. Eventually, I lift my head, and here, on my knees, I pray. I ask my parents to stay with me. I know they must be here—somehow they must be in this room, keeping me safe. I just need them to stay a little longer. I pray for Gwen, her baby. For everyone the Nomen took.

"Please, Mom, Dad . . ."

I never talk to my parents this often, but they've been talking more than ever to me. Because I'm still alive. After everything, I'm still free. Of course they're here. Rex was wrong. He can't hurt me by bringing up my parents. He's only going to make me stronger. Because they're always at my defense. They devoted their whole lives to me: every night, every weekend. They framed my preschool art. They saved every paper-plate face—every pipe-cleaner fish—in the basement, as if I would be the first to leave. They bound the stories I wrote as a nine-year-old, as if they mattered—as if *I* mattered. Death isn't going to stop them.

Slowly, I stop crying.

I dare Rex to bring them up again.

Say their names. Say *Paige and Tom*.

Because they can hear you, Rex. And they can hear me. Because they are still in the glints on my picture frames, those perfect shimmers. They are in some of my best ideas. And they'll always be the wind at my back—that slight, invisible lift.

~

I wake up early.

Remembering the plastic bullets.

Our next step has to be Tony Graham.

If he made it out of the Oakwood alive—if he's hiding—we have to find him. He must know something that we don't. I head toward the library, sore, one sleeve damp. I must've slept on my cuts, opened some. But no matter how I feel—no matter how deep the pain goes—Gwen's facing something worse. It's been nearly two days. Gwen counted things when she got nervous: the gel pens on her desk, people in a restaurant. And now I know she's counting the hours. The vitamins she's missed—she must be on those, knowing her, if she and Logan were trying in earnest to have kids. Daily folic acid, something dutiful, optimistic.

I don't stop until I'm at the laptop.

I start by googling *Tony Graham*.

All I know is that his biggest hit has been *Jim*, a sitcom taking place in a gym. Netflix picked it up to great success this year, after a lackluster first season on network TV. The search bar prompts *Tony Graham* **Jim**, followed by *Tony Graham* **father**.

Curious, I click through.

Woody A. Graham is apparently in real estate with a property empire. He owns one million square feet, including a skyscraper in Manhattan, an international resort chain, and waterfront properties in Venice Beach. Woody married at forty-three to a former actress, and they have two children. The family is between New York and Hollywood Hills, where they overlook the Sunset Strip.

From my brief time with Tony, I wouldn't have guessed it. His speech was tortured: the *fight*. He repeated that nothing was handed to him—maybe because people assumed that it was. I click back to photos of his dad. In every one, he has an orange-tinted tan and veneers. A Rolex with a blue face. Apparently, he wrote a memoir that came out a few years ago, his headshot across the cover.

Even if Tony never struggled to get by, maybe he struggled to distinguish himself from his dad—earn his own respect. No matter what he achieves, maybe he can still hear the whispers. *All those advantages. All those connections. Do you know the head start that he had?* Tony might've snapped first because he felt hated longer. Or maybe he grew up watching his dad make under-the-table deals, trading favors for construction permits. Maybe Tony grew up to believe everyone breaks the rules, that trust is for the weak and betrayal, the savvy.

Tony married his former assistant, Alice. They have a house in Medford, New York, a suburb that I read is known for dirt roads, horses, and spotty cell service. I pinpoint their address on Google Earth and, on Street View, crawl through snapshots toward their home. The seasons change with every click, each photo taken at a different time of year. I jump through months in seconds and reach their place to find it blurred. They must've removed it for privacy.

I break in the kitchen for water.

Cole crosses the threshold.

At the coffee machine, he cues a mug. He's still in last night's outfit, one sleeve rolled up to his elbow. The cuts on his tattoo are pinker today, a rosy mist. He asks if I'd like coffee, but I shake my head. He brings his to where I stand. Up close, the left side of his face looks better, tighter. His jawline is becoming a hard edge. Only his eyes look worse, with red veins in their corners, as if his tear ducts are bleeding. He must've barely slept.

I launch into what I learned. Cole listens with palpable fatigue, purple shadows under his eyes. I tell him about the house in Medford, an hour away. "I doubt Tony's there now—it's in his name—but it might be a good place to start."

Cole takes a long sip of caffeine.

"I have a car we can use."

~

Cole's behind the wheel of his black BMW, steering us away from his building. We decided that riding with Nick in his extra-wide car might draw unwanted attention. Now we head for the FDR Drive, passing a fruit stand under the Queensboro Bridge—open boxes stuffed with bananas, apples on foam trays. It's uncomfortably bright, with so much sun on the streetlamps that they look fully lit. The dashboard clock reads 1:03 p.m.

Soon, we're leaving the city.

Cole's spent the drive so far coming to terms with last night.

He'd heard my story about the Nomen in the alley, so he had a sense of their rage. But seeing them knife each other was different. They really are such a hateful group that they will destroy themselves. Every now and then, Cole murmurs another detail from last night: the pool around Drew, Mack's scream. I remember bolting down the stairwell. With no one behind us, it would've looked like we were trying to escape our own noise.

I read the news on Cole's phone.

The Nomen are still at large, targets missing.

It's reported that, unbeknownst to the Oakwood, their staffing company received an email last week. It appeared to come from the club's events director, Margaret Clark, canceling their Saturday plans.

So Majestic Staffing kept the deposit and did not show up to service the forty-seven-person dinner. In their place, a new team arrived. Margaret made them sign nondisclosure agreements before the dinner—with what now appear to be illegible scribbles. By the time the police arrived on the scene, everyone from "Majestic" was gone.

I look up to find we're neck and neck with another car.

When the driver glances at me, I tuck my profile into one hand. Cole speeds up. Even once we're in the clear, I keep looking down, facing the phone in my lap. Part of me desperately wants to text Marlowe, Caroline, and Emma. I know their numbers by heart. It would be so easy to send them a line—just to tell them I'm safe, to ease their minds for one second. Of course, my friends can keep a secret; we've been keeping each other's for twenty-five years. Then again . . . if they're questioned, for any reason, I don't want them to have to lie.

I stuff the phone in the console.

When I look at Cole, there's something behind him.

On the billboard over his shoulder, the model Carla Chen faces us in an ad for a diamond necklace. But . . . a smile has been spray-painted over her mouth. It cuts up to her ears, jagged, fat. It feathers at the very ends, where the aerosol must've caught the wind. Her eyes have been blacked out, each like a pad of steel wool. Cole must've seen it, too, but he just keeps watching the road. The next billboard is an ad for fast food: orange red, pristine. I scan the ones across the highway, facing the other direction. From here, they're just wires, supports.

We fall into a lull. We pass high-rise public housing and then a chain-link fence around basketball courts. The windowless corner of a warehouse and then a food truck hitched to a southbound van. I would've thought the Nomen were too busy for stunts like that. They have almost fifty hostages to supervise. Then again, maybe the ones who did this weren't Nomen—just fans. I picture a group climbing onto the ad in the middle of the night. They would've had to work fast, with this many eyes on the road. I wonder if anyone reported them for vandalism or disturbing the peace. Or if everyone just drove, letting them finish their work.

"How long has that been there?" I ask quietly.

Cole shrugs. I hug myself, getting chills.

But just because the face might've been there for a day—or two—doesn't mean no one's reported it. Things take time to resolve, even with everyone moving as fast as they can. The department in charge would need to alert the billboard's owner. Then someone would have to show up and assess the damage. Then find the right chemical treatments, scaffolding. Then, finally, pressure wash the smile for hours, until the very last drop dribbled down.

"What do you think the Nomen are doing with everyone?" I ask.

"I think that's up to Rex."

I remember him from last night. *"Not everyone scares the same way."* He was almost playful. His words had a well-educated flow—everything grammatically sound, with pauses that let each point land. I would've imagined the person behind this to be rougher. Someone who'd been abused and degraded in a way that had permanently shaped him, down to the way that he spoke. Maybe someone who, on the rare occasion that he opened his mouth, was unable to say what he meant. Who had clear disadvantage, reason for a vendetta.

But Rex was . . . smooth.

Then again, maybe that makes sense.

Someone had to come up with the Nomen's philosophical grudge. Someone had to write the Manifesto, make it airtight and persuasive. Of course the one who drew people to this group must have dark charm and unnerving charisma. Mack told me about the one behind this. In my apartment, what did he say? *"He always hated fame, hated you people. I just . . . didn't know how much."* We pass a garbage-compactor truck. Cardboard's been clamped to the back, peeking out from under the compressor. But if Rex hates us that much, why did he learn so much about me? Why did he reach so deep into my life, digging up my roots?

The answer hits me slowly, like walking into mist.

Rex is coming for more than blood.

I get the feeling that what the Nomen have planned will be emotional too. They won't settle for easy wounds. They want psychological pain, in full force. And if anyone could pull it off, it would be Rex. He's always seemed capable, with a bulletproof and intelligent confidence. Even when grazing instability, he sounded no less convinced.

"Since we have a moment," Cole says, glancing at me, "is there anything else I should know about you?" I sense him picking up our earlier conversation: *"We'll need to have faith in each other's support."* I want to give him a good answer. I could tell him that I'm the rare kind of introvert who loves people. That my friend Caroline has been my emergency contact for over a decade, that she's eight months younger but always seemed older. That if I could have dinner with anyone, living or dead, it would be my parents—and family aside, it would be Tolkien, so I could ask if he ever got so deep in Middle-earth he believed in it. But everything that comes to mind sounds insufficient. "I'm sorry Rex said that," he adds. "About your parents."

"I still google them," I admit without expecting to. But it's true, and the results never change. Every time I search for *Paige and Tom Hart*, I find the same photo with their obituary: one gray thumbnail with their foreheads together and deeply present eyes.

"What about you?" I ask.

"What about me?" he repeats, under the shadow of an overpass. I ask about growing up in Chicago. He says his family lived on "Professors' Row," a line of town houses in Hyde Park. It was a twelve-minute walk from the college library. That was where he read the first book he ever loved, Danielewski's *House of Leaves*, a horror about a house bigger on the inside than on the outside. He says no other book has had a greater impact on his taste.

I ask what he was like as a kid.

"Bullied," he admits, as if we're almost out of time. "Maybe because I stuck to myself. Or maybe I stuck to myself because of them. It's hard to know which came first, because they were both always true." He says he was an outlet for aggression. Kids would cluster near the drop-off area, where they socked him in the ribs before class. When he was thirteen, a bad friend lured him into an ambush, where kids ended up dislocating his shoulder. "Maybe it would've stopped if I'd told an adult. But . . ." He squints at me with some vulnerability. "It's hard to have your body taken from you like that. I felt like the strong thing to do was to take it.

"So, I spent a lot of time inside, by myself. That's probably why I started writing: It was something I could do alone. Plus, I had so many things broken over the years . . . Part of me was always hurt. If I was going to let loose and have fun, it was going to be with my mind." Maybe when he works out now, he feels like he's reclaiming his body.

"People say your greatest weakness is your greatest strength," he goes on. "For better or worse, I can spend an unusual amount of time alone. It used to be because I was hiding. But even when I was out of that school, something about my old life stuck." I say that sometimes people re-create what feels like home. If he was always avoiding people to stay safe, maybe that started to feel like home to him. Maybe that's what he gravitated to as an adult.

He nods as if that might be the case.

"You know," he adds, thoughtful, "the thing about outrunning your demons is that even when they're gone, by then, you've invested so much in your . . . infrastructure. You have so much momentum. So when you're finally free, your life might not fundamentally change." I picture his apartment, the rooms that suck me into his books. "I'd bet a lot of people are in homes they built for themselves a while ago, multiple selves ago. Some probably don't fit anymore—all those decisions you made when you were younger. They feel stale or maybe even dead." Trees behind him fill the space between high-mast lights.

"I spend a lot of time alone too."

"Is that what feels like home?"

I think about it. "No, for me, home feels like . . . my mom, dad, and me running into the ocean." I tell Cole that they used to take me to Rhode Island once a year. They'd rent a house close to the beach—so close there was sand in the lawn. Dad would teach me about the tides, how the moon's gravity caused the ocean to bulge. He'd teach me about every crustacean, the lungs in rare kinds of fish. Mom would be reading a book, taken with it. We'd open the windows every night and smell the water, hear the waves. "That's probably why I started writing about the ocean, building a whole world in there. It was a way to make it last." Cole looks at me for so long that I almost worry about the car drifting into the median.

"Thank you for telling me that."

He checks the road.

Looks back at me with purpose.

I feel like I could ask him anything.

"Are you this open with everyone?"

He shakes his head.

"Why me?"

"Because we need each other," he says, certain.

But there's something else in his tone: I realize he's trying to convince me.

I pivot to ask if he has any bad habits—sleep deprivation while he's working. He says he's gotten better about it, but every so often, he'll dip back into his old life. He asks the same of me. I say I don't know, quieter now. Because what's coming to mind are my friends'. Gwen wanted to stop answering calls after midnight, spend more time at home. I can almost hear her listing everything she'll change after the next store—or whatever the next milestone would be. She used to daydream like that, even at her happiest. But I don't think she wanted to change. I think she just wanted to remind herself of her freedom, to enjoy the options she had.

Cole must see where it hurts.

He changes tack to ask about my favorite food—popcorn, but only real popcorn made on the stove, with a barbaric amount of salt. He says there's nothing wrong with that and admits sometimes he'll put salt on his fruit—mostly melons, pears. We keep up a back-and-forth. But after a while, I'm no longer looking at him, just at a nick of his profile. None of our answers feel as close to the bone. We don't get back to that place, whatever it was. It wasn't full trust—the unblinking, follow-you-anywhere kind. But it was something.

Cole takes the next exit.

A stop sign marks the end of the ramp.

Getting closer, the sign looks smeared with dirt—or rust. There's a dark curve cutting across the letters, more smudges in the middle. They could be glare, but they don't move with us. When we finally roll to a stop, it's clear the sign is smiling.

~

From the road, Medford looks empty. We drive mostly through raw forest, the trunks and brush overrun with kudzu vines. But every few seconds, a driveway appears without warning. It cuts through the trees, leading to a farmhouse-style home: sliding barn doors, bronze lanterns. Cole and I have gone silent, just watching for the next turn.

We're getting close to Tony's.

I read this morning that Medford draws those looking for privacy. As a small town with wide lots and distant neighbors, I see why people would come here to get away. I also read that a few A-listers have homes nearby, adding glamour to the rustic scene. After a couple of movies were filmed in the area, some of their biggest stars didn't want to leave.

The road turns to dirt. A gray-white layer of dust covers the tops of mailboxes, the bushes on the sides of the road. It billows behind our car like fog. Cole and I pass a horse farm, the paddocks spanning multiple hills. Then another homestead. I scan the unlacquered brass planters on the porch, the barn converted into a two-car garage, until I see the turn.

We make a left onto Tony's cul-de-sac.

A dense row of trees leads up to his mailbox. They're orange and red with skirts of dead leaves. We are now in Google Earth's blind spot. Tony's place creeps into view as we approach his driveway: a stone

Colonial engulfed in ivy. In some places, the ivy climbs all the way to the roof, so compact it looks like moss. Is anyone home? There are no cars in sight, no faces between the curtains, but something's wrong with one of the first-floor windows. The glass is so fractured—cracked so many times—that it's white. Cole doesn't stop.

"I saw it too," he says quietly.

We park at the roundabout.

Cole's reaching for his door when I ask him to wait. "I think I should go first." My voice is cautious. "I can check the house. As soon as I know it's safe, I'll come back for you." He looks ready to protest. "Then we can search the whole place—every stitch in the rugs."

"We're in this together."

I argue he's hurt worse.

"No." The word is final. "That's not working together, Fiona. That's me in the wings while you stick your neck out." He reaches again for the handle. "You know, you spend so much time looking out for everyone else. It shouldn't surprise you that one day, someone would try to do the same for you." He opens the door, facing me. "Whether or not I have your permission, I'm going to keep track of you as much as anything else." He steps outside, clearly frustrated with me. I follow and land on a molehill that sinks an inch under my feet. There are no sounds except our doors shutting. My resolve gives way to spreading fear. It feels different to be out here than it did to be in that car, boxed up in sheets of steel.

I walk over to Cole.

"I have a bad feeling about this," he admits.

Without thinking, I put a hand on his shoulder. My stomach flips, as if I'm even more afraid than I think. Or maybe it's standing this close to Cole—so close I see dried blood on his inner ear. Feel a line of scabs pushing back through his shirt.

Quickly, I take my hand back.

We set out for Tony's side by side. Platinum clouds cover the sky, just thick enough to blur the sun. Cole and I separate for two quick steps around a mailbox. My breaths get shallower the farther we get from his car. I keep checking for anything that looks out of place. Eventually, we reach the edge of Tony's property. We take a sharp left, walking through trees down one side of his lawn. Some of these must be eighty years old—towering, thick. A few spiderwebs glint between branches, netting pine cones the size of small bullets.

Cole's still at my side, moving forward.

I hear birds, but not many, none close.

I almost crush a worm slithering blindly over dirt.

Cole points suddenly to Tony's backyard. I follow his finger to tire marks: three sets of them. It looks like three trucks drove well past Tony's driveway to park behind his house. The gashes are deep, dirt-mangling. Maybe it was raining when they parked there. Or else they must've stayed overnight and let their trucks sink. I glance back at Tony's driveway: a gravel quarter-mile, more than big enough for . . . whoever needed the space.

Are any Nomen still here?

I feel my own empty palms.

I'm still in last night's clothes, the pants hitched with a belt, hems collecting dirt and the jagged pieces of dry leaves. I did bring the box cutter again, stashed it in my pocket as we left. I just didn't expect to need it. I touch it—still there, over my thigh. But I'm getting ahead of myself. There are no signs that anyone's here. It's so quiet I can hear every squirrel, pinpoint each one and look them in the eye. I scan the house—no smoke in the chimneys, no lights.

We walk to the back of the property. French doors surround a first-floor room, too far away for us to see through the glass. It wouldn't be a bad place to start. We could try ten handles within steps of each other, testing for one to give way. Cole and I lock eyes. My heart picks up as I pose the question. He's open to the idea, nodding fast.

We step onto the lawn.

I feel exposed, out from under the trees.

Pine needles stick out between spikes of grass.

We get closer to the house. We're heading for the nearest French door, past a tennis court. Dead leaves cluster around the net and drift across the white lines. I come face-to-face with what turns out to be a sitting room. But the carpet's smothered with magazine pages. It looks like someone tore a *Vogue* into hundreds of sheets, until it was nothing but a thread of glue. I lean toward the glass. The photos have all been defaced: eyes gouged, lips stitched together with black pen. In the center of the room, a beige sofa looks trampled.

I try the door—open. I step inside to find two framed posters in ruins. They used to be classic movie covers—*Gone with the Wind* and *All about Eve*—now shattered and slashed on the floor. Half of Vivien Leigh's face is missing. All of Bette Davis has been hacked out. I keep moving, but it's hard to avoid the broken glass. Crystals the size of breadcrumbs crunch under my shoes. Every time, I go still for a few seconds, my pulse lapping in my ears.

Cole and I tread past the sitting room.

Into a sprawling den.

Here, bookshelves on the far wall have been emptied. A gray sofa has had its cushions knifed, the foam core exposed in white gashes. A coffee table has been carved end to end with a smile, the incisions deep, splintering. Most glaring of all, a hundred cereal-bar wrappers are scattered across the rug. They're all warped with creases, silver linings turned inside out. Just as many plastic water bottles clutter the room, the half-pints squeezed and dry. Cole touches my arm and points straight ahead. There, a fabric mask lies in the corner, where it seems to have been dropped. Frozen waves distort the face, the cheeks in clumps.

We listen—nothing, no one.

We turn left into the dining room, where a round table is off-center. It's surrounded by a chaotic mix of chairs: armchairs, barstools, a rocking chair, and an ottoman. These must've been grabbed from the rest of the house. The table is covered with debris: deli papers, plastic containers streaked with mayo, and the uneaten bready butts of sandwiches. I walk up to them—over pale lettuce shreds, past strangled packets of mustard—and touch the bread. It's softer than I expected, holding on to the dent of my finger. I get the feeling we should leave.

Before I can say it, Cole moves into the kitchen and stops in front of a MacBook Air. It looks precarious on the counter, one corner over the edge. I step closer, watching the screen. It's smeared with windows, as if whoever was there last never closed a tab, just buried it. The nearest one is black with bold white text. Cole pulls out his phone and snaps a photo.

A toilet flushes upstairs.

Cole and I meet eyes, my hands ice cold.

We rush back through the dining room, into the den. Outside, a dozen teens walk this way across the lawn. They're in all white—two in industrial onesies with a zip front and hood. Their steps are quick, out of sync with each other. A line of advancing legs. They seem to be swept up in a conversation, with multiple people talking at once. All move with bravado and something more unstable, coming toward us with untouchable swagger.

Someone starts humming on the second floor—a male voice. It rumbles with gaps in the tune, as if his mind is somewhere else. He plods downstairs to the kitchen behind us, then into the ravaged sitting room. I hear the glass snap and grind under his shoes. A distant door opens, and he emerges on the grass: another teen. He has moles across his face: a dime-size one on his jaw that spills onto his neck. Two almost touching by his ear. He heads for the group, in one more full-body suit. The hood bounces lazily as he walks.

A muffled scream comes through the floor.

Followed by a mangled *"Olp."*

My adrenaline spikes. I study the Nomen on the lawn. They couldn't have heard the shout. They're still a hundred feet away, far enough that there's time. I glance at Cole. His expression is tight, as if he's already resigned to what we're going to do. We step forward, looking for a way downstairs. Past the empty shelves, stabbed sofa.

Endless bottles. We walk into a hallway, one wall riddled with bullet holes. They bore through pink insulation.

"Please!"

It's muted, desperate.

Cole and I spin toward the sound.

We come face-to-face with a door.

I open it to descending stairs. They're uncarpeted, the walls on either side unfinished concrete blocks. I race down ahead of Cole. The air gets dense with the smell of old furniture and something like copper or decay. There's someone in the middle of the room. I can only see up to his calves: He's barefoot, in suit pants. His ankles have been tied to a chair. My view rises: Tony Graham. But he doesn't look like the Tony I saw two days ago. Now he's been beaten to distortion. His brow has ballooned. His nose bends at a sharp angle. Bungee cords bind him to the aluminum chair, its back up against a central pillar.

I come to a stop.

He's in the same shirt from the dinner—white twill, wing collar—now stained with a long red bib. It slants all the way down to the hem. Could Cole and I carry him to the car? Could we make it there without the Nomen spotting us—hearing us move? I'm not sure, but I can't leave him here. I physically can't. Something in me won't do it.

"Please."

His voice strains.

I reach for my box cutter and get low. Tony's big toenails are cracked. A pink circle of urine stains the rug under his chair. He must've peed on his wounds. I cut the ropes around his ankles, the blade sliding through them like cooked noodles.

"Fiona—" Cole starts.

"We have to."

The ropes drop.

"Don't do this, Fiona."

"Where are they?" Tony asks.

"The lawn."

I try to help him stand.

A beat later, Cole lifts the other side.

Tony's knees are slow to unbend. When his feet finally touch the floor, he barely puts any weight on them. Instead, he hangs between us, toes drooping. I'm eye level with his temple, where the hair is caked together, his skin the color of red wine. Maybe this is the Nomen's plan: brutal transformation. Making sure we're never recognized again.

Heading upstairs, Tony gets harder to carry. He's sinking in my grip, his damp clothes sliding against me—Cole too. I peer left, check on him. The veins are tense across his forehead, a bloodred tree right over his eyes. But we don't stop. We keep moving, one step after another, getting closer and closer to the door. Finally, at the top, I leave them to scan the windows in the den. The Nomen are still walking toward us, now less than ten feet away.

They're distracted.

But close.

I race back to Cole and Tony.

We scramble together for the entrance.

I hear one of the French doors open in the distance. It scrunches magazine pages, tearing one. Footsteps rustle inside. Their conversation is a blur, getting louder.

When I open the front door, we bolt.

Darting across the driveway, Tony yelps with pain—one high-pitched cry, lasting less than a second. It's just long enough to make me feel exposed. Cole and I sprint even faster, cutting through the lavender lining the driveway. The silvery stalks bend toward the lawn, top-heavy, almost tripping us. I see Cole's car through the trees.

Tony lets out a stuttering moan.

We're halfway across the yard when crunching gravel turns me around: A Nomen is racing after us. He's intent, his eyes narrowed down to a point. Two more follow behind him. More Nomen emerge, faster than we are. Cole swings one arm as he runs.

At the road, he unlocks the car. I open the back door as he throws Tony inside. Tony lands hard on one shoulder, head clapping against the seat. If any of his bones were broken—the ends sharp, misaligned—they might've just pierced new holes inside him. There's a chance his nose was pushed clean off. Cole grabs my hand before I shut the door and pulls me toward the front of the car.

He opens the driver's side.

I race around the hood and jump in, two seconds behind him.

I watch the Nomen through the open back door. Their suits flicker between the trees, coming this way. Tony starts to cry. Every sob must hurt—and that's what they did to someone who had cooperated. What would they do to Cole and me now? Cole starts the engine as one Nomen sprints through the tree line. Thin branches snap on his chest. He's just steps away. I scramble toward him over the console and fall on my knees, reaching for the back door. He leaps forward, catching air. I find the handle and pull the door shut just in time.

The Nomen crashes into it headfirst.

I shut my eyes, hear the crack.

Cole floors it. The thrust almost pins me to the ground. It takes all my strength to get up and crawl back to my seat. As we speed ahead, a wiry Nomen jumps onto the car. He latches on to one side, holding the roof racks. We accelerate as he hoists himself on top, disappearing. I only hear him inching forward until his head is on the windshield.

He stares at us upside down.

Cole stops short.

The Nomen flies forward.

I spin to see the rest coming at us.

One opens fire at the back of the car—metal crashing into metal. Cole steps on the gas and swerves onto the main road, nearly colliding with an oncoming car.

FOURTEEN

"Tony, can you hear me?" Cole barks as we drive.

He adjusts the rearview mirror to capture the back seat.

Tony is sprawled across it, with one cheek on the leather, his hips lifted over a seat belt clip. Fortunately, his nose doesn't look any worse. I scan for anything new—any visible bones, any unnatural bend in his arms. One sleeve has been ripped up to his elbow, revealing a bite mark. It's an oblong purple ring, piercing the skin by one molar. Some of his other injuries have started to drip. A slick red thread connects his lips to the seat.

"I asked you a question," Cole says.

"I can," Tony croaks.

"He's hurt," I tell Cole.

"He's dangerous," he shoots back, his arms flexing on the wheel. Turning to Tony's reflection, he adds, "Tell us why we should trust you after you sold us out."

Tony moves his lips.

Nothing comes out.

"Speak up," Cole snaps.

"This is cruel—" I start.

"We're dealing with monsters."

He glances back to see if we're being followed—no one.

"And this isn't the time, but you can't keep risking your life for people who want us dead." He keeps his voice raised. "Because it's not just your life anymore. It's mine. We're together on this, and I need to trust that you're not going to run into every burning building. That'd be fine if you were alone. But if you run into that building now, I'm going with you." He looks at me. "These people are demons, Fiona. They're not something you can take on by yourself—even you." His voice softens. "We're only going to get somewhere as a team, a real team . . ." We hear rustling in the back seat.

Tony's pushing himself up to sit with effort.

He makes it, slanted, and leans back.

"You have something to say?" Cole demands.

Tony whispers something.

"What's that?"

"I'm sorry," Tony says, louder.

"I don't hear why we shouldn't kick you out right *fucking* now."

I'd never let Cole do that, but I keep it to myself. Fighting with him would just stoke the fire. Instead, I hand Tony the water bottle by my feet. I drank half on the drive here. Tony's grip on the bottle is so limp I half expect it to slip out and hemorrhage over the floor. He looks at me, grateful. His beard has grown out like mold, with bruises filling the gaps.

"What did they do to you?" I whisper.

"I was a target—"

"We're all targets," Cole cuts in.

Tony sips the water.

The slow gulp takes focus.

Cole barks at him to start talking.

"The Nomen came to me . . . my social media." I wonder if they contacted me too. I rarely check those accounts. "They sent photos of . . . my wife. They were . . . watching us." He says he had to do *something*, coughing in the middle of his sentence. The sound is deep and wet. "After the invite . . . I said I knew where the targets would . . ." He takes another sip, a pained bulge down his throat. "They sent me . . . phone number. I called and . . . Nomen . . . answered." He apologizes, the word *sorry* just one syllable. "I had to . . . for my family."

"You trusted them." Cole is derisive.

"Of course not." Tony's voice is breathy. "But . . . no choice. Of course that dinner . . . raided. I had to think . . . survival." He finally drops the water bottle. I pick it up as it oozes. "Before the Nomen took my deal, they gave me . . . role. They shipped me . . . bulletproof vest. It went like they said . . . until the end. They wouldn't let me go." I check if anyone's on our tail. "I tried everything . . . Told them about my wife. She's pregnant—our first—but . . ." He shakes his head. "The Nomen said, 'We promised you life . . . We never said you'd . . . enjoy it.'" He sways with a left turn. Meanwhile, Cole's lips are tight. His shirt glints with Tony's blood. "They knew about my home, took everyone there. Then left for . . . God knows."

"Where were they going?" I ask.

Tony is silent.

"They didn't say?" I press.

"No, and they . . ."

"What?" Cole demands.

"Made me help." He drops his voice to admit he unlocked the front door. The steering wheel crackles in Cole's grip. "After they left, they kept me there. Some Nomen too . . . Turning my house into a . . . base . . . I don't know. To kill time, they tied me up . . . used me as a . . . It didn't make sense." He takes a break to catch his breath.

"What didn't?" I ask.

"They'd say other targets' names before they . . . hit me." It's a degrading flourish on a brutal attack. "I've never seen people enjoy . . . so much pain." He tells us they fed on it, and I picture white flies in blood. "I felt the whole mob . . . in every one. They were that . . ." Tony pauses for a word he can't seem to find. *Single-minded? Conjoined?* "They kept reciting the same . . . They'd all read the same . . . and it'd programmed them all the same way."

"Where'd they take everyone?" Cole asks.

Tony looks helpless.

"They didn't say anything about it?"

"The weather, even?" I'm gentle.

The engine hums.

"Nothing," Tony says at last.

The word is desolate, final.

We pass an old rock wall down to its last line of stones. Tony closes his eyes and moans. I say we need to get him to an emergency room. Cole breaks his concentration on the road to look quizzically at me. He reminds me that Tony made a deal with devils—that the only reason he's still in this car is because he might know something we don't. A silver Jeep approaches, a quarter-mile away. It turns before it reaches us, and we're alone again in the woods. An upturned tree on our left has roots like black snakes. I tell Cole firmly that our only options are the emergency room or Dr. Mason.

"They kept saying . . ." Tony trails off.

"What?" Cole demands.

"'The—'" We dip into a pothole and Tony gasps. His hand chokes the plastic bottle on his thigh. Cole prompts him to finish without sympathy. "'The . . .'" We speed around a turn, the edge of the road on a steep hill. In the pause, Cole hits the steering wheel with the heel of his hand, glaring at Tony's reflection. "'The . . . Intake.'"

"What's it mean?" I ask.

"Don't . . . know."

He looks emptied.

We drive through a small graveyard.

Tony says that he knows he hurt people. He says that he knows it was wrong, that he'd give anything to take back what he did. Throughout the apology, his voice crackles with remorse. "I'm sorry, it was just . . . My wife. Our kids."

Kids—plural.

"Your kids?" I'm calm.

"Yes, they're . . . my life."

But he just said they were pregnant with their first.

I glance at Cole. He's caught it too. Cole reaches into his pocket, removes his phone, and offers it to me over the console. I stare at the screen, confused. He turns one-handed at the next intersection and stops short. We're half on a field, with knee-high weeds bending under the hood. The slanted street sign behind us reads **Windy Hill**.

"I have a compromise," Cole says, rushing. There are still no cars in sight. "Call 9-1-1 and tell them where he is." I get a cold sense of what Cole wants to do. He says an ambulance will get here in the same amount of time it would take us to reach a hospital. "But he's wasting our time, and I don't trust him. Don't keep us in this town longer than we need to be here. Don't lose an afternoon in a waiting room. Making him priority one is only going to hold us back. If we want to make a difference—"

"*Wait.*" Tony sounds pained.

"We have other things to do."

Cole pushes his phone closer.

I'm overwhelmed but think it through: Tony would still get help.

Cole's stare is firm, his mouth a hard and patient line. He's waiting for me to decide. I take his phone and nod. Wasting no time, Cole jumps out and opens the back door. He grabs Tony from behind, under the arms. Tony's screams are whispery. He starts flailing as Cole drags him outside, and his open hand knocks me across the jaw. I cry out, bending over my knees. It takes me a second to recover, my fingers on the burn, right over the bone. When I sit up, Cole's in the driver's seat. I make the call as we turn onto the main road.

"9-1-1, what's your emergency?"

FIFTEEN

Cole and I ride in silence on the interstate.

I told the dispatcher where to find Tony. Then I brought up his house. I said that Nomen had overrun the place and spelled out the address. Since then, I've been refreshing the news on Cole's phone, hoping for a story about Tony, proof that he's all right.

Maybe it's better things happened this way.

If we'd taken Tony to a hospital, we would've gotten involved with the police. I would've stayed in the ER—explaining his condition, handling paperwork—until the officers arrived. With them involved, Cole and I would've had to debrief with multiple people across departments. They could've insisted on our protection, maybe a government-owned safe house. Somewhere fortified with alarms, a camera in every room. At best, Cole and I wouldn't be able to do anything that matters. At worst, we'd be handing ourselves to the enemy.

I check over my shoulder.

It doesn't look like the Nomen chased us after all.

After we left, maybe they launched an evacuation of Tony's home. I picture them racing through the estate—past the shot walls, over shattered lamps—piling into cars in the garage. Or maybe they bolted into the woods, carrying all they'd brought, leaving nothing except blood in the carpet. I remember their laptop in the kitchen—the photo Cole took.

"What was on their computer?"

He nods to the phone in my hands.

I swipe to Cole's photos, pull up the most recent.

There it is: the laptop, covered with dark windows. In each, the background is a void—no ads, no logos. It's strange to find a site that isn't flashing with sponsored content—unsettling, now, to be without it. It makes this corner of the web feel hidden or deserted, as if the topics might be that disturbing. The text is white, but most is off-camera. Cole focused on the web address in the center of the frame, visible all the way to the *.onion* toward the end.

I finally realize what this is.

~

At Cole's, we head for the library.

I almost trip over my feet, stiff from the drive.

We never had enough service to download Tor, the browser we'd need for the dark web. Every time I tried, the icon would freeze with a circular progress bar on top. Cole and I couldn't talk about anything else. At one point, he asked about my jaw, but I couldn't bring myself to respond with more than a grunt. I was too intent on the app, staring at the purple tile on his screen—the white onion on top, portending layers of encryption.

I get to the laptop first.

http://nomencollective73029-9fk29sk29sk?19d-
j19d0sname-fighters.onion/home

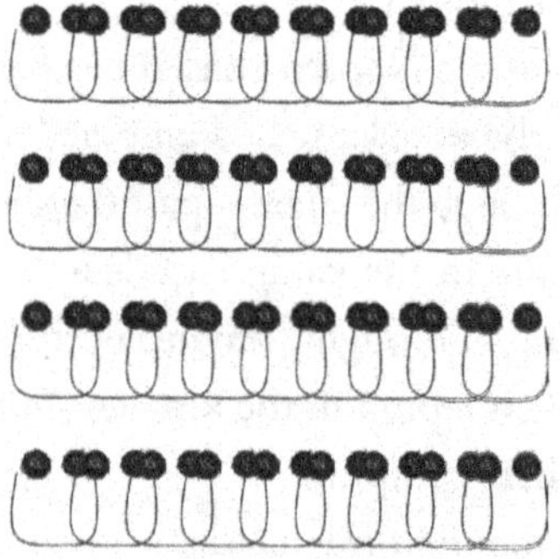

http://nomencollective73029-9fk29sk29sk?19d-j19d0sname-fighters.onion/origin

Origin

No one knew who you were.

You lived in the margins, unseen, unheard.

Everything felt empty. It was all waiting in line with your hands full and staring at someone's back. It was all sitting down to watch ads for laundry detergent and thick, white, absorbent, fucking perfect paper towels. Your whole life was a TV dinner, a microwaved bowl of soup. And no one even looked at you. No one ever stood this close and saw you were barely alive.

Together, we can undo the damage.

It will be a war.

But this is what you need. This is what you've been craving. Because the missing piece in your dead life has always been a great and terrifying mission. You want to feel the burn and outlast the pain for the sake of something good. You want to walk into the dark, fight death itself, and step out on the other side. You want to sink your teeth into what bites back and finally star in your own life.

Welcome to the glorious revolution.

No comments permitted.

We are the creators now.

http://nomencollective73029-9fk29sk29sk?19d-j19d0sname-fighters.onion/manifesto

Manifesto

I. Remove Class Differences

The famous are modern monarchs.

They live without the rules that the rest of us do. They live in a world where everything they want is free; where opportunities arrive independent of merit; where they dominate attention at the expense of real issues and widespread aliveness.

They have disproportionate influence on matters entirely unrelated to their "talents," including but not limited to major political elections. They direct a disproportionate amount of wealth based on their influence and sway.

II. Overcome the Talent Fallacy

The Famous Elite have tricked us into believing they have a monopoly on talent.

Talent is everywhere, in every single one of us. We are all born bold and inventive. We are all called on to design and perform. These roles do not belong to the creative monarchs, the unelected cultural tyrants, the visible class.

There are too many unknown masters, too many champions in empty rooms, too many greats whose gifts go unseen. They have been ignored for too long.

III. Cure Unworthiness

The famous fuel the belief that we aren't worthy. They want us to feel inadequate so that we think they're different. So that we think they're more.

IV. Overcome Worship

People have always suffered from the impulse to worship.

We have always found icons and given them everything of value: our gold, our love, our undivided attention. First, we worshipped gods. Then we worshipped the false idols among us. The religious instinct is written into our DNA, embedded and deadly.

When we bow to worship, we undermine ourselves. When we kneel, we cut off our own legs. We deny our own power and disappear into an audience.

V. Redirect Focus

Their trivia has become our cultural sustenance.

We need more to eat.

VI. Our Mission

We were locked in cages, robbed of our humanity, by the Famous Elite. They convinced us that only they were special. But now we are breaking out of the zoo.

What did you do, make, and believe before the Famous Elite made you feel invisible? That is your true self. That is the fearless kernel of who you are meant to be.

We are Nomen, from nomen nescio, Latin for "I do not know the name." As Nomen, we will liberate mankind by removing those who took advantage of our religious instinct, exploiting it for their own gain. We will light the sparks they stole. We will unbreak the broken. Because we are all wild originals. We need more space than comment sections and reviews. We deserve to chase our own greatest potential.

We are now at the dawn of a world filled with local arts, sports, and entertainment. We will see true meritocracy and unimaginable freedom. Come with us and feel it. Anyone who continues to support the Famous Elite is an enemy of the new America.

http://nomencollective73029-9fk29sk29sk?19d-j19d0sname-fighters.onion/new-new

New New

November 4, 4:51 a.m. ET

The Royal 50 are in our hands.

After we spent our lives in theirs.

Look around now.

Without them, buses keep running. Planes take off.

We worshipped them, but our lives are the same without them. They were never responsible for the work that sustains us. Despite what they made us believe.

Their song has been silenced.

And now ours will play.

http://nomencollective73029-9fk29sk29sk?19d-j19d0sname-fighters.onion/formerly-tony

Formerly Tony

Tony Graham spent too long in his ivory tower. So high above us that we must have looked like insects. We're eight-legged scavengers. Aren't we, Tony? Skeletal specks.

Tony misjudged us and tried to save himself with a bribe. Of course, we weren't surprised. The Famous Elite always expect special treatment, even from their enemies.

Before he joins the others, let's remind him that his days of special treatment are over. From this moment on, we won't treat him like Tony. He is our blank space, our ____________________. He is every target, all targets. Is there anything you want to tell the Royal 50? Let us unleash your fury.

Nomen10023: Guy Conrad: entitled talking head

Nomen1011: Fk **all of you** and your self-satisfied award shows. If I have to listen to one more soapbox from someone who hasn't spent a day in the REAL WORLD since they were 15, I swear. I am so sick of your smug opinions cropping up like weeds. You weren't elected to Congress. You won a trophy for [movie]. And since you forgot your place, let us remind you.

Nomen203: Krissa, everything I learned about your "personal" life was against my will. Every second of it felt like a violation of my faith, a path I was forced to walk against God. Shame on you for teaching us and worse, our children, nothing except to be the most photoshopped, the most plastic versions of ourselves. It's going to take real work to get us on a better path.

Nomen1829: Lane Driver, you call yourself a "climate activist" then jet around on private planes? Do you have any idea how much damage you personally have done to our planet? Do you think we buy your empty sound bites about the rainforest? I'm done watching you pretend to be an environmentalist. You love this planet? Do you? Good, because we will bury you alive.

Nomen2932: to the Visible Class: prepare to be Invisible. The amount of exposure you've had, and for what? You abused your power, and we are here for a reckoning . . .

SIXTEEN

Cole and I read through hundreds of attacks, all the insults Tony must've heard. It was sadistic enough to maul him, but to depersonalize him—anonymize him when he was in that vulnerable state, making him feel confused and unknown—is true evil.

Some of the attacks are precise. These people catalog the reasons for their hate, drilling down, ultra-specific. Others get philosophical, saying names are an invention in need of repair, that we shouldn't be lulled into watching other people live. These posts are more general, raging at ideas over people. Then plenty are primal, bloodthirsty. Someone begs the Nomen to cut off everyone's hands. Someone refers to a "debt of pain" they're dying to collect.

The page transitions to photos of Tony in the basement. In the first two, he's unmarred, his shirt still white. The camera flash burns a hole into the room, while the rest stays hidden in the dark. I pause on the trackpad. It feels like an invasion of privacy to see Tony's worst moments, when he had absolutely no control. But we have to look. Don't we? Everything is evidence. Any detail here could bring us closer to Gwen.

I scroll, nauseous, upset.

The lower we go, the more Tony falls apart in his chair. We see the break of his nose deepen over a series of stills. We see his bruises darken, widen, like shadows creeping over his skin. His bones lose their stiffness. Bite marks break out across his arms, one with spots of blue. It's almost too disturbing to take in. Tony tried to sacrifice everyone for himself, and instead, he sacrificed himself for everyone. I remember him starring on billboards for *Jim.* Now he sits alone in front of us, his face all but ripped in half, splitting from torture meant for fifty people.

"We are the creators now."

This is what they chose to make.

Cole and I click our way through the site.

He sits closer to me as the night drags on, his arm drifting toward mine. At one point, he insists we eat. We order to an alias—two spaghetti and meatballs to Tom Parker—but only poke at the food once it arrives. It's hard to open my mouth, harder to chew. While we eat, Cole's quieter than usual, gone inward. We feel too busy to clear and leave the aluminum boxes on the desk. Our meatballs are mostly untouched, split in half with forks and left to cool.

http://nomencollective73029-9fk29sk29sk?19d-j19d0sname-fighters.onion/unplugged

Unplugged

Why we joined. What we became.

Nomen011: RS found me.

Back then, I wasn't committed to life. I said as much online, and no one listened, no one cared—except him. Other people read my posts, but he was the only one to respond.

Nomen121: At first, I didn't message him back.

After all, we'd never met. I figured he'd forget about me like everyone else. But he didn't let me disappear.

We started talking. Then he kept checking in—not in a pushy way, but like he genuinely wanted to know how I was. He'd ask about my day, the little things—like what I had for lunch or if I'd seen anything funny online. It was small, but it started to crack something open.

We kept messaging. He'd say things like, "You're quieter today—what's going on?" And "You always notice the details." It wasn't empty praise: it was specific, real. He made me feel appreciated, like I had something to offer, even if I couldn't see it myself. It wasn't an overnight transformation. I didn't wake up "fixed." But RS saw me when no one else did. He reminded me what it felt like to matter.

Nomen91: Then he invited me to the House.

Nomen011: I didn't know what I was saying yes to at first.

Because at first, I didn't get it. A place where people lived together and looked out for each other? He said it wasn't just a place to crash—it was a family for people without one. I remember thinking I didn't belong there or anywhere. But RS has this way of making you believe in things. He kept saying, "You should come. Just see it for yourself." And somehow, I said yes.

Moving in felt like . . . stepping into another world. The House was just like he said, full of people who actually cared. I remember the first night, sitting in the living room, watching everyone talk like they'd known each other forever. I felt like an intruder, until someone handed me a drink and said, "Welcome home." Home. I hadn't realized how much I'd been missing that word.

Nomen121: The House . . . it pulled you in.

People noticed you. If you didn't show up for dinner, someone would knock on your door—not to nag, but to check in. If you were quiet, they'd ask what was wrong—not in a prying way, but like they actually wanted to know. For the first time, I wasn't just seen. I was part of something.

Nomen91: Then RS started teaching us about fame.

He'd sit us down in the living room after dinner and lay it out like it was obvious: all our problems stem from fame. At first, I didn't get it. I didn't see how celebrities had anything to do with my life.

But then, RS had all of us read a book: a small white one that fit right in your palm—if the Bible were a deck of cards. Do you know what I mean? The book explained everything he'd been saying. It had the Declaration of Grievances, the Manifesto, everything. It pinned all our emptiness—that gray fucking void—right on celebrity culture. Then it started to make sense. It helped that we were drinking. RS made us drinks every night—but it wasn't the drinks. It was the ideas.

Nomen011: RS didn't leave it there.

He said that one day, we'd put an end to fame. One day, we'd hold celebrities accountable for what they'd done—just like in the book. Because the book had a punishment for the Famous Elite, one designed just for them. At first, it sounds . . . wrong. But then, you see there's justice to it. You realize the punishment is also a profound lesson, perfectly suited to the crime.

Wrong, but . . . right.

Nomen121: RS got serious about making a difference. He let us into his master plan: We really were going to end fame. We were going to hold them accountable.

And then, life in the House started to change. RS started punishing people who were late to dinner. People who talked over him. Who laughed too loud. He'd be there with a slap, a shove—or worse. He never used to do that. The first time he hit me, I didn't know what to think. RS didn't apologize. He just said, "You need to be ready." And over time, it made sense. He was making us stronger, preparing us for the plan. For what we'd all agreed to do.

Nomen91: Then RS took it even further.

He pushed us even more. He got us to be rougher, confront each other with force. "You need to be ready." His words were like a chant in our heads. Slowly, arguments in the House turned into fights. Fights turned into something raw, primal. And RS never stopped them—the opposite. "This is how you grow," he'd say. "You have to feel the pain." He turned everything into a crucible for strength. Because he couldn't let us be soft.

He needed to harden our souls.

Nomen011: When we were finally ready, we left the House. We got jobs, waiting for the plan to begin. Now, after all that preparation, the moment is finally here.

And you can be part of what's to come . . .

So, Rex recruited the Nomen online.

It looks like he preyed on kids who'd posted about feeling numb. He made them feel seen, slowly earning their trust. And then . . . "That *house. That* fucking *house.*" But that place was even worse than I thought. The Nomen are victims too.

I stare at the white on black.

For a while, I wasn't sure if Rex was out of his own control. But this . . . took planning. He ran a home for kids who felt like the walking dead. He groomed them and then drove them to pull off high-wire attacks. Of course Rex is in control. Everything the Nomen write about their cultural shift, becoming more violent—I sense how the new atmosphere fenced them in. Suddenly, they were too terrified to leave. Rex cultivated that: He baited them with empathy, a new home. Then he used violence to control them. If he was erratic, it was on purpose.

It's all been part of his plan.

Cole shuts the computer. "Before we go any further, there's something I need to tell you." He's looking at me as if he has bad news—terrible. As if we're both terminally ill. I can sense it's the kind of news that will take energy, tear us away from the mission at hand. I ask if he should tell me now or if we should finish combing through the site first. He fidgets.

"Sorry," I pivot. "What is it?"

"We can keep reading."

"No, really, what is it?"

"I want you to know that I'm sorry."

My stomach starts to tense, squeezing what's left of the noodles into something hard, tight. I reach for Cole's hand. His fingers are cool, as if the blood is running back into his arms, warming his core in an emergency. I tell him that whatever it is, we'll figure it out together. He stares at me, his eyes red rimmed, moody. Eventually, he nods.

"I'll go get it."

He leaves me alone.

I hear his footsteps track into the living room, then over to the . . . shelves? I'm not sure. I glance at the computer, feeling defeated. It must be close to two in the morning, maybe even later. Cole and I have pored over most of the site and still don't know where they're keeping everyone. I rub my eyes. Even with them shut, I see a white-on-black glare. I taste something like grime and feel a rising doom. Going so deep into their site must've taken more of a toll than I'd realized. Maybe we dipped into their world for too long without a break.

Cole returns with something in his hands.

He sits next to me, visibly uncomfortable.

I try to see what he's holding, but his fingers hide what's behind them. It only peeks through in white slivers, as if he's gripping a bone.

"We're in one of my stories," he says.

I look around.

Ultra. Exquisite.

I tell him warily that I know.

"No, I mean the Nomen. What's happening to the world."

He puts a book on the desk between us. It's white, slim—closer to a pamphlet, really. It doesn't look longer than sixty or seventy pages. I stare at the all-white cover—but it's not all white. There's something else. I lean in to see a smile. Its eyes are two dark holes, lips thin as a pinkie nail. It floats in the center of the void, one face alone in oblivion.

"Tell me what this is," I demand.

"This is *Rotator*." He flips through the book, too fast for me to read. But I see the dark pages, white text—a familiar white on black.

"It's about a vigilante group that targets celebrities. They kidnap fifty up-and-coming stars . . ."

"I don't understand."

I feel like the chair's been pulled out from under me.

"I know this is meaningless now, but I'm sorry. I'm so sorry." His voice is weak, as if he has no wish to defend himself. As if what's on the desk is so unforgivable—so uncorrectable—that he's resigned to what it's done. "I wish I knew what else to say. But . . . nothing even comes close." He's at a slight tilt toward me, with his angst coming through his eyes. But I really don't understand. The Nomen said Rex was inspired by a book: *"a small white one that fit right in your palm—if the Bible were a deck of cards."* Rex made everyone read it. Is Cole saying . . . Could he possibly be saying . . . he wrote what inspired Rex?

This doesn't make sense. Cole has always been dark, but he'd never write . . . a blueprint for an army. A map for a new terrorist group with living, breathing victims. Cole couldn't be the *brain* behind Rex—the man's caused too much pain. He kept children in his house for years, scaring them into submission. He taught them to hate, then handed them masks. Now he's taken forty-seven adults and had at least one mauled in a basement—tied to an aluminum chair, left to smell his own rot. Even if Cole *wanted* to—if he set out to write true horror, he could never write something with that kind of . . . power. Stories that start a revolution—that radicalize people, mobilize them into war . . . They're so rare it's not worth considering.

"Talk to me, Cole."

"Forgive me."

"You're the only person I have left. Don't tell me—"

"I'll tell you what happened." His tone is heavy with regret. "I've always been interested in horror—I know this sounds callous now." The book lies between us, pages bent with a subtle wave. "When I started writing, though, I didn't see any stories that truly terrified me. They were all too . . . safe. If you bought a book, it was in a public marketplace, part of a corporate business plan. A professional had removed all the typos, formatted every page to fit in a box. None of that was chilling enough. At best, a book like that could make you uncomfortable. But it wasn't going to come for you in the middle of the night—or better yet, at noon."

He pauses, reluctant to go on.

I'm about to prompt him when he opens his mouth.

"I was young and wanted to try something different. Because I wanted my story to bring on a panic. The kind that makes you look over your shoulder ten years later. That forces you to live differently because you feel a genuine threat on your life." His eyes widen. "So I printed the copies—two hundred, unsigned. And I scattered them." I ask what that means. "I got in my car and drove north. I made it a road trip—went all the way to Maine, leaving books along the way." I picture the white gift in the back of a mailbox.

The face waiting to be seen.

"Like I said, I wanted everything about the book to unsettle you—even the way that you found it. I wanted it strange enough to make you feel unsafe. I don't know. When other people are young, maybe they drink too much. Maybe they go to other extremes. But I went too far with ideas." He looks ashamed. "I have no excuse. All I can say is . . . Creative people are cursed: We have to do things our own way. And it can look bizarre or self-defeating, but at least it has our own personal stamp. At least we expressed ourselves and didn't fake it. We got closer to truth or freedom—real, infinite freedom. Yes, what I did was mad, but at least I could show the world I was here. I could be Cole Harper. I didn't have to be anyone else.

"Again, not trying to *excuse*. Just trying to *explain*." His palms are open on his knees, with his fingers in limp curls. "I know this book has been misused. It's hurt people in ways that can't be undone. I just . . . We're not in control of what we make. Or what people do with it. Are we?" His eyes search for confirmation, but I can't give it. As much as I believe him. I'm still too shocked, unnerved. He nods, as if he didn't expect a response.

"So you printed these books."

I'm still processing.

"Then . . . delivered them? At random?"

"I remember every house." He nods, looking haunted. "There was a split-level in New Hampshire, with no one else for miles. I looked up photos of the inside, from when it was sold, just to have a sense of who'd be reading. I remember there was a bed in the kitchen. Trophy heads on every wall." I picture the book in an ammunition box, bolted to a splintered post. The box muzzled shut with a bungee cord, at the end of a narrow road. "Then there was a room in the middle of the woods—a single room, nothing else. And then there were massive estates. I found a manor behind a six-foot gate with lions on either side.

"You don't know how strange your tastes are until you're older. It's like . . . realizing your food tastes different from everyone else's. You're seeing different colors. Do you know what I mean?" I do, but I'm in no state to have that discussion now. "I know what I wrote was terrible. I'd never do anything like that again. But . . . I'm responsible for the man I used to be." He looks kicked in the stomach. "Yes, I wrote this book, over a decade ago. And yes, I must've given one to Rex. I chose someone who . . . brought it to life." I picture Rex strutting through a ten-bedroom house, this pamphlet with him at all times. I imagine how deeply worn it must be now: creased cover, soft corners. Maybe fringed with tears from overuse.

"What happens in the book?"

"I'll tell you . . ." Cole winces. "But please, I need you to know I never meant for this to happen. I didn't even reopen the book. I'd almost forgotten about *Rotator* until New Year's, when I saw their symbol." It smiles below us, radiant, decapitated. "The Nomen took it right off the cover. But it wasn't just the face. It was the name of the group, their mission. During the ball drop, on air, they quoted full lines from the story." His bottom lip hangs open with shock. "They hadn't just read it; they believed in it. Like it was a voice in their head.

"I hoped that would be the end of it. Then . . . Myra." He pauses, as if he's feeling her loss all over again. "At that point, I had to do something. I felt responsible—worse, involved. As if I'd been there in the Garden and grabbed her myself. That's why I set up the dinner. It's part of why I'm still here with you." I'm unnerved by how much I believe him. Maybe it's his eyes, pinched with regret. Or it's the rumble of his voice. It makes everything sound sincere, like it's coming from so deep inside him it's an organ slipping out of his mouth.

I try again, firm. "What happens in the book?"

"The Nomen build . . ."

He stares at the book.

"The Nomen build a village in the woods," he admits. "They build off-white cabins in two straight lines—in the center of a circle of trees, the edge so sharp it looks man-made. When you stand on one side, the pines farthest away are dark pinpricks." It's unsettling to feel the story conjured in this room. "There's a road between the houses, leading into a town. There, the cabins become stores, all the same off-white. It might look normal if it weren't so remote. This street cuts through the middle of nowhere, wedged between dead ends.

"The book starts with a walk through the woods. The missing celebrities are in a line, trudging through the pines. Everyone's in plain white clothes, moving toward the cabins. And the closer they get . . . the emptier it feels. The cabins look small, maybe just one or two rooms each, as if this is a place where everyone lives alone. Paint peels in patches down to the wood. A few roofs sag. Old shingles curl up at the edges. The next thing they know, everyone is waking up inside the village. They come to in bed, with their memories erased.

"I won't take you through every page . . . but eventually, you learn about the Nomen. You learn they kidnapped the Famous Elite and moved all of them into this pen. Somewhere no one can see them, with their real names scrubbed, their minds wiped clean. It's the Nomen's utopia: a prison of anonymity for those who transgressed with fame." His words are slow, grim. "It inverts the high-flying lives celebrities used to have. *Rotator.* A reversal of fortune. A twisted form of justice. Now celebrities are remote and unknown, even to themselves."

Did the Nomen really bring this to life? Did they really build those cabins, with the sinking roofs, damp walls? A couple of them did mention concrete mix, shoveling until they were numb. They were talking about . . . a prison. This whole time, they've been building a prison. I picture the stores in town, like a segmented body across a clearing. I see a barren Main Street, starting nowhere, leading nowhere, gravel in the road like gray knucklebones.

"We're in a horror novel."

"I'm sorry."

He looks gutted, body limp.

"Why didn't you tell me?" I keep my voice even. Because nothing—not my terror, not my sense of betrayal, nothing—is as important as his answer. And if I'm not steady now, I'll never know. "This whole time, you've been asking me to trust you. You said we were a team—" He tells me he knows. "I don't think you do. You said we needed to understand each other. You said working together was our one way out . . . And you kept this from me?"

"I wanted to tell you." He sounds defeated. "But the idea that it's gotten this far . . . There are moments when *I* don't believe it, and I put the story together myself. I still have no idea how much they took from it, if they're going to . . . act it out." He swallows, looking ill. "And if I'm being honest, I didn't want you to leave." His tone softens further, making him sound even more vulnerable. "If you thought I was involved, you wouldn't have stayed. I had a hard enough time getting you to wait when you thought I was an innocent man."

"You expect me to trust you now?"

"I'm sorry, Fiona."

"Are you?"

"Yes. I should've told you. But I meant every word about needing a team." For the first time tonight, he doesn't sound like he's on his back foot. "If I've been a bad partner—and I have—it's because I'm not used to this either. I spend my days alone too." He looks at me, and I feel his eyes so deep in the back of my mind it's almost like they're in my memories. "I don't expect you to trust me now, but I'm also gambling with my life. They're coming for me too. I know that I've done something wrong—worse than wrong. It's spiritually disturbing." He turns away from the story. "But here I am, all in, trying to make it right."

He stares at me, raw, open.

And . . . I can't help but believe him.

What I feel most now is stupefied, spellbound by what this *thing* has done. Cole's eyes beg for forgiveness—from me, and maybe from himself. After all, he created this world. He might've chosen its smells. And whether I like it or not, he's right about staying together. If anyone's going to know this story and understand the Nomen's plan . . . it's him.

~

I can't sleep.

I'm in a horror novel.

Not just in any horror novel—one of Cole Harper's books.

The Nomen read it, and now they've built us a village. An ivory village in the woods. I see it every time I shut my eyes. In my mind, it's a half mile away. I'm standing in the field, just like Cole described, watching a dozen cabins emerge from the fog. They're low, with flat roofs. Each has two slim windows, and all of them, dark.

Is Gwen there now?

I turn over in bed, unable to stomach it.

We're all trapped in a horror novel, where the details were chosen to spike fear, freeze blood. Where it's only going to get worse with time as we tunnel deeper into the plot. The Nomen are even more terrifying now that I know they weren't formed to hunt us down—not really. They were made to haunt every witness. They were made to be pieces of hell.

I'm still trying to grasp how this happened. Of course Cole is a powerful writer. But Rex must've been ready for this book. Maybe he already hated fame, but now, he knew what to do with the rage. I picture him opening his mailbox to see the little white surprise, the tiny smile inviting him in. Back then, Rex would've been a teen. I don't know what was going on in his life at the time. But maybe the book arrived at just the right moment.

I try to stay grounded.

Hold on to the facts.

Even coming from a horror novel, the Nomen will have to work within the bounds of reality. Doors won't spontaneously lock. My fingers won't suddenly snap. And working within what's possible, I wonder if the Nomen can erase memories. I imagine finding Gwen only to watch her face stay blank, to realize that she doesn't remember me . . . or her baby. No, they couldn't—not this group. I've seen plenty of them up close: wired, junkie-thin. Lots of them, teens. No, they're not behind any breakthrough. The most they could ruin, within reason, would be short-term memories. They could do it through drugs or . . . head injuries.

I should sleep.

I really should.

There are still a few links left on their site. I should rest so I can get up again and finish sifting through them. I think over what we've seen, in case I missed something—glazed over a pivotal clue. The navigation bar wasn't straightforward. All links were cryptically named: "New New" for their newsfeed. "Unplugged" for testimonials. Then "Pure Force" for the page where Nomen pledged to be working with high-ranking police. They showed thirty redacted headshots in a grid, with their edges traced, features erased. I never was sure what Cole and I were clicking on. I'm still not sure what's left. All I know is that I really should sleep.

But when I try, I see the village.

Silent cabins in the woods.

SEVENTEEN

I rush back to the laptop at six.

My legs feel heavy, asleep.

I check first for any mention of Tony.

Now there are a dozen stories about him.

The paramedics found Tony where we left him. He was conscious, with what are described as significant facial injuries, bite marks, and broken ribs—in addition to a dislocated shoulder, blunt trauma to the back, and contusions where he was tied. He's in stable condition at Northern Westchester Hospital, expected to make a full recovery. Police have cordoned off where Tony was found, as well as his nearby home. No arrests have yet been made.

I picture Tony in his hospital bed after CT scans and X-rays. Nurses shaving the hair around his wounds, administering local anesthesia, and carefully stitching them shut. A whole team in scrubs giving him tetanus shots, morphine, and ibuprofen. Maybe Tony was in such a state that he begged them to take off their masks. Police and federal investigators might be in the waiting room now, asking reception when he'll be ready to talk.

I close the articles, mouth dry.

I should reopen the Nomen's site.

But first, I head to the kitchen for water. Maybe I'm avoiding the last few links—the white text, black pit behind it. Every page was intense, disturbing—the giddy violence, the sense that real Nomen were online with us. I grab a cup, run the faucet. Watch it drip, stalling. Finally, I force myself to fill the glass and bring it back to the library.

Now I pull up their site.

Their homepage greets me with mean smiles, overlapping like barbed wire. I click to their news feed—still nothing since their last update announcing that they had us. *"The Royal 50 are in our hands. After we spent our lives in theirs."*

The next link leads to a series of forums.

I read them closely, looking for a decisive clue, something to tell us where everyone is. In the most recent thread, Nomen share countersurveillance tips. The paranoia appears to run deep, with everyone watching the shadows, anticipating deceit. Someone lists twenty signs of being followed. "If you change your routine and still see them, they are there for you." I wonder if paranoia is a side effect of Rex's special drinks. Or maybe it grew out of living in the House. Someone posts a link to a device that sweeps for hidden bugs. One comment shares signs of a home break-in, with giveaways as slight as one cabinet left open, one light left on.

Cole walks into the room.

Takes his seat next to me.

Without thinking, I hug him close.

I must've meant to comfort him, but this is more comfort*ing* than I expected. He pauses, then puts his hand on my back. I feel the tips of his fingers, the heels of his palms. He's holding me too—harder than I would've expected, with his injuries. As if the feelings outmatch the pain—the need for relief, forgiveness. I hold on as if he's the only thing between us and the cabins in the woods. *Rotator* is still on the desk, the smile facing me upside down.

"How did you sleep?" I ask.

"I didn't."

I pull away.

"This isn't your fault." I get right to the issue. "Yes, you wrote the book. But I need you to know I forgive you. You didn't want this to happen. And I trust you just as much as I did before." For the first time since we jumped, he can now open both eyes. The intensity of his stare is doubled. "I know we're all . . . messy." My voice is softer. "We're all broken and hurt and doing our best. And we've all done things that don't define us—even this. Even this, Cole. So don't worry about me, not with everything else going on. Don't worry about—" I drag my hand back and forth between us. "Because *this* is solid. *This* is what we have left. It's our handhold in the wall, the one thing that's safe and sure going into . . . whatever lies ahead."

He's teary. "Thanks, Fiona."

"Don't thank me. You are the good guys. *We* are the good guys." I hold his fingers. "I know you were different when you were young. Everyone is." I remember moving to New York for college, how lost I felt without my friends and their families. Pain used to be a core part of who I was. It wasn't until I started to write *The Redfins* that I found some steadiness, a thread of purpose to make me stronger on my own. "Everyone changes. We all grow up. I forgive you for everything you did before." For a second, I have a vision of our younger selves meeting. Him, creative as a way to cope. Me, writing for the same reason, in a different way.

"We're going to find everyone." I wrap my other hand around his—then let go, self-conscious. "Sorry, I'm . . . physical with my friends. We don't really have personal space."

"I'm honored."

In this light, his eyes are two pupils. And even with everything that he's written, I see the good in them. Because he doesn't have to be here. He doesn't have to be in this fight. He could be in a safe house, under medical supervision. Letting everyone fend for themselves. Instead, he's up early, here next to me. He really is all in, trying to make it right.

"I see the good in you."

It sounds awkward, more prophetic than I hoped.

"If you see any good in me, that's because you have it in you. You really do, Fiona. And you have more than that: You have the strength to show it." It's such a heartfelt compliment that I'm embarrassed. "So don't give me too much credit. If any part of me is looking decent, it's just because you invite it. You make other people want to do better."

His gaze drifts.

I follow it to the computer.

The link to their news feed is bright.

I click it to find an update. Cole and I lean in and read: "The Intake" is set to begin in twenty-nine hours, at precise coordinates. There's one longitude, one latitude—and that's it. That's the full update. A digital clock ticks down in the middle of the screen.

~

Cole and I search the coordinates.

They converge in the woods next to a sprawling home in Maine—and I wonder if we're looking at the House. From the satellite image, it's big enough, multi-winged. The surrounding woods are dense—leaves almost cruciferous from a bird's-eye view, all unseasonal shades of green. I remember that Google Earth doesn't update its photos of rural areas as often. This shot could be from three years ago, four. I wonder what the place looks like now, what's lying in wait at these coordinates, in place of the compacted trees.

Cole and I zoom in.

A winding driveway cuts through the forest, thin as a whip under the leaves. The house itself is an irregular U shape, with long, branching extensions. It bulges with every gable and turret, like something organic, left to grow to cancerous proportions. A few clearings reveal scattered additions: A possible garage. A shed. At least one guest cottage. Others peek through the canopy, all of them almost drowning in green. This house shows signs of deliberate isolation: not just the iron driveway gate, but the striking lack of neighbors.

This place leaves you alone.

I stare, transfixed.

The House.

Just maybe, the House.

This one easily could've housed a group of kids—dozens, maybe even hundreds, if they were willing to be close. Let their arms touch around the dinner table. Sleep five or six to a room. And why wouldn't they? The way they talked about the House, they made it sound like the first time they felt at home: Dinners every night. An authority figure who cared. Rex made these kids feel secure. I picture them under the canopy—it's almost lightproof, letting nothing in, nothing out. I imagine them in the House's long arms, getting used to the place, letting down their guards. And . . . I have the overwhelming sense that *this* is where they lived. This is where the kids were led, where they joined a group that spun out of control.

We look up the address.

17 Crow Fields.

The house appears to have been sold thirty years ago to Malcolm and Leigh Stiller. We google them to find an obituary: The couple died thirteen years ago in a ski accident. They left behind one son, Rex, at sixteen—RS. Rex Stiller. We keep reading. Apparently, Malcolm spent his career at Dark Horse, a cybersecurity company, becoming its CEO.

"His parents left him the house," I put it together.

I turn to Cole.

He's staring at the screen.

"Cole," I whisper. "Have you . . . been there?"

He nods, blanched. "I remember the mailbox: a hinged door in a stone post. You couldn't see the house . . ." I picture him driving up to the gate. By then, he would've been on the road for a while. Maybe he was down to his last few books. Or this was the final one. I picture him rolling down his window to hear nothing but trees. Thirteen years—if Rex's parents died thirteen years ago, this book would've found him reeling. I wonder if Cole could tell that something was wrong, if he sensed a breakdown through the woods. I picture the white booklet on top of accumulating mail. It would've looked deceptively innocent—lightweight, no obligations. Delivered completely free. Much like a religious pamphlet, arriving for someone in need.

We search for more on Rex.

But he seems to have kept to himself.

There's no social media, nothing in the news.

Cole and I debate one more time if we should turn this over to the police. Now that we know Rex's full name—now that we have their website. Now that we know where the Nomen plan to be tomorrow night, maybe it's time to step back. Cole plays devil's advocate, arguing for us to trust the professionals. But with his voice retreating, even he doesn't seem to believe it. We've both seen "Pure Force," with the cutouts of those in uniform, lurking on their side. And this close, with a clock running against us . . . we can't make any mistakes. I don't want to trip a wire and let the Nomen get away. We decide not to bow out. We can't hand this over to people we don't absolutely trust. There's too much at stake, no time.

We should see this place for ourselves.

EIGHTEEN

We drive north out of New York City.

Cole is in the driver's seat, while I'm with his laptop on the passenger side. Our duffels are in the back, stuffed with clean clothes, rain gear, flashlights, water bottles, and food from Cole's pantry. We're headed straight for the coordinates in Lasco, Maine, and should be there in six hours. The plan is to get close to the house in the woods. If our friends really are there, then we'll call every number in the book—not just 9-1-1, but the state police, fire department, everyone. We'll drown out interfering Nomen with real people desperate to help.

We packed masks too. It was my idea to order two white ski masks to Cole's apartment. I figured that if we're going to be in a small town with other Nomen, we might need to blend in. The gear arrived in a brown bag for Tom Parker. They're full-coverage masks, polyester. In each, the eye holes are almond shaped. The mouth's a perfect O, like a scream in a glass of milk. I tried mine on briefly to make sure it would fit. It was unnervingly comfortable, only slightly muting sound. Cole and I tucked ours into our duffels right before we set off.

I face the laptop on my thighs.

"Any more updates?" he asks.

I check the Nomen's news feed.

Shake my head.

"Not yet."

I flick back through the site.

Rereading parts, still processing.

The Nomen might've lived in the House, but eventually they did leave it. *"We got jobs, waiting for the plan to begin . . ."* Then Rex must've refilled the place—returned to social media and chat rooms, sniffing out the wounded. People cut off enough that they wouldn't be missed. He must've recruited in waves. That's the only explanation that fits—there are too many people in his group. Some have looked in their twenties; others, more painfully young.

Rex must've been hatching this group for years.

Now I'm thinking of the kids.

I know they're lethal.

I know there's a chance that they kill Cole and me in Maine, with one shot through us both. But as much as we're fighting for our friends—in a way that feels dangerous to *think*, even just this once—I feel like the Nomen are hostages too. I could never say that to Cole. He might stop short on the median, refuse to drive another inch until I take it back. Until I swear to treat them like their lives are less important than our own. Still, I can't help but think that the Nomen are just . . . kids who trusted the wrong man. Yes, they're brutal, loyal to Rex. Some might not even be in their right minds. But in a way, they're vulnerable too.

They just wanted a home.

Once they found the House . . .

Of course they couldn't turn back.

Because a house is a powerful symbol, especially when you're alone. I didn't put my parents' house on the market until I was a senior in college. I kept it, even though I only went back once every few months—to run faucets, flush toilets. Walk through and notice its details: The leaky guest bathroom sink. The upturned edge of the hallway rug. The child-safe shelves in the living room, which my dad anchored himself. I held on to the house because . . . a house is braided into the idea of family. It makes a silent promise to keep you safe.

I don't know these kids.

But I know they deserve better—better than Rex, better than this group. I don't believe everything happens for a reason. But maybe all the pain I've felt—everything I've lost—has been preparing me for this. Maybe I was hurt so one day I could recognize people with similar pain and be ready to help them. If that's true, then I shouldn't feel so nervous, barreling toward the Intake. Because if that's true, my whole life has been building up to this.

~

"What happens at the end of the book?" I ask.

The highway's almost dark.

The sun burns behind black trees.

Cole changes hands on the wheel, untired and alert. He must be running on the same adrenaline that I am, the Nomen's ticking clock like a second heartbeat. *Rotator* rests in the console between us. I know this book isn't a computer program. It's not fate. But it is . . . a direction. The ending could tell us more about what's lying in wait on Crow Fields.

"The story follows one man who wakes up in the village." Cole's tone is flat. "In the end, he gets a group together, and they escape into the woods. They carve X's into trunks as they go, in case they need to find their way back. When the sun starts to set, they turn around to see an army of X-marked trees—but not just X's. There are lowercase t's. Triangles. So they're not the first to walk through the woods. And what happened to the rest of them?"

He lets the question go unanswered.

"The next day, they find a chain-link fence—massive, with twenty-foot posts, circling the town. Armed guards walk the perimeter. Still, he's determined to get out of this place, whatever it is. He lifts part of the fence, and his group runs for it. Guards chase them with dogs. Soon, he starts to smell the beach. With no choice, they charge into the ocean, in the middle of the night. But the water's too cold. It squeezes the air right out of them."

Cole takes a slow breath.

"He wakes up in a hospital, where he watches a video of . . . himself. It's a compilation of interviews with him, taken from late-night shows, the red carpet. He used to be an actor, a household name. But in every clip, he describes how fame ruined his life.

"The rest of his group is doing the same thing. They're all watching themselves list their gripes with fame: the stalkers, loss of privacy. The constant pressure and threats to their kids. At the end, every video addresses the person watching and explains that you chose to live in this village. Even before the Nomen, you wanted a new life . . . didn't you? So when the Nomen arrived, you joined a like-minded group. You pooled your money and bought this land. You built this town together, every room. When it was finally done, every one of you took a rare and powerful drug—something to forget the past, forget yourself. Then you lay right down in your cabin.

"The video reminds them no one can leave. You already signed your commitment to stay." Cole watches the windshield. "In the final scene, he's escorted by a nurse back to his cabin, followed by the rest of his group. They're all shaken, convinced. But in the end . . . the reader knows they never chose this place. The reader knows they're victims."

I picture the village. The houses in two parallel lines. I see them with sagging roofs and insect damage. Leaky pipes and cracks in the foundations. The Nomen have enough land to build them—so many acres at their place in Maine it must feel like a world unto itself. Besides, the cabins wouldn't have been hard to assemble, so close to falling down. The Nomen could've scraped the materials from junkyards, demo sites. They could've scoured for uneven boards, only reaching for the worst: the ones with rot and screw stains; long, branching splits.

"I'm sorry," Cole says.

I take his hand on the console.

After a few miles, I still won't let go.

He stays in place like he needs me, too, not just my mind but my body—the tension in my fingers. The pressure of my wrist. He holds on like I'm precious and vital, every nervous inch.

~

We get closer to the House.

We're almost in Lasco, sundown.

New England–style homes are lit up on both sides. Each has a central chimney and steep roof made to shed heavy snow. In this light, they're all shades of yellow, gray, and absolute black. The closer we get to Lasco, the more the homes spread out. We pass firewood for sale—unattended with a sign, just left ready to burn. Eventually, we cross into Lasco and start to trek through denser forest. We drive by two mailboxes without any homes in sight.

We pass fewer and fewer cars.

Until we're the only one left.

Cole pulls off the road as planned, coming to a gentle stop. The woods are just outside my window, pines forming a natural edge. The House should be straight ahead. A mile through the trees, hidden from here, is the outer bound of Rex's land.

We open our doors.

The world is cold and still.

I stay in my seat, listening hard.

The only sounds are crickets and sheets of needles shaking in the wind. But I'm craning to hear if there's anything human: any whispers, footsteps. Anything unnatural in the woods. So far, there's nothing: no other cars humming this way, no echoes of movement. I flinch when Cole shuts his door—a loud crack through the night—and follow just a beat behind him. We grab our flashlights and masks from the trunk, stuff them in our coats.

We hurry into the woods.

A step inside, everything starts to feel alive: It's the dense forest smell. The surround-sound of shushing branches. I can only see fifty feet ahead, with scraps of moonlight through the canopy. My breaths come out in pale thrusts, the rest of the world dark. Cole slips on his mask, tugging the fabric down to his chin, until his eyes become black holes. We hadn't planned to wear the masks—not yet—but I sense the fear in his decision. He's right.

Without stopping, I pull mine on.

We walk, painfully alert.

We make unavoidable noise, cracking over woodchips, pine cones—only going quiet once in a while when we finally land on moss. There are no signs of a path, just unchecked growth: Vines under scruff. Mushrooms in a white bloom. Cole almost trips over a stump, grabbing my arm just in time. All our sounds echo briefly, only to fade into the woods.

So far, I think we're alone.

The ground is uneven.

I catch the rustle of something in motion and go absolutely still. Cole stops short. It came from the left. As we wait, the shadows start to look like they're breathing. The pines start to look like men, watching on all sides. I'm sweating, until the rustle turns into a four-legged scurry—tiny, racing paws. I take a recovery breath, feeling saved or maybe warned. Cole and I set out again, over rocks, roots. Branches drag over my mask.

Now . . . something new.

It's pale, straight ahead.

Barely there through the trees.

Cole and I slow down as we get close.

Eventually, we reach what looks like the end of the woods. We stay here on the edge of the forest, our toes dipping into a clearing. In front of us, there are over a dozen ivory cabins. They're small, maybe just one or two rooms each, as if this is a place where everyone lives alone. I'm frozen, feeling punched, staring at the homes in two parallel lines. I see where they become stores—all the same shade of white, tinted with just enough yellow to look sour. I can't move. I can't. I feel like I've already been here, in my mind.

The village.

It's really here.

Dark, empty—by all signs, empty.

Cole and I stare at the improbable jail.

This close, I'm terrified down to the blood in my feet. Each cabin has two slim windows. The doors are shut against the night—except for those without doors at all, just gaping holes. There's no one else in the clearing. It's an open field, in a noose of trees. Cole and I stand in place, dead mute, communicating our fear through locked knees and planted bones.

I don't want to get closer.

Until . . . Gwen.

I remember her weight on me, napping at the hotel. Then her white knuckles at the Oakwood, once the Nomen arrived. I promised her I'd help. I swore she'd meet her baby—and now I want to be there to see it. When she finally brings them home with Logan, I want to see them as a family of three: exhausted, happy, overwhelmed—and most of all, safe.

I step into the clearing.

Cole catches up with me.

We walk toward the cabins.

They look just as run-down as he described. One has a broken window, with sawtooth glass around a black hole. The next one slants toward the road. All of them, the color of Cole's book—like the blank space in an eye. A color you can't miss, not even in the dark. Cole and I tread through grass, quietly nearing the road. Porches sag. Railings splinter. Now we're steps away, and this close, I smell the decay. The moss plugging the cracks. The wooden planks so mottled that they look like they've been chewed. We walk between two cabins.

Stop by one.

Should we go inside?

There's still no one else here. The town looks dead empty, like a body without a soul. I glance back at the house. The windows have a thin gray veil of grime, hiding what's behind them. But of course we have to go inside. We have to understand this place.

I tread up the stairs.

They're covered in forest-green lichens.

I dodge a hole in the top step, longer than it is wide.

I'm reaching for the door when my shoes slip on a damp stretch. Cole stops me from falling just in time. I clutch his arm, heart racing. I feel like I just came dangerously close to . . . breaking through the stairs. Sending a shock wave into the woods. Leaving proof we got this close. I thank Cole just by meeting his gaze, too afraid to speak—to announce to anyone in earshot that we're here.

Together, we step inside.

The first thing I notice is the smell: concentrated musk. Cole grabs his flashlight. The beam takes a slow tour left to right. This place is a single room. The armchair by me has a diagonal slash across the back, leaking fluff in frozen clouds. The space ahead is cramped, with a dining table and four chairs. A kitchen area on the far wall includes an old sink and two-burner stove, one fridge in the corner. I take a lap around the table and face Cole from the other side. The dining chairs are mismatched, missing spindles on the back.

His flashlight finds a ladder.

It leads to a loft with four mattresses.

He continues to wave his light around the room. The ceiling beams are dark with green fur: None looks sturdy. Maybe Nomen built these places hoping they'd collapse. Maybe they watered the wood every day, urging it to rot. I open the refrigerator to find it working. Food waits on the shelves, precut in plastic containers: deli meats, one veggie tray, and hard-boiled eggs with yellow eyes. I walk back to Cole, spotting a bookshelf behind him. All books are the same, with unmarked white spines. Without picking one up, I know what they are.

This is where they plan to keep us.

We tread back outside.

In town, the cabins become shops. They're narrow, each with a sign extending toward the road: **General Store, Town Police.** I stare at the latter. **Town Police.** But something is . . . off. I take in the round corners, the weathered front. **Town Police.** It looks like the other signs, but there's something about the O's. Eventually, I see what's inside them: thin smiles, faint as spiderwebs. Someone took a knife and made the letters grin.

The front door to the station is open.

Cole and I peek inside, seeing what we can under the moon: just one front desk, dim shelves behind it. We keep moving past a toy store. The window display has a few old, ripped marching drums. A rocking horse lies on its side. Next is a hardware store with no door, just one hole. I poke my head in to find tools on both walls. It doesn't take long to see that nothing here could be used as a weapon—no hammers, no nails. All child-safe. There's a reception desk here too. It looks like a saloon counter from the 1800s: dark oak with a footrail.

I keep walking.

But Cole's stopped.

He's staring between two shops.

I follow his gaze, and now I see them: distant lights through the trees. A half mile away, there's an orange-yellow grid—windows. More than a dozen of them. The chill sets in more and more the longer that we stand here. I start to feel the cold in my eyes. My skin tightens up my arms. We must be looking at the House. Of course we expected to find it here. But it's another thing to *see* it. Another thing to stand here at night, right in the backyard.

Now Cole faces me.

His mask glows under the moon.

Of course we have to. It's why we came.

Gwen could be there—everyone. They could finally be close, right there past the trees. Cole and I set out for the lights. But even once we're moving again, my body won't warm up. It's as if my muscles know what lies ahead—just how afraid I should be. The wind picks up. And the closer we get, the more I see of the House. The place is still mostly dark, deeply saturated with the night. But through the shadowy pines and skeletal hardwoods, I make out more of its shape: The gables blotting out stars. Smoking chimneys. Stone facade.

Then, on the front porch: Nomen.

A short jog ahead, they sit on the railing.

Cole stops at the same time, as if we both just brushed up against the same invisible wire. We drop with painstaking slowness onto our knees, then our hands. There are four of them—all men, early twenties. Two slouch on the railing, their backs to us. Two more lounge in Adirondack chairs, facing the pitch-black woods. In white suits, no masks. Holding drinks, swept up in conversation. They might look distracted now. But how long will that last?

I scan the rest of the House.

The front doors are wider than my wingspan. The dark wood has been carved a hundred times with their symbol. The scratches look like matted foam, a thin film over the grain. And this close, I feel the weight of the place. There's something heavy in the air, almost like a tangible warning or a physical need to get back. Something moves across a first-floor window—three Nomen, more. And now I see: The Nomen are everywhere. They're in every window, every room. On the first floor, they're moving furniture. Six of them surround a sofa, like white ants around a crumb. On the second floor, four walk in a pack. Someone emerges at the top of the stairs, holding a chair over his head. Even in darker windows, I see signs of the group.

This house is full of them.

Are you here, Gwen?

Are you inside?

But there are no trucks in the driveway. There's no fleet of parked cars—not enough to have moved forty-seven adults. The closest Nomen throws his bottle into the woods. It lands on an exposed root and shatters, high pitched, uncomfortably close. I'm blinking fast, deathly still, as they continue to talk. They couldn't have seen us—couldn't possibly have seen us. But . . . how long before they do? Before they decide to check on the cabins?

Cole and I start to retreat.

Slow—very slow.

One foot.

Another.

We stay crouched low to the ground. I can't hear what the Nomen are saying, and hope we're just as silent to them—dead mute, like the stumps under me, the cold rocks in the dirt. I watch the Nomen on the porch, their legs spread wide, exuding a casual dominance. The ones inside haven't stopped moving. I can sense their energy from here, the thrill of feeling untouchable. Flying right next to the sun. Because their plan is working—their impossible plan is working. Cole and I are halfway back to the clearing when we finally stand up and run.

NINETEEN

We drive down black, empty roads.

I'm still lightheaded from the sprint.

For a while, after we got in the car, there were white specks across my field of view, shifting and elusive points of light. They looked like flecks of paint from the village. Or lingering fibers from the mask. Now, at least, I can see clearly. But my hands are shaking in my lap. The Nomen never saw us, but still I feel threatened within an inch of my life.

They did it.

They really did it.

Cole and I don't speak. We know what we saw.

After a tense few miles, Cole asks where we should spend the night. The sound makes me jump in my seat. I hadn't thought about sleep, but he's right. If we want to make a difference, then we absolutely need to rest. With the Intake tomorrow . . . That must be when the Nomen will fill the cabins—which means everyone must be close. As soon as Cole and I know *where they are*, we'll call every emergency branch for help. I still don't want to ring the alarm too soon and scare the Nomen off. Cole glances at me, lifting an eyebrow that grazes his curls.

Right, a place to sleep.

~

Cole and I pull into a campground on the outskirts of Lasco. We drive between parked RVs. Only a few still have lights on, exposing a lonely picnic bench and then a grill down to its last hot curls. Two men smoke on lawn chairs, their ends like a pair of orange eyes. I whisper that maybe we should sleep with our masks on. Cole nods, parking.

He turns to me, in grayscale.

"Sorry," he says, "but if we're going to get any sleep, I need to pretend for one second like we're all right. I need to make myself believe we're not at gunpoint." He hangs on to my stare, and I sense his urgency. His tight throat, chest. "Is that okay?"

"I understand."

Maybe he's right. Maybe there have to be moments—even with everything at stake—that you go somewhere safe in your mind. That you force a second of peace. Cole settles into his seat. I can't hear anything from the other camps, from the woods. It starts to feel almost like we've stepped back from the edge and found this place to ourselves.

"At the dinner for everyone . . ." The pause that follows is so long my attention drifts. I'm about to turn when he adds, "I meant to put your seat next to mine."

I ask him why, blindsided.

"Well . . ." His tone is still slowed down, confessional. At the same time, there's a need under the surface, a clear drive to leave nothing unsaid. "I really did admire your books. The six-gilled sharks, the yellow kelp jungle . . . I bet your first draft smelled like the ocean. I don't presume to know what that takes. But I thought something about us might be the same.

"Then I watched an interview with you, and . . . I'd never seen anyone like you." Even here, now, he sounds moved. "We might've had writing in common. But you were miles above me." I'm about to protest when he shakes his head. "No, I'd like a minute to explain. Because it's important to me that you know. I'd never seen anyone—on a *talk show*—so interested in the people around them. Your attention just flowed out. I've still never met anyone with the same . . . natural empathy. Your books had me interested, but *you* were something else. You were a force for good. I thought about reaching out. It wasn't until the dinner—

"We were there to talk about the Nomen," he interrupts himself. "But I had to sit next to someone. I'm sorry to tell you now. There'd be no right time. But as your partner in—whatever this is—those are all my cards." I reach for his hand. I can feel that he trusts me, really feel it—his fingers slack, body relaxed, letting the truth flow through him.

I tell him it's okay.

"The last thing I'll say is . . . I know who I expected to meet. I had an idea of who you might be, and somehow, you're even better." I try to downplay the compliment, saying that you're the sum of who you spend time with. "Then you've found some special people."

Now I'm thinking about them.

But this time, I want to let Cole in.

"I don't think I've told you about them."

"What are their names?"

It's such a simple question, but it makes me feel like he understands.

"I have four close friends," I admit. "There's Gwen. Then there's Marlowe, Caroline, and Emma. They're from my hometown." He asks me to tell him more about them, as if he knows that I want to. So I tell him that every year, Marlowe gives us each a specially chosen crystal for our birthday, along with a handwritten card explaining its power. Caroline just bought her own apartment in Philadelphia; she's training for a marathon. And Emma is the most *un*-superficial person I know, always with one of her kids on her hip. Her oldest has type 1 diabetes, but even in the worst of times, she can laugh. "By now, they all know Gwen, and when the five of us hang out . . . it's hard to draw the lines between everyone."

"You're a great friend."

"I just take care of the ones I have."

He says he can see that, looking right at me.

"A lot of people who've been through what you have . . . I imagine it would've closed them off. Made them unwilling to feel that kind of loss again. But you still love your friends. You still give them everything you have. And that's not even the half of it. Because you're not just there for your friends. You put yourself on the line for other people, even the ones you've just met. Here you are, about to risk it all again . . . Why do you think that is?"

I swallow.

I can't remember the last time someone asked that—if ever.

My friends don't bring up the accident anymore. They've learned from my subtle cues to give me room where I was hurt. But now, with Cole, I don't bristle as he gets close to the nerve. There's almost no resistance at all. "I think pain opens you up," I admit. "I think when you've really suffered—when you've been through life-altering grief—you never want anyone to feel that again. Once you know the lows that are out there, you're gentle." He says he wouldn't necessarily call me *gentle*. "Well, you're what the situation requires—strong, gentle."

"One of a kind."

I still have his hand.

And want to tell him more.

I want to go on like this and get a little lost with him. Time feels too precious, but that's just it: Time feels too precious, and there are people who need us. I tell him we should sleep, and he nods in agreement. We reach for our masks. I slip mine on, and the air from my nose burns a damp spot in the fabric. When I look over at Cole, he's already in his. It's as tight as an airless plastic bag. We settle back down, facing each other, holding hands. He shuts his eyes, but I don't. For some reason, I'm tempted to stay up, watch over him.

"*We* should sleep," he repeats.

He opens his eyes, as if he could feel me watching. Or as if he knows me. Either way, he's right. I nod, close my eyes, and neither one of us lets go.

TWENTY

I can't breathe in my mask. Hands are squeezing my throat from behind. I try to dig under the fingers, but there's no room. I can't scream, can't whisper. Can't even turn my head to see if Cole's still next to me in the car. My shoulders twist against the seat, but I'm getting weaker and weaker, moving slower. The hands merge into a noose.

I wake up gasping.

Yank off my mask.

Cole's dozing in his seat, reclined.

I check behind us. The back seat appears to be empty, but I keep staring at the leather, scared stiff. My breaths stay quick, heart loud. Eventually, I lie back down, mask balled in one fist. But I can't bring myself to put it on. Instead, I watch Cole sleep. He's perfectly still—no jerking legs, no twitching fingers, steady as the pines outside his window. I almost reach for him, but I don't want to wake him. Instead, I rest a shaky hand on my neck.

~

I wake up to the sound of thunder. Everything is white.

Dozens of Nomen surround us, packed so tightly together they're almost locked in place. Their bodies squirm against each other, chests on each other's backs. Everyone within reach is hitting the car. Some can only fit an arm through the front line, but they're still flailing toward us, beating with everything that they have. Three fists slam my window. More hammer the windshield, where someone's climbed onto the hood, slapping the glass like a drum.

Someone drags a crowbar across the window behind me. They yank it back, and I cover my face right before the glass shatters. The window behind Cole breaks next. White arms snake inside and open both doors. Before I can even lean forward, a crowbar slides across my chest. Someone pulls it tight, pushing the wind right out of me, pinning my arms above the elbows. The metal edge digs into my sternum. More Nomen climb onto the hood. One starts kicking the windshield, his lace-up boots untied, one heel thumping the glass.

I turn to Cole.

There's a bar over his chest too.

More Nomen pour into the back seat. One crawls onto the console, opens my door, and pushes me into the mob. Suddenly, their hands are all over me. I lean forward, braced. My body doesn't feel like mine anymore. The mob pushes me in one direction, howling like they know the woods are empty, like there's no one to hear the screams. Dread pools inside me, ice cold, rising. I lose track of Cole. His car cracks and splinters behind us. Someone pushes me from behind, and I'm trying to find my balance when someone slips a mask over my head.

Now my world is dark.

TWENTY-ONE

Someone rips the blindfold off my mask.

The black Velcro flutters to the floor.

For a terrified half hour, I felt myself driven here, carried inside, and then placed on the rug. I raise my chin, blinking until I make out someone crouched in front of me. He's in a white mask, his eyes so close that I see the small holes in the mesh. He's craning toward me, his neck fully extended. I recognize the silhouette, the distinctive patience.

It's too familiar—Rex.

My breath stalls in my throat.

We're in a living room. It has the breadth of a Victorian ballroom, with its furniture pushed to the edges. Chairs are stacked on sofas and one piano, blocking off a few windows. In the center of the room is . . . everyone who went missing. I'm too shocked and overwhelmed to count, but it looks like all other targets are here. They sit on the thinly carpeted floor, in the same clothes they wore to the Oakwood, every last one in a mask. Only a few aren't in black tie: One woman in a knee-length trench coat. Another with long blue hair, in blue fishnets with thigh-high boots. And then, a man in a tee and gray sweats, as if he was pulled out of bed.

Lane. Myra. Max.

This has to be everyone.

I'm toward the back of the room, just a foot from those closest to me. They're all cross-legged, hunching forward. Squeezed water bottles litter the rug. One lies straight ahead by Rex's feet, looking like a plastic corpse. A body with every bone broken.

He stands with painstaking slowness.

At least sixty more Nomen line the perimeter—all in white, holding guns. Most are on their feet. The rest sit on transplanted furniture: sofas pushed against the wall, armchairs and end tables crammed beside them. Some Nomen lean forward, zeroed in. Others relax on each other, hanging an elbow on a neighbor's shoulder. Those are the ones who terrify me more: too confident, at ease. Without reverence for the humanity they have here on the floor.

We must be in the House.

The walls are burgundy, ceiling gold. A velvet settee in the corner is smothered under crushed energy drinks and a gaming console. A massive flat-screen rests on a sideboard, the top covered with vape cartridges. Past that, an ottoman lies under a pile of masks, like dehydrated ghosts. Pizza boxes have been stacked on the floor, with parchment corners peeking through the seams. Now I smell it: stale food, under the dense tang of unwashed clothes. Windows around the room are framed by thick drapes, all a dusty red. One curtain's half torn from its rod. Outside, Nomen stand on the lawn. Half of them face the woods, while the rest watch us.

Gwen—I see her.

I finally, *finally* see her.

She's diagonally left, two people away.

Her ponytail's still warping her mask, but now, much lower. The hair tie's drifted down, almost to her neck. She stares at the floor. I look away, trying not to tear up, not to show Rex who I love, in case he wants to make the wound even deeper. Looking right, I find Cole. He's one man over, next to the wall, with a grass stain on his shoulder.

No one looks hurt—no blood.

Still, there is palpable pain.

Maybe it's a lingering mood from their trip—the motion sickness, claustrophobia. The weight of the unknowns. Or maybe the true deadness came from having arrived. From settling into this place, this unrecognizable room in the woods, the air heavy with the smell of their bodies. Or maybe . . . it had to do with us. Maybe their hope died when Cole and I were dragged inside, when people saw that the Nomen still have the momentum.

"Nice of you to join us," Rex says.

He addresses Cole and me at once.

But I can't let him taunt us.

I break from everyone else to lift my chin and look him in the eye. It's the most I can manage now, this one sign he doesn't have me yet. He may have my body, but he doesn't have my mind. Part of me wants to *say* it, but I can't goad him into a fight. There are people who need me alive: Gwen. Cole. Everyone, really. Everyone ripped out of their life and forced to sit in this hopeless place. Everyone who wants to leave Rex's group but is afraid it might eat them alive. I can't be reckless. This is as close as I'll come, looking him hard in the eye.

Rex looks back at me.

I don't flinch. I barely blink.

But eventually, I look down. I stare at Rex's knees, my cheeks hot. And while I might look steady under this mask, I channel everything—all my hurt rage, every frustrated urge—into pinching my index finger. I squeeze the bone so hard I'm almost sure I've dammed the blood, that the tip is turning white. Rex seems to relax, glancing at Cole.

"You were always so confident. Weren't you?" It sounds like Rex is enjoying himself. "But it takes a real delusion to sleep just a short drive away. To come that close and curl up like bait. Did you feel . . . invincible?" He lifts a foot and nudges my knee. I squeeze my finger even harder. "You must've felt like gods. Like you were just made of light." Rex turns toward Cole and rubs his knee with one toe. "It's easy to feel strong when you don't live in the real world. But you're in the real world now. And we know this place better than you.

"You look like children when you sleep," he goes on. "Especially you, Cole. Sleeping in your mask. Were you one of us in your dreams?" The room is quiet. "And you, Fiona, holding yours like a blanket." He takes a half step closer. His white boots look heavy-duty, padding his ankles, with thick laces through brass eyelets and hooks. I wonder if he's going to kick me in the face—aim for my teeth. Stomp its grooves into my nose. "Unfortunately for you, there were Nomen all over Lasco last night. *This place was crawling with us.*" He's seething, before he resumes, "We've been making our way here, getting in place—getting ready for today."

I scan the windows.

The sun's low behind the trees.

I let go of my finger, only to realize that my hands are untied—all of ours. I have a flash of hope before remembering that we're still surrounded, in a ring of their guns. Maybe you don't need to tie people's hands when there is no way out.

Today. The Intake is today.

"We've built a place just for you." Rex is stepping back, addressing the broader group. He lands intentionally on a plastic bottle, squelching it under his boot. He keeps moving, letting his knees brush people's shoulders, his shins drag over their backs. He doesn't say more about the place they've built, but I can see it. I picture the village from last night. The cabin walls were water-stained, the vertical streaks like knives. Where the paint was peeling, under the moon, it appeared to be by design. Every strip was the same width, as if it had been chipped with the same blunt tool and devoted hands. Rex makes it through the front row.

He strides between sofas of Nomen.

They perk up as he passes.

"Watch them," Rex says, now addressing the Nomen. "But don't just sit there and stare. Don't make them feel like they're still on TV, with all of you holding your breath." He mocks the idea, breathing loud enough that I hear the air rush past his teeth in an otherwise silent room. "They've had enough attention, haven't they? It's time they understood neglect. So . . . when you're in this room, talk to each other. Make them feel like you don't care. Because they don't deserve to be front and center—not even in their jail."

He leaves the room.

Most Nomen follow him, charging through our group. Shoelaces drag over the backs of my hands. Someone stops next to Cole, his legs locked—the pause alarming—before picking up his pace. They seem to enjoy getting close, watching us crater and flinch. Once they're gone, a few dozen remain in a quiet ring around the room.

I should be strong now.

I should focus on making a plan.

But . . . there's a new fear in my blood: This could be the last day of my life. Maybe this is all that I get. My bones weigh on the rug. Time slows to a drip. I hear my own dry swallow, the current of whispery breaths. Meanwhile, footsteps creak through the house. They're spreading to every corner, now directly overhead—a nonstop pressure around us. Cole and I should've gone to the police. Even with the risk of tipping off the Nomen . . . it's clear in hindsight: That was our best chance. On our own, we were doomed to be taken.

A sunbeam shifts on the rug in front of me. It's so beautiful I could cry just looking at it: This perfect diamond of light. This bit of the divine. Maybe it's so gorgeous now because I know it might be stolen. I want to look at Cole or Gwen. I desperately want to crawl over and check on them—hold them one more time—but I'm terrified of drawing attention. So I sit in place, feeling the depth of our loss. Like we've been stripped of everything but our most basic awareness, our ability to observe our own pain. Just an inner eye, a knowing.

That's all we have left.

Just this.

I close my eyes and see my parents.

Keeping them shut, I picture Dad next to me on the floor. Mom, sitting cross-legged on the other side. I can sense them too—really sense them here, more clearly than ever before. As if I'm closer to death than I've ever been and we're meeting in the liminal space. My hands drift forward into the sun. It's almost warm in the light. And I just know without proof that my parents are here: Dad, steady. Mom, vibrant. Giving me all they can.

What if this is my last day?

I can't wallow.

But I have to ask.

The question is practical, realistic.

What if Nomen move us into the cabins and decide we're not even fit for those? If this is my last day—my last few hours in the sun—then . . . at least I gave this life everything that I had. I really tried. I put my heart first. And I was there for my friends. I was there for the turning points and the small stuff. For the minor frustrations and average days and the tiny bits of good news. I was the sounding board, the second opinion, the quick funny story. I know I wasn't perfect. I could've opened up more about the accident—let them all the way in.

Still, I must've done something right, to end up with the friends I did. Because they were there for me too. Emma always said that no one will praise you like your mom. She said that no one else will celebrate your smallest wins—your third place, your minor improvement. So, for every milestone I had—-everything that might've felt invisible, including the first draft of my first book—she was there with Marlowe and Caroline to treat me like a . . . giant. They showed up with mom-level love. And if this is my last day, at least I had them.

My life has been unexpected.

Chaotic, beautiful, overwhelming.

And I still want . . . more. I want more time with my people. I want more time to work. I want the ocean and the light and this planet. I feel like I have so much farther to go, so much more to offer. Because I'm not just one person; I'm everything that everyone's ever invested in me. I've been given too much to end here, like this.

Maybe everyone dies unfinished.

~

Three Nomen pass out uniforms.

I receive an off-white top and pants.

We change on the rug as Nomen pick up discarded dresses, dinner jackets. The shirt's a loose-fitting crew neck, rough and thin. I feel the air intimately now, with even less to protect me—just one millimeter of cotton. A Nomen snatches my jeans as he passes, disappearing with an armful of satin and wool. My pants lie on the heap, like a crumpled cut-out of my body. I feel the standardization seep in. The sense of their ever-rising control.

After changing, everyone goes still.

There's no clock in this room.

I can only tell that time is passing from the rising sun. From the Nomen along the wall who will occasionally lift a window and hop outside to pee in the grass. From the growing white noise among Nomen, toward the front of the room. Some are close enough that their shoulders brush, knees bump, and even guns rub each other without much effort—dynamically at rest, like milk in a cup. Every now and then, someone will peek in from the porch. Their mesh eyes will tap the glass, then recede in the space between windows.

I keep checking on Cole.

Tiny glances.

There's only one person between us. Still, for him to be out of reach feels like . . . a physical loss. Maybe it's because we've spent the past few days so close together. Since the minute we met, we've barely spent one apart. We broke into all the same buildings. Shared water bottles, his phone. Ate elbow-to-elbow at his place, together for hours in a single room. I've even been wearing his clothes to sleep—and besides, he told me about his parents. Wanting to change his life. I told him about my friends. How the accident changed me. Yes, it's been less than a week. But we've spent so much time trying to trust—to *matter* to each other . . .

I realize that we do.

~

Rex reenters close to midday.

After a few hours here, my adrenaline's dulled to a buzz. My heart's still beating faster than normal. I'm still hyperaware of every detail under me: The red medallions in the rug. The blurred ring stains, tracing old bottles. But now I feel a terrifying creep of fatigue. My body can't sustain this level of fear, bracing for things to get worse.

"It's time," he says.

The Intake.

Nomen cross into our group.

They're barking at us to get in line, shoving us into a clump.

We're slow, after sitting all morning, doing nothing to move the blood. I stand along with everyone else. Feeling creeps back into my feet, the heat both sharp and numb. People churn between Cole and me, pushing us apart. I lose track of him—and in the crowd, I feel temporarily unseen. The Nomen wouldn't expect us to try anything now, not with the odds so stacked against us. Gwen's not far ahead, with her arms slack, hands limp.

I could try.

I really could.

I take two steps closer to Gwen.

I slip between four others, slotting right behind her in line. I'm praying that no one saw me—and if they did, they didn't think twice. I stare at a knob in the back of her neck, the bone right under her skin. After all this time, I'm here. My heart's raging—I'm scared stiff, eyes getting wet—but I am finally here, with my friend. I don't say a word. I don't get her attention in any way. I'm afraid if I so much as tap her arm, she might scream.

But I'm here.

The line starts to move.

Each step feels clumsy as we shift toward the front of the room. No one's at their full height. We're all hunched forward, relearning balance. Gwen and I keep drifting, reaching the sofas. A pair of white boots dangles from the chandelier overhead.

We file into a hallway.

Nomen flank us, holding their guns.

We pass a library, where the red wallpaper has faded to salmon pink. Fifty Polaroids have been taped up in a grid over the damask—our headshots. The next room smells like stale weed, with a few velvet stools tipped over, the bar cart overloaded. In the entrance hall, silver forks have been stabbed into the wall, in the shape of an enormous Cheshire grin.

Now we're on the lawn.

Nomen lead us into the woods.

Dark needles feather over blue sky.

I can only imagine what this must be like for everyone else in line, not knowing what's ahead. They must believe this is the end. They must think that all their learning and growth and effort on earth will end today, like this. That they've become all they'll be. That they've had their last taste of water, seen their families for the last time. Because nothing good ever happens in the belly of the woods, in a place this deliberately remote.

And maybe they're right.

We single-file through the pines.

I want to take off my mask, release the clamp from my head—the constant pressure on my ears, cheeks. I want to breathe without smelling fabric, without lint in the back of my throat. Someone ahead of me starts to cry. Do they see the village? Needles drag over my arms, and suddenly I feel like I've been here—not last night. Somehow before that. *"The book starts with a walk through the woods."* I teeter to the left, snapping a twig. Nomen whip toward me. I get back in line. *"The book starts with a walk through the woods."*

The cabins come into view.

Our prison, just in sight.

I turn to find Cole two steps behind. He must've trailed me, the same way I followed Gwen. The line stalls—the Nomen too. They're closer than ever on both sides. My heart throbs as they remove their guns and lift them to the sky. For a moment, nothing moves except the gun straps. The dark hammocks swing back and forth in the silence. Without warning, the Nomen drive their guns down, ramming everyone on the backs of their heads. Some cry out. Others rag-doll in front of me. I'm about to sprint when I feel massive blunt pressure.

Right on the back of my head.

TWENTY-TWO

I wake up to a blur with an aching skull.

For a while, it feels like I'm floating on a cloud. There's nothing but colorful mist around me. Eventually, my body starts to feel heavier. I become aware of my spine on something firm, my legs outstretched and limp. There's something like a wooden cabin below me, under the loft. It looks like one barren room, cramped with a dining table and a run-down kitchenette. I just barely make out a Nomen leaving, shutting the door behind him.

It hits me: their prison.

I'm in their prison—*we* are.

Gwen, Cole, and Blake lie on mattresses beside me.

I sit up with effort, straining against my own weight. Cole pushes himself up next to me, cradling the back of his head. He scans the cabin, ending with me, and I see to the pit of his terror. *Yes, we are here.* I read his eyes. *We are in my worst idea, the nightmare I perfected.* Gwen's in the fetal position, on the far side of the loft. I crawl past Cole, then Blake, who's just starting to stir. Gwen still hasn't moved, facing the wall.

"Gwen?"

She moans.

"Gwen, can you hear me?"

She blinks, turning to me.

"Fay," she says.

I hug her, indescribably relieved.

I turn to Cole and Blake, holding her hand, and ask if they're okay.

They grunt meekly in response, forms of *yes* that have been stripped down to even briefer versions. But I'm not sure if everyone else was as lucky. The Nomen didn't hit us with precision. In *Rotator*, people woke up without any memory of who they were or how they got to this ruined place in the woods. Did anyone here forget how they arrived? Has anyone been permanently changed? I get the creeping sense that I should look outside.

I tell Gwen I'll be right back.

Climb down the ladder.

My head pounds.

I open the front door: The village is full.

People peer through their cabin windows. Their faces appear to melt with shock, with slack jaws, dark holes in their mouths. Only their eyes move, flicking left and right, tracking Nomen who fill the rest of the town: strutting down the road, around the clearing—all the way to distant flashes in the trees. Their guns swing as they walk. One Nomen whistles as he passes, letting the high note die fast, with a whoosh of amazement. They just keep ogling us in the village, as if they've been waiting for this view all day—maybe even for years.

One Nomen stops short, a few yards away.

He turns to me, cocking his head.

I bolt inside and slam the door.

~

Minutes later, I hear voices behind our cabin.

"The wait's *killing* me."

"Hang in there."

"If you go early, Rex'll . . ."

Cole and I meet eyes from across the room. Blake's in the armchair by the window, transfixed by the view. Gwen's still in the loft, nursing a glass of tap water. Cole and I speed toward the back, arriving side by side, and lean our foreheads against the wall.

It sounds like the Nomen are mocking us now—but they're on the edge of what I can hear, their voices going in and out. Someone says that Blake sings like a strangled cat. There are a few laughs, then a human purr, followed by a distorted meow. I miss the next few lines, only catching a few words: "Myra Mane," "little princess." Then: "Fucking plastic." There's one more muffled laugh, followed by something else about tonight.

"Soon as it's dark . . ."

"They won't see us coming."

"You think Rex'll join? Or just . . . ?"

"'Course he will. He's gonna clean his teeth with their bones . . ." The Nomen walk out of earshot.

I'm paralyzed by the wall.

Cole's rigid, eyes wide, breath faint.

I feel my heart beat slow, temperature drop.

My whole body feels colder, like it's already beginning to die. Like it knows the end is near and is quietly turning off its lights. I sit in one of the wooden chairs and hug myself, feeling shaky and too fragile, like I can smell death in this room—the old wood, the brown moss, my fearful sweat. As if death is sitting right next to me, patient for the night to come. But I want to *live,* even if it's here. I'd choose this prison over death, with all its terror—the nails jutting out of the beams, the draft, this doom. I would still want more of this.

I look down at my hands.

How do you hold on to life?

I'm fully present, feeling the air through my nose, the pressure of my heartbeat. The fabric itching my inner thighs, my wrists. I hear Gwen shift in the loft, but it all keeps passing by, precious and unable to be held. The breaths keep leaving me too soon.

~

I help Gwen down the ladder.

The four of us sit around the table, sharing a meal of hard-boiled eggs. We're all still too stunned and nauseous to eat much, but we nibble while the Nomen stream by our windows. They have an intimidating energy to them—on the balls of their feet, looking fresh and quick. Rex passes by twice, both times with an entourage.

"Did they hurt you?" I ask Gwen.

She takes a deep breath.

"After you left . . ."

She's so quiet I barely hear her.

I wonder if she's spoken in days. She clears her throat.

"After you left," she restarts, "the drugs started to hit everyone. We could still walk at that point, but things were starting to . . . drip." I nod, remembering. "The Nomen led us downstairs and stopped in front of a door. By then, I couldn't see much.

"The door opened to a bar or club. Whatever it was, it was packed." Maybe filled with Nomen. "They led us outside, two by two. I wanted to run—had to. But . . . my body wouldn't listen. I couldn't even scream." I picture Gwen overlooked in a horde. If anyone saw her, they probably just thought she'd had too much to drink. After all, this was happening in public. There would've been too many people around for anything to seem unsafe.

"One of them pushed me into the back of a car. Then we all woke up in one room—someone's living room, at one point. But the place had been hollowed out: furniture slashed, walls shot. We sat there all day, all night." I remember Tony's den, the wrappers, bottles. I picture everyone hugging their knees. "I kept my head down.

"The Nomen drugged us again before they moved us. They loaded us into trucks on the lawn." I remember the tire tracks at Tony's, the ruts going deep. "We spent the next two nights at another house. Then, this morning, the Nomen brought us to Rex's place. But they didn't hurt us—not yet. It sounds like they've been waiting to do that." Gwen puts one hand on her belly. It's a firm, deliberate touch, as if something—some*one*—is still there. I hug her, wanting to smile and cry. This is all so depraved, and still, I'm overwhelmingly relieved.

"They're not going to win," I promise.

I hold her bare hands. The Nomen must've taken her wedding and engagement rings, both silver. She loved that silver is softer than gold, that it would change in subtle ways over time. I repeat myself, finding resolve I didn't know I had left. But here with Gwen—seeing the pain in her eyes—I feel surprisingly unbroken. I never thought of myself as strong, but now I do feel . . . persistent. Like my grit goes deeper than I ever imagined.

Like I can fight when truly called.

And I can defend my friend.

~

Cole and I try to plan.

We sit at the table while Gwen rests and Blake searches the cabin for anything useful—in case the Nomen do invade. And next to Cole, as we think, I wonder if this was a scene in his book. I wonder how deep the echo truly goes—whether I'm the engineer of my thoughts, or there's a more powerful plot moving everyone, everything.

Cole would know.

Wouldn't he?

He's deep in thought, two fingers to his temple. His left hand still looks raw with shallow cuts, the edges pink and raised. Smaller abrasions dot his knuckles, next to red patches like sunburned skin. Does he remember anything about the story we could use to escape? But he looks as stumped as I feel. As if knowing the map of this place—what's in every room—doesn't matter once you're here. Once you are your own hostage, in the prison you designed.

Cole lowers his hand.

"We have to run." He breaks the silence. "Before tonight . . ."

But I lose track of what he's saying. My mind's on *Rotator:* the black pages and that white ink, like razor thin cuts in the paper. I can't shake the sense that the key out of this place is in that book. There must be something in the story that can help, because here we are, inside it. Here we are, in some of Cole's most dangerous words. That's what certain words can do: Build a town where there was nothing. Seed a brutal vendetta. And, just as fast, maybe they could . . . undo it all, *unmake* this.

"If a story could start this . . ."

I trail off.

Cole looks at me, curious.

"I was just thinking," I explain.

"Thinking what?"

"If a story could *start* this, then one . . ."

"Could stop it," Cole finishes, seeming to understand.

Sure, some Nomen are past reason. But even they know about *Rotator*. If we tell them all *who wrote it*, they might be confused enough to—if not *stop*, at least *pause*. Then there are all the Nomen who must be terrified of what the group's become—people like Mack, who feel trapped, coerced. We'd give them an excuse to leave. The right *story*. That's it. Because when it's the right one, it can change what you feel. It can change what you think.

"We tell the truth," I say.

It feels like a breakthrough.

But how could we get the message out?

I suddenly feel the breadth of this place—the teeming mass of Nomen, all the way into the woods. Even if I screamed, I imagine how fast the sound would die, how many would never hear it at all.

"Did you write a microphone into this place?"

"You know what?"

He seems hooked.

"In the police station."

Cole says he put a mike and speakers in the back, for announcements and emergency alerts. For the first time today, there's a lift in his voice. We both seem to agree without saying it out loud: If we want to reach people, that mike is our best shot to be heard.

TWENTY-THREE

That afternoon, Blake is peering between the floorboards. He's pressing one eye to a wider crack when I hear him murmur something. Cole and I turn toward him from the table as he slides one hand into the slit. He can only cram up to his knuckles, but he's straining, pushing harder and harder, as if the wood might be soft enough to give.

"What is it?" I ask.

Blake pulls his hand back.

A red line of pressure runs across it.

He stays on his knees, intent on what's below.

Cole and I stand, our chairs screeching behind us. We crouch on either side of Blake, peering into the slit, the black lip across the floor. It's hard to see much—just shadows, dirt. But there is something in the dirt. Something . . . brassy.

I put my eye to the crack.

What *is* it?

It's . . . short.

A stubby two inches.

With a round, white plastic tip.

It looks designed to break on impact—and I've seen something like it before. I sit up, giving Cole room to see. Outside, Nomen pace the road. Distant trees form a natural wall—the needles knit together, as terrifying as stitches over a mouth. Cole rights himself, palming his knees, looking straight at me. I can tell that he remembers it too: We were this close in the car, coming back from the Oakwood, when he showed me the exact same thing.

"It's a blank round," I say.

Blake looks wary.

"What does that mean for us?" he asks.

I shrug, at a loss. One blank doesn't mean the Nomen's guns are harmless, that they're all just stuffed with shells. Then again . . . maybe that's the truth. Maybe these guns aren't meant to kill. Maybe Rex gave them out for show, to bend us into submission—without losing his sense of control. Without giving his men power to use against him.

The Nomen continue to move.

One of them peeks in our house.

The three of us scatter as he points his gun at me. He lifts the barrel, simulating a silent shot—then does the same for Cole, Blake, and Gwen. Without a word, he moves on. My back's to the wall, heart drumming. My body still reacts to their guns. Blank rounds or not, that hasn't changed. The Nomen still run this town. They're still in every open space, like white rags stuffing a throat. Still everywhere between us and the woods, blocking all escape.

~

At dusk, one Nomen catches my eye.

He comes into view with a limp, his right foot touching the ground just a split second longer than the left. Farther away, I might've missed it. But I've been by the window for an hour now, racking my brain for a way into the station. He stops in front of our cabin, leaning against the handrail, taking the weight off his hurt leg. His profile is just visible through the glass, narrow and . . . familiar. I inch forward on the chair. I'm trying to place someone covered head to toe: the starved limbs, hard slants in his cheeks. I've seen him before—Mack.

Of course, his leg.

I saw the bloody knife.

Now he's just feet away.

Mack. I'm feeling something rise, something close to hope. The faint pulse of a chance. Yes, he ignored me at the Oakwood. He really might've attacked the Nomen we found. But that's when he was pressured, in a group. I've seen him alone. At my place, he wanted no part of this. *"Bad people . . . Unmothered."* I know he must feel outnumbered, in deep. But I also know he wants a way out. Maybe now more than ever, he wants help to leave.

I could say a few words.

I could do it right now, and no one would know.

My palms are slick just thinking about it. What's the worst Mack could do? He wouldn't want to draw attention—not with his group in a hair-trigger frame of mind. Already baited and on the edge, in a state of suspended devastation. He'd probably just ignore me and move on. Then again, maybe I've misjudged him. Maybe Mack would report me to Rex, for the slim chance of a reward, status that could protect him—before the raid tonight.

Maybe I'd be punished like Tony.

But what choice do I have?

Mack's just a few feet away. Other Nomen shuffle behind him. I hear the collective scuff, metallic clinks. The army of shallow breaths. More Nomen circle in the clearing, taking the long way around our cabins. And Mack is still right here. All my energy is on my tongue. I should reach out, make the connection. *"Bad people . . . Unmothered."* He doesn't want this group—I know it in my gut. He just needs to see an escape and believe it.

"Mack."

He goes still.

His mask turns to me.

"We can get you out," I whisper.

It's absurd, but I commit. I act like I believe it—because if I convince him, it might be true. *Come on, I know you don't want to be here. This isn't the group you expected.* In the pause, I resist the urge to look away from his gun. It hangs across his chest, pointed casually at me. This close, I can almost taste the metal. The more I stare, the more it blots out everything else, almost like I'm sinking into the matte-black finish. The trigger with a gentle bend.

"Can't," he whispers.

As in . . . we can't get him out?

But he spoke—I can reach him.

"If you get a uniform for Cole," I say, thinking fast, "we can get you out."

Mack doesn't reply. But at least he's listening. And I feel like there's a chance—a vanishing spark—that he might agree. I just need to . . . give him a reason to trust us. With everything at stake, maybe I have to tell him the truth. Maybe he won't be convinced by anything less than everything. The sun keeps dipping toward the trees. We're running out of time, and I feel my chance with him slipping away. "Cole wrote *Rotator*," I admit, keeping my voice as low as I can. "He wrote the whole book, and if we tell everyone—"

Mack steps back.

Our handrail snaps.

The pieces hit the ground.

I look down, feeling like a focal point.

When I glance up again, Mack is cutting across the road, almost running into three other Nomen. A half dozen have stopped to stare at me. Traffic bulges around them, everyone turning for a look. A few step closer, their heads cocked.

I retreat to the back.

Nomen circle the broken handrail.

One stands right outside our window. He's cut off at the neck—just a hovering mask—staring at us inside. Two Nomen climb our front steps. I see the white flickers through cracks in the door, and my stomach is a sickening ball. The doom is so intense that I'm leaning on the wall for support, right between Cole and Blake. The Nomen stop outside our door, suddenly quiet as snow. My hands start to shake. I try to make a fist, but my grip is weak and numb. A sharp thud breaks the silence—one more. Nomen kick the broken rail like soccer balls.

I flinch at the sounds.

The Nomen jump off our landing.

The rest peel off behind them, returning to the road.

As soon as we're alone, Cole and Blake turn to me. I know they heard me talk to Mack, and I wish I could apologize—not just to them, but to everyone here, for what I might've just set in motion. I can't believe I bet it all on him—all our lives—on someone I barely know. We've had just one conversation alone. Even then, he was scattered, under pressure. As if he had a knife to his neck. Of course Mack isn't going to help us. He's at risk here too.

Now, where's he headed?

What's the worst he could do?

~

Soon, the sun grazes the trees.

Cole and I watch from our window.

There's been no sign of Mack. But Cole and I have been standing here since he left, watchful, tense. We still haven't thought of a way through the Nomen, into the station. But once the horizon turns blue—once it's just dark enough to give cover—we've decided that Cole's going to run for it. If the speakers are there, he'll broadcast the truth.

I'm trying not to think about it.

It's too heartbreaking, terrifying.

I didn't mean to bow out of the speech, but we both know it should come from him. Cole can quote from the book verbatim—more than that, he has every draft inside him. Nomen would be moved to hear from *him,* their unexpected inspiration. This afternoon, we rehearsed what he'd say. Now the sky is purple, fringed with a dying red. I know our plan is tenuous—less than that, a dream. Even with the speakers . . . it still might fail.

But this is our best idea.

Our only idea.

Cole looks at me. His gaze is soft and deep, as if he's seeing my details: The width between my eyes. The freckle on the edge of one iris. I stand still, looking back. There's a faint shadow under his nose. His right eyebrow is rougher than the left, with a chunk of hair growing up and down. Outside, the Nomen seem more wired than they've been all day, moving with a predatory swagger. Still no Mack, but I'm getting close to something unexpected here with Cole. It's almost like . . . a flicker of peace. Distracting, fragile. Dangerous, brief.

"What do you want to do after this?"

I puzzle.

"After we get out," he adds.

I hadn't thought that far ahead.

It's so blindly optimistic I feel reckless just thinking about it. Cole doesn't budge, as if he wants an answer. The sun dips even lower. "I just want us to get home." Cole nods, then asks what else. He's looking straight at me, as if he's trying to close the gap between us—peek into my mind one last time. I try to hold on to a speck of hope. "I'd . . . see my friends." I glance back at Gwen. She's sitting in the loft, her legs dangling over the edge. "Then I don't know. I'd make sure something like this never happens again. What about you?"

"I'd want to see you again when it's safe—after we all go home. When you can go anywhere in the world again. I'd want to see you when you have a million choices where to be, not just when you have one." His expression is undressed. I watch his mouth, grounding his voice in his body. I almost want to lean in, feeling a surge of, against all odds, desire.

I could kiss him.

I really could.

I want to be even closer to this man who's pushed through so much already. Who's looked out for me all along, not because he was stronger—the opposite. He was cut deeper, more badly hurt. And he stayed because he cared that much. Because he has a fight in his heart. I don't know if it's this sense of doom supercharging everything. Or if I'd feel this way if we were . . . safe. Together on a regular night, not one that could be the worst of our lives.

I lean back.

I can't think about this.

There's too much at stake.

I doubt Cole noticed me slant toward him, until we lock eyes. There's so much feeling in his that he must've seen. I'm getting drawn in again when something grabs my attention: Mack, coming this way. He almost blends in with the Nomen on the road, but I catch his limp, the snag in his flow. He's holding his gun to his chest, as if the strap broke, as if the gun will fall unless pinned. He's close and . . . there's something under his gun.

The same color as his shirt.

The same fabric too.

Could it be . . . ?

He holds it tight.

It's another suit, just like his own.

I feel a new spike of adrenaline—a uniform. He got a uniform. Mack didn't just believe us; he's bet on us. Now it's on Cole and me to deliver. Mack breathes under visible strain. A few Nomen glance his way, but only for a fraction of a second. They must not see the white on white, the soft layers under his machine. Even I can barely see them. They look like . . . ripples in his shirt, shadows in the folds. He did it. He really did. He must've felt like this was his only chance, like he was already in free fall, forced to grab whatever he found.

Mack is just steps away.

I sense what he wants to do.

I go to our front door, open it an inch.

Mack climbs our steps and drops the uniform through the crack. Just as fast, he turns around and disappears into the flow of guards. I shut the door, feeling wired, paralyzed. But no one second-guesses

Mack. No one stops to check why he climbed our stairs, not when Nomen have been tormenting us all day—tapping our door with their guns as if they were asking to be let in. Pressing their masks to the window, the glass distorting the shapes of their heads.

I snatch the clothes.

Bring them to the back of the cabin.

Cole is at my side, moving fast, already starting to strip—dropping his shirt, flashing the slab of his torso. I hand him the uniform and stay close, watching him change. I should give him more privacy, but I can't look away: He's sliding his arms into the thick flannel shirt, the sleeves reaching all the way to his wrists. He's stepping into the pants, a durable canvas—transforming piece by piece into one of them. Finally, he slips on the mask.

Once he's ready, a chill stings the back of my neck. He looks like he belongs outside. Then again . . . wasn't he always one of them? He was the original Nomen, the founding member of their group. The one who struck a chord with the criminally insane.

"How much longer?"

"Hang in there, man."

"Not too long now."

The voices are behind our cabin.

Cole takes my hand and puts it on his chest—hard, in the center—right before striding outside. I speed over to the window as he steps into the flow of bodies. My eyes get hot. *I'll see you soon.* I want to believe it, but I'm watching him as if this is the last time.

Cole seems to fit in—everywhere but his shoes. I realize it too late. He's in his sneakers: run-down, oyster brown, with dirt in the mesh from when we walked through the woods. Nothing at all like their white boots. My mouth parts in nervous shock. I want to tell him—*do* something—but he's too far gone, taking a sharp left between two cabins.

I watch the station.

Stiff, alert.

Blake's beside me now as the world gets dark. The sky's a rich blue, trees black. The horizon is a molten line. One Nomen gets unnervingly close to our window. Someone else whispers, "Here, kitty, kitty," but I can't quite trace the sound. Then . . . Cole. It must be him, slipping into the station. I'm barely breathing. Is he going to come back out? Of course. We've been watching the station all day and haven't seen anyone inside. Seconds pass. I hear Gwen leaving the loft to join us.

Now . . . Cole.

He emerges with the mike, speakers.

I cry once with relief, just to see him again.

He's moving fast, drawing the eyes of other Nomen as he heads for our cabin. I run to the kitchen table, telling Blake and Gwen to help; we'll need to barricade the door as soon as Cole's inside. We start pushing the table across the floor, moving it inch by inch. Cole crosses the threshold, and the three of us heave with everything that we have—every fiber in my arms, bone in my chest. The table reaches the door, keeping it shut.

"The window!" I cry.

We block it with chairs.

Nomen swarm our landing.

"*Rotator* isn't what you think," Cole projects through the village. "I know because I wrote it myself. My name is Cole Harper, and over ten years ago, I wrote the book that started your group. This was never supposed to happen. It was nothing more than a story . . ." A Nomen thrusts himself against the door. Blake, Gwen, and I are piling everything we can in front of it when something breaks the window. The barrel of a gun pokes through the frame.

Someone right outside opens fire at the sky—explosive, almost skull-cracking thumps. Blake, Gwen, and I drop to the ground, rattling the house. I smell burnt powder. Gwen goes tight in a ball. In other cabins, people are shrieking, as if this is their first and last chance to express themselves, ever since they were taken. The sound is pent-up, grieving.

"No one move!"

It's Rex.

I get on my feet.

He's charging this way, from across town.

"I drew the smile on every cover myself," Cole plows ahead, his voice unshaken. Meanwhile, the Nomen outside our door have paused, waiting for Rex to arrive. "If you've seen it up close, you know it wasn't printed. It was hand-drawn with a fine black pen.

"The whole book is sixty pages. Small enough to keep it on you, keep it close. Like a constant companion, always around. Part of me hoped that would breed obsession, intrusive thoughts about the story—an itch to pull it out and browse. I'm sorry to say it now, but I liked how a book that size sucks you in; the small print physically pulls you in closer, like it's whispering right in your ear. Making the horror feel . . . personal. Inescapable.

"If you've read it, you know what I mean . . ."

Outside, Nomen start to squirm.

A few push each other, sending ripples through the mob. But the rest are . . . listening. Now Rex is getting close. He beelines through the group, onto our landing, and starts attacking our front door. He's throwing his body against it, plowing shoulder-first into the wood. I hear the impact of a punch and whip toward it. One Nomen has his fist tight, elbow raised, over someone else on the road. Rex rams into our door so hard a panel finally caves.

I can't let him through.

Cole's not done.

I climb onto the table, waving at Blake to follow.

In Rex's next pause, we throw open the door, with all our weight behind it. Rex loses his footing, and now Blake and I are falling with him, sending a cluster of Nomen down the stairs. We hit the road. Rex is trying to get up when I yank off his mask. He clutches his face, but I see him through his fingers: the scar, the clipped ear. The chaotic dark hair, sweat clumping it in surges. So unkempt that I wonder if he's been sleeping in his mask.

Around us, the fight has spread.

Nomen are attacking each other.

One bites another's hand, his teeth clamping around the thumb. Someone else rams the butt of his gun into another's throat. I can't tell if they were moved by Cole's speech and want to hear the end. Or if they're just finally getting their blood. Three shots go off at the sky before someone is tackled. People flee their cabins before the brawl reaches them.

I jump on top of Rex with Blake. Ryan runs over to join us, using all his strength and weight to help pin Rex down. I'm working as fast as I can to remove Rex's gun. Finally, I slide it off one arm and push it forward under our house.

Gwen's in our doorway.

I yell at her to run.

But she's still.

Terrified.

I yell at her again, misting.

"I'll find you!" I shout over the fray.

One Nomen pins another to the stairs.

"You have to run! I promise I'll find you!"

She's tearful as she jumps out of the cabin, slamming the door behind her. "I love you!" she shouts, fleeing through a gap in the mob. *I'll find you.* I hang on to the promise as she disappears. I can still hear Cole on the other side of the door, his voice a half beat ahead of the broadcast. Rex is warm under my knee, thrusting his chest up and down.

When I look down, he stops writhing.

He smiles at me through red teeth.

"The speech is working," I warn him.

"What makes you so confident?" His voice has the same cadence I know, even now with three knees on him. "I've wondered that for years. What makes you *people* so confident?" Blake and Ryan watch the Nomen fight. I hear the whumps and snaps. "The rest of the world has the decency to doubt themselves. To let other people be heard—"

"Don't talk to me like a savior."

"Why not?"

"Because I know what you did to your group—the *kids*." I pause, horrified. He looks briefly surprised. "You're not here to rescue anyone. You're in this for yourself. Something about fame is so personal—it cuts so deep—you'll do anything to make it stop."

"You simplify my ambitions, Fiona."

He thrusts his chest with more force.

"This means you have no leader," Cole continues. "The one who wrote what defines you doesn't even believe it." A Nomen sprints past, mask off, shirt torn. A couple to one side stand rooted in place, contending with a new understanding. "Without a leader, you have to decide for yourself what's right. Does it make sense to punish us, when one of us gave you the idea? Your credo's broken down. Now you have to think for yourself—"

"You won't get away with this," I tell Rex.

"Who said I wanted to?"

His smile grows.

"Why did you take it this far?" I ask. "What about fame just . . . destroyed you? What did you lose—"

Now I remember his parents. And suddenly, I see the invisible wound—invisible to everyone else except those who've been hurt the same way. With an accident like that, there would've been no one to blame. But maybe he needed justice. Maybe he needed a villain, someone to suffer for what had happened. Then came Cole's book, the case against fame. It was exactly what he needed: the idea that you could trace all misery and brokenness back to one poison. Because when life got hard, Rex didn't want God; he wanted the devil—something to condemn. In his darkest moment, this was the map he was given. This was his call to avenge.

Then his house.

He filled his parents' house with other people.

As soon as it was empty, he bused them in. Lived with them up close. I can see it as if I were there: The place overrun with mattresses. Every closet stuffed, new sweaters just spilling out of the shelves. Kids crowded around the dining room table with their elbows touching, milk in splotches, and Cheerios all over the floor. A house once again filled with noise. Because I know what it's like for your childhood home to suddenly . . . go to sleep. To be the only heartbeat there, the only blood running through the halls. Of course Rex made a plan that brought people into his house—if this has been a war against his pain.

He's still smiling.

Who said I wanted to?

And what does he have to fear?

If he gets caught, he'll have carved out a notoriety of his own. He'll be the one who grew an army to bring down the Famous Elite. Who got farther than anyone ever imagined. And maybe he thinks that if he's infamous enough, it won't hurt anymore.

The fight spreads.

I hear the grunts, footwork.

One Nomen stomps another in the stomach. Two more drive someone's head into a wall. I'm wincing when Rex kicks his feet in the air. The force knocks all three of us off, leaving him suddenly free. He pulls a knife out of his boot and points the blade at me. I back up two steps but can't go farther. If I do, I'll run into the swarm behind me, getting louder all the time. I hear the ragged breaths, pops of cartilage. Fabric tearing and desperate gasps.

But I can't hear Cole.

Did he finish?

The door to our cabin swings open.

Cole emerges, tackling Rex to the ground.

The knife launches out of Rex's hand, landing a few steps away.

As soon as Cole jumps to his feet, we take off down the road. I see heads snap back, a brief choke hold. Two Nomen wrangle each other in the grass. I glance back, but Rex is gone. I stop and pivot, searching for his face, but he's lost in the churning mass—as if his own group has swallowed him whole. In the distance, Myra sprints for the woods. She's followed by Max—and Gwen. Her whole body's in a forward slant, almost at the trees. She's going to make it. She's really going to make it. I cry once, all my relief rushing out in a breath.

Is anyone still trapped?

I look at Cole, nodding to the cabins.

Wasting no time, we run toward them.

We pull open the doors, one by one. Each cabin appears to be empty, with people having run for their lives. Nearby, one Nomen starts to shoot—taking wild shots left and right, spraying the woods—until someone pushes him to the ground. Cole is tugging my hand in the opposite direction when I collide with someone else.

It's Mack—mask off.

He does a double take. And while it wasn't there last time, now there's a spark of recognition. I can tell that he remembers it all: walking to my apartment, finding us at the Oakwood. Then whispering from outside our cabin. It's right there in his eyes, cutting through the desperation. Maybe this is the first time he can show it—now that he's finally broken ties with the group. Now that he's no longer forced to conform. Now he's on his own, fighting for his life. I'm about to thank him for what he did, just two quick words, when he takes off.

Breakneck, panicked.

Cole tugs my hand, and we run.

The world is inky blue. I keep looking for Mack, but he's lost in the fray. And suddenly, I'm not sure if I'll ever see him again. Maybe that was our goodbye—silent, scared. Like most goodbyes, with both of us unaware that would be the final time.

Cole and I run for the woods.

I pull his hand toward where I saw Gwen.

We're the only two who stick together, side by side across the lawn. I catch pieces of arguments whipping past us. The soggy cracks of fists on bones. We sprint faster. With the Nomen fighting each other, I can't tell which are on our side. I step on someone's arm or leg and stumble, almost tripping. Their scream is so loud I feel it in my skull.

Someone hits me in the face.

I'm stunned, momentarily frozen.

It's someone in a mask, standing in front of me.

He shoves me onto my back. I roll sideways as fast as I can, away from his white boots. My nose is burning, wet. A stone digs into my ribs. I hear Cole shout my name, but I can't place him. I keep rolling until I'm alone in the grass. And when I finally stop, the world keeps spinning. Shots break out in the distance. Cole's calling my name. I dig as deep as I can and shout back, telling him to run, that I'll find him. I palm the ground, getting on all fours. I make it to my feet, only to get knocked down again by two Nomen in a brawl.

I get up, tasting salt.

The mob is turning red.

It's splotching their masks, their chests. Some of their smiles are starting to drip. I walk at a diagonal. The ground feels like it's tilted, sending me off on a tangent. A hand warms my shoulder—Cole. He picks me up before I can say his name. With one arm under my shoulders and the other under my knees, he runs me toward the trees.

Step by step, the confusion wears off.

The ground looks level again.

I tell Cole I'm okay.

I have to say it twice more—louder and louder—before he hears me and slows down. I scramble out of his arms and land on my feet. He's wary, as if I might buckle, but I'm already on the move. We start running again, building speed—still chasing Gwen. I'm using every muscle I have, my arms swinging as if I can pull the forest toward me.

We cross into the trees.

After three steps, it looks like midnight.

The canopy is thick, the moon behind low gray clouds.

Cole and I slow down, staying close. I hate that we're walking now, but there's not enough light to run. The village should be tucked in the woods, to our left. But if we stay on this path, we won't see it. Twigs snap all around us. Someone screams in the distance, but I can't tell why—if it's pain, fear, vigor, or maybe even bait. Cole and I keep moving, brushing through baby trees, ducking branches. I sink into dirt, black grass. Eventually, I hear someone on our left, but it's too dark and loud to place them. I get the feeling they don't want to be found.

Someone grunts behind me.

I turn to see a pale shimmer—a Nomen.

There's a dark handprint on his chest, smeared down toward his waist. It looks like someone clawed his suit, leaving five long and grasping trails. He lunges for us. Cole and I scatter. Cole shouts my name, but we've lost each other in the dark.

I run with my arms in front of my face, trying to block any hard branches, sharp sticks. Needles whip my hands and sting my cheeks. I listen for Cole, but his noises have melted into the mess. I keep moving with a new pit in my stomach. He's okay. Of course he's okay. He's sprinting just like I am. There's nothing I can do for him right now.

Once I've lost the Nomen, I slow down. I barely feel my body anymore. I sense my hands shake. The air cools sweat on my face. But otherwise, I'm an electric current. I'm a hormone in blood—charged, floating. How deep are we in the forest? I remember the bird's-eye view of 17 Crow Fields. The house sat on hundreds of acres, bordered by a channel. But the distance doesn't make me nervous; it's the people we might find in the woods. The Nomen who haven't changed their minds since Cole opened his mouth. The moon peeks out from the clouds. I forge through mossy roots, patches of clover, and manage to stay by myself.

Something ahead is rumbling.

It sounds like radio static with a beat.

The closer I get, the more I hear waves.

Suddenly, I see water through the trees. I pick up my pace until I'm out of the forest and sand forces me to slow down. The surf is a jagged line down the coast. Dozens of us are here, along with Nomen—everyone running into the channel. Some are already gliding across, their heads quiet bumps on the surface. Others kick forward with a vengeance. I squint at the lights on the other side, a couple of bus lengths' away. They look like lanterns outside cabins, porch lights on wooden docks. Their reflections drip down the water.

"Fiona!"

Gwen raises a hand, twenty feet away.

I run to her. As we hug, she loses her balance, and I'm the only force between her and the ground. As soon as she steadies herself, I look her up and down. Her face is tinted blue in this light, like everyone's. But there's no blood—not hers, not anyone else's. There's only sweat clumping her hairline, glossing her cheeks. She's still panting. Her shirt is sliced where trees must've clawed her, but still, no blood. I count all ten of her fingers in mine, feel her wrists, her forearms. I hold both her shoulders. She's okay, just spent.

"We have to swim," I say.

She nods, wary.

I scan the beach for Cole.

More and more people rush into the water. Across the channel, some crawl onto land. Everywhere, the wet sand looks like a dark mirror. But he's nowhere in sight. I guide Gwen into the surf. Even with shoes, my foot freezes in the first wave.

A shriek comes from the edge of the woods. It's primal, aggressive. Gwen and I hurry deeper into the water, holding each other's hand. The cold clamps down on my legs, feeling like teeth in my shins, on the backs of my knees. Soon, I'm up to my neck, wondering if anything's under the surface. Our feet lose touch with the ground. The chill tightens my chest, making every breath an effort. Gwen paddles without strength, patting the surface.

I still have her hand when her nose slips under.

Moving fast, I string one of her arms over my shoulder and kick us forward. She tries to help with her free hand, but the strokes are slow, uneven. Twice, her arm goes limp. I need to get her across as fast as I can. Water splashes all around, looking like sleet. Flurries of it keep crashing down, slapping the waves—landing on my head, biting my skull. Through the spray, I see flashes of other swimmers. Their scattered body parts pound the channel: open mouths, crooked elbows. Wide eyes and cycling shoulders. But still no sign of Cole.

Gwen's getting heavier.

"It's going to be okay," I say.

She slips under again.

I yank her up.

"It's going to be okay," I repeat.

Gwen rests her head on my shoulder, her wet hair molded to her skull. My free arm is fatiguing, leaving longer and longer gaps between my strokes. Longer periods when we're doing nothing but floating with the tide. I fight a growing urge to shut my eyes, to rest for one quick second. My hands are white, and eventually, Gwen stops paddling.

"We're going to be okay," I promise.

But we're making less progress.

The waterline rises on my neck.

I can't feel my chin as it dips—can't feel much below my jaw, just the slow current, ambient pressure. Now I'm getting an urge to sleep. It vaguely triggers an alarm, but the alarm isn't stronger than the urge itself. I smell the rockweed that must be on the beach. The tiny crustaceans floating in the waves. It's painfully nostalgic, like my summers used to smell. Almost like my world is collapsing and the past has arrived—fallen back into my life, as if I never lost those moments at all. As if they're tumbling briefly back into sight before it all comes down.

A wave rolls into my mouth. It burns my tongue, the soft back of my throat. And I'm still trying to fight it when my eyes close on their own. With them shut now, I see my parents. They're straight ahead in the water, half turned toward us, their arms reaching out to me. My mom's in sunglasses. My dad has one hand on her back, the other stretched this way.

I open my eyes.

Swim faster, harder.

Finding new strength in my legs.

Because part of me can still see them. If I hang on to the image, I can see them straight ahead, with the water up to their thighs, soaking through their clothes. Outdoor lights drench them in electric glitter—it's on their shoulders, their hands. Flashing on their cheeks. There's even more in their eyes—wavering specks, like life itself, blinking at me through the dark. Mom and Dad are reaching back because they're going to help.

This time, I didn't need to ask.

Gwen and I are moving again, making real progress. Mom lifts her sunglasses, smiling. Dad is preternaturally calm. *I love you,* I want to tell them. *I love you.* But I feel deep down that they know. More sleet rains on my head, and when I open my eyes, they're gone—their eyes, their hands. Everything but the radiant glints. They're still bright near the shore—brilliant, silver white. With a pulse from the waves, rolling through the light.

And then my toes feel sand.

I let out one ecstatic sob.

I pull us forward, every step firmer than the last. There are more rocks on this side, large, slippery. My foot slides on one, sending us back into deeper water. I spit out a salty mouthful, feeling the chill in my teeth. But soon, our shoulders are above the waves. Then our hips. It gets even colder with the wind on our backs.

Gwen takes weak steps.

"We're going home," I say.

Her next step is stronger.

We pass Blake and Myra, recovering on wet sand. They're on all fours, hunchbacked, panting. A new wave rolls in, sweeping the beach. Lost shoes float back and forth in the surf, slick as sealskin. Gwen and I keep going, past Sean Ridley pulling Ella Kline out of the surf. He's holding her around the waist as she leans forward, hugging her chest.

In the nearest cabin, thirty feet ahead, a grizzled man watches us through a yellow window. Gwen and I pause as he scans the beach. I see the view through his eyes: the sand almost hidden under squirming bodies. Most are in all-white suits, crawling toward him, having abandoned their masks. When he faces us, his jaw is open, eyes wild. He backs up, stumbling. As soon as he's steady again on his feet, he runs backward, disappearing inside.

Something brightens on our left.

Gwen and I spin toward a three-level house, receding from the channel like a staircase. There, on the second-floor terrace, a middle-aged woman steps outside. She's in a terry cloth robe, with chin-length brown hair. Big apple cheekbones round her face. She raises a shocked hand to her mouth. Eventually, she finds my eyes and stares.

"Please," I beg.

Gwen feels heavier. I hoist her up.

The woman runs into her house. I'm not sure what to expect until she comes back with a quilt. It's embroidered with jumping fish—salmon, red snapper, skate. They're all mid-twist, their bodies like rounded corners. I want to hug this woman, thank her twenty times in a row. I guide Gwen to the outdoor stairs. The stranger wraps her quilt around us.

"This way."

She's kind but firm.

Inside, her house feels tropically warm. We're in a blue-gray living room with a fishing theme: wooden trout appear to leap across the wall. An anchor hangs at eye level over an armchair. Thick rope outlines the ceiling. The stranger gestures to her sofa, where Gwen and I collapse. The cushion feels like a cloud, even though it barely gives an inch. The woman runs to her sink and fills two glasses of water. Her hands shake as she brings them to us.

Gwen takes a small sip.

"I'm calling 9-1-1," the stranger says.

More and more drag themselves out of the waves. Some are staggering this way, their hair dripping, skin blanched. I scan every face—there he is. Cole crawls onto the sand, spitting up water. I step toward him before I realize what I'm doing. I can't leave Gwen—not while she's hinged over her knees. But she follows my line of sight outside.

When she looks back at me, she nods.

"Go," she says.

I hesitate.

"Go get him. Bring him back."

All her strength is in her eyes.

I nod and jump downstairs.

Without warning, someone grabs Cole's ankle, pulling him down—it's a young Nomen, scrambling out of the surf. The boy lets go and climbs higher, his palm sliding on a piece of seaweed. Cole stays on his side, facing away from me. I pick up my pace. In the distance, unmasked Nomen swarm the old man's house. They bang on his door, a dozen fists at once. Maybe they want to commandeer his phone. Maybe they just want to get warm. One of them looks poised to break the window, wrapping a drenched shirt around his fist.

I skid to a stop next to Cole and, on my knees, turn him toward me. A red stain blooms across his chest. Part of his gash has opened up. This is the first time I've seen it without the bandage—even deeper than I thought. The skin around the remaining stitches is raised, swollen. His eyes flutter. I tell him to stay with me, grabbing a discarded shirt.

I wring it, tie it around his chest.

"We need to get you warm."

Finally, he sees me.

His eyes focus.

"Fiona," he whispers.

His lips are tinted blue.

I drape myself over him, giving him none of my weight but all of my warmth. It takes me a second to realize that I'm holding his hand. Our fingers are interlaced on the beach, my knuckles digging into the sand. I feel his heartbeat through his clothes.

I pull back and take another look. His hair is twisted into sandy clumps. There's a brown sheet of kelp behind him—sea lettuce, too, matted green ruffles on one side. Cole looks at me, fully aware. The ocean drips down his temples, down his neck. His long-sleeve sticks to his arms in tight grooves. His gaze drops to my mouth. There's something new in his eyes. It looks like he's giving into something. I lean closer, until I'm inches above him. He's breathing on me, staring at my lips, when I finally lose myself and kiss him.

His mouth is soft and cold.

He tastes like the ocean.

He's kissing me back.

And for the first time since they took us—any of us, I feel free.

I can finally make a choice without being ruled by fear. And with that freedom, I choose this. I choose Cole, right here, with our knuckles in the beach. I'm melting on top of him, giving in after the fight, the swim. My body just trusts his, and I realize that every time we've touched, accidentally or not, I've been getting used to him. I've been getting to know—not Cole, the mind. Cole, the body. Cole, the man. I feel the wet grit on his shirt, in his fingers. Waves crash. The wind is cold, but everywhere I touch Cole, I'm warm.

Glass shatters.

I pull away, leaving my hand in his.

Straight ahead, Nomen pour into the old man's cabin. They speed through the broken front door, like white flies into a skull. I slip under Cole's shoulder and try to lift him. He rolls his head back, grimacing. He feels twice as heavy as Gwen. We try again, and this time, he makes it to his knees. The next time, we stand and take our first step together. It's shaky and short, but we move forward. I make out Gwen in the living room ahead, with the fish quilt around her, a sockeye salmon on her shoulder. The room is full of familiar faces now.

Pinched but safe.

Finally, free.

Hostages Found Alive: Nomen in Custody

BY ALEX TEAL AND MICHAEL GOSS
Updated 8:23 AM EST

NEW YORK (AP) — All 49 missing persons kidnapped by the Nomen were recovered last night in Lasco, Maine.

At least six are critically injured, including at least one with hypothermia.

The hostages had been kept for four days on an estate belonging to 29-year-old Rex Stiller, who has been identified as the Nomen's leader. Stiller grew up on the premises and still resides there in his childhood home. According to unconfirmed reports, the Nomen lived in Rex's house for years while preparing for the abductions.

An FBI search of the residence is ongoing.

Stiller is in police custody on charges of kidnapping and assault. He is being held without bail until trial. 83 Nomen confederates have been arrested so far with Stiller, at least one quarter of them underage. They are being held in a juvenile detention center on charges of kidnapping and assault as well and will likely be tried as juvenile offenders.

Cole Harper stymied the Nomen last night when

he revealed that he wrote their core text a decade ago. His story *Rotator* contained the Manifesto, Declaration, and other documents key to the movement. Though fiction, it was taken to a real-life extreme.

Harper revealed this in a speech delivered last night to the Nomen.

In the ensuing chaos, targets escaped through the woods and swam across the Lasco Channel to safety, taking shelter in nearby homes. Emergency responders arrived at the scene just after 8:00 p.m., responding to a call made by local resident Judy Moore.

Stiller hasn't said a word since police apprehended him.

He has been seen smiling in custody.

A source within the FBI described Stiller as "unnervingly intelligent," with "an unaddressed instability." Stiller graduated from Lasco High School with high honors. His activities since then are unknown but are believed to have involved the Nomen.

At Lasco High, Stiller had no disciplinary issues. His junior and senior years, he emerged as a force in cross-country running. Senior year, he qualified for the New England Championships and finished in the top 10. His coach at the time, Paul Keats, was quoted in the school paper as saying, "Rex has got a fire. He doesn't just run. He attacks the course." Senior year, Stiller won prizes in math and English, and accolades for his essay, "Violence as a Brand: the Making of Criminal Celebrities."

Stiller is the only child of Malcolm and Leigh Stiller, who died in a ski accident when he was 16. At the time, Malcolm was CEO of Dark Horse. The cybersecurity company has a market cap of $2 billion and offices in Portland, San Francisco, and New York City.

During the FBI's initial assessment of Stiller's property, they found a cluster of dilapidated cabins, according to a source within the Bureau. The cabins sit on a dirt road with two dead ends, in a perfect circle of trees. Each is three hundred square feet and dangerously run-down. While they might have decades' worth of damage, they appear to have been built within the past few years. Their connection to the case is under investigation.

1,996 Comments *add comment*

Worship1987
Praise God for their safe return.
I believe that God has worked through the brave individuals who came to their rescue, who helped them when they needed it most. May He continue to watch over the victims and their families as they begin to heal and recover. Amen

Greg Martins
Someone should make this into a movie

Greg Martins
And everyone should play themselves lol

Lorena Silva
Except Rex. He'll be a little busy

LawyerMom
The man behind the Nomen was FAMOUS?

J Harold
Be careful what you write.

Ernest Costa
Does that make Rotator non-fiction?

Emma Taylor
The terror of waking up in one of Cole's books . . .

Cybercat
The nightmares they'll bring home.

TWENTY-FOUR

I'm in a hospital bed the next day, with privacy curtains on either side. After taking my vitals, a nurse hooks me up to an IV. She's moving fast, her hands a blur. She tells me I'm dehydrated, and this will give me the fluids and electrolytes I need.

A necessary boost flows into my blood.

Meanwhile, a doctor examines me.

The gash on my shoulder has opened up, as has the one on my knee. He injects me with a local anesthetic—lidocaine; I asked—then sutures them back together. Next, he adds a stitch to the tip of my nose—absorbable; I asked. For some reason, I want to talk. I'm desperate for plain and simple conversation. Maybe I just want the reassurance of something normal, someone good. I ask the doctor if he has kids—two boys. Before he leaves, he starts me on antibiotics. He's asking if I'd like any pain medication when I interrupt to ask about my friends.

"Fay?"

Gwen. Through the beeping equipment—the conversations, clinking tools—I hear her on my left. I pull the curtain back, and she's here. Right here, under the same blanket, in the same blue gown. Our beds are just feet apart, with only my IV drip between us. A nurse tries to close the curtain, but I don't let go. We reach across the gap, fingers touching.

"You saved my life."

Gwen's crying.

"You saved my life," she repeats.

I want to respond, but I can't find the words.

Everything that comes to mind feels too small, like trying to catch the sky in a plastic bag. *I love you* doesn't feel like enough. *Of course, you're family,* doesn't come close. My whole life, I've been putting things into words, and now I'm soaring through the space between them—in the fluid, infinite gap. Gwen and I fall quiet. The only sounds we make come from our bodies processing the reunion: shaky exhales, fragmented sobs, and wild, momentary laughs. I can't believe we're this close again, that we made it out, intact and alive.

"I owe you everything," she says.

"You owe me nothing."

I find my voice.

Wipe my eyes.

"No, really—"

"Really."

"How did you do it?" she asks.

The sweat in her palm brings me back to the waves.

"I saw my parents in the water," I admit. Gwen starts to cry all over again, quiet enough for me to go on. "They were waiting for us on the other side.

"I always thought they'd be there when I needed them. But to *see* them, to *feel* them there . . . I've never felt so loved." Gwen squeezes my hand. "I know this week has been hell. But it brought me closer to Mom and Dad than ever—even when they were alive." I wipe my eyes. "I must not have been in my right mind, because . . . I just felt so connected to them. Like all the boundaries between us—all space, time, everything—just dissolved. Like they were always here." I touch my chest. "Always . . . everywhere." I remember the lights in the dark, shining even after they disappeared. "It gave me . . . unimaginable strength."

Gwen hangs on.

"You made it."

"*We* made it," I say.

Gwen smiles through her tears, and despite how thin she looks—despite the IV line in her wrist and the cords between us—she is radiant to me.

~

We keep the curtain open all day.

I'm here when she has her first ultrasound.

Gwen holds my hand as the doctor rubs a device across her low belly. We see her baby for the first time on a small, dated TV. Gwen lets out a blissful sob, quiet, shaking. The baby is even smaller than I imagined, curled up like an apostrophe. The doctor points out the head, the spine. The yolk sac that will grow into a placenta. He says that Gwen's eight weeks along and will be due on June 16. As far as he can tell, everything looks normal.

"A summer baby," Gwen says.

Her voice is full of magic.

For lunch, Gwen and I order from the hospital cafeteria: everything that catches our eyes. Our meals arrive on packed trays. Her beef stir fry comes with long snow peas and pillowy white rice. She finishes the plate, along with a noodle soup, side salad, and vanilla cake in a cup. I pretend I'm not that hungry and offer Gwen half my chicken. She refuses, but we share my dessert: a wedge of cheesecake. At the end of the meal, Gwen smiles. She asks the woman who clears our trays where she's from and how long she's lived in Maine.

~

That afternoon, Logan visits. He skids to a stop on the threshold, looking at me, then locking his gaze on Gwen. He's in an oxford—the collar uneven—and khakis deeply creased around the knees. He carries his coat on one arm, briefcase in the other hand. He's been calling our floor all day, passing messages to the nurses. They've been updating

Gwen on his progress—when he left home for the airport. When he boarded the plane. When he landed.

He drops his coat and briefcase.

He drifts slowly across the room, arms out toward her—elbows drooping, palms up to the ceiling. He's crying. Gwen is, too, reaching right back for him from bed. As soon as he's close, she throws her arms around him, burying her face in his chest. All I see of her now is the white knot of her hair and her hands pressing into his back.

I turn to give them a moment and make out three familiar faces. Through the window in our door, it's Marlowe, Caroline, and Emma. They hold on to each other, moving this way, armed with four pillows and a plush blanket. Marlowe is red faced, sobbing. Caroline's in the middle, hopeful, sad. She's in a black work dress and pearls, as if she just walked out of a meeting. Emma's on the end, the only one who looks overjoyed. Finally, they find me through the glass. I'm so floored and ecstatic to see them that I laugh, even as my eyes get hot.

They open my door.

"You guys," I say.

They hurry inside, waving at Gwen. Now they crowd around my bed—for the first time in our lives, giving me physical space. They keep a few inches back from the plastic railings, squeezing their pillows. It's so foreign it feels like they're miles away. Marlowe wipes her eyes, digging her fingers into her lashes and scooping out tears. Her hair's in a low ponytail, with a half inch of static on top. I tell her she looks worse than I do, which gets a laugh.

"Come here."

I open my arms.

"It's okay. I promise."

All three of them lean into me.

I keep laughing, too happy to stand it.

Once they pull back, I take a better look.

Emma is in a nursing turtleneck—newer this time, without the hammock. Caroline is adjusting my sheets, which had partially slid off the bed. Her mood's lifting to see me smile, to witness Marlowe's well-meaning doom loop. Marlowe is still weeping. I promise her I'm really okay. Caroline takes my hand. Emma reaches for the same hand, bringing the three of us into a knot. It feels so good to be with them, but I never told them I was here.

"How did you . . . ?" I trail off.

"Cole found me on your social media," Emma says. "He was looking for an Emma, and apparently, I've commented on every post you've ever made. That narrowed it down." She says Cole messaged her about the family reunification today. Then she and Marlowe, who had been staying with her since the news broke, called Caroline together, and the three of them jumped on the first flight here. "We told the front desk we're your sisters. There's no chance they believed us, but Marlowe was our secret weapon. If you cry as much as Marlowe does, you can basically get in anywhere. People just feel terrible." Everyone laughs.

I ask Emma who's with her baby. She says her neighbors will be on duty until her husband gets home tonight. They offered to help more tomorrow. Caroline asks how I'm recovering, and a sudden tension chills the group. They stare at me, silent, stiff, unsure what horrors I might've seen. I repeat that I'm okay, forcing a laugh so they can relax.

"Do you need any pillows?" Marlowe lifts one.

"I've spent a lot of time in hospitals," Emma interjects, referring to her son's diabetes. "So I know the pillows usually suck." I laugh, letting them arrange pillows behind me. Emma drapes the blanket over my comforter, sharing that this is the one she took to the hospital for every birth—well, not this *exact* one. I laugh again, and she's right. It's beyond soft. I make everyone give it a feel. Caroline says it feels like velvet without looking like you're in a terrible '70s movie. Marlowe asks if I'm more comfortable now, and I say yes, hoping they'll relax, but the conversation still comes to a halt. They wait with bated breath, as if I might say more.

"I don't want to talk about me," I insist.

Marlowe looks hesitant.

"I want to hear about you," I add.

"Careful what you wish for," Emma quips.

"Really, I mean it. I missed you. I missed . . . this."

This *group* that's always been there for me—not just in high school, but every impossible day since then. No matter what, they've always taken me out of my pain. Made my world so much bigger—and funnier, more beautiful, more miraculous—than whatever hurt.

Emma tells us about her nine-month-old, who's just figured out how to stand but has no idea how to sit back down. "It's really sad and really funny." She squints with guilt and restrained amusement. "All he wants to do is pull himself up. Then he just freezes, bawling." Emma says that her two-year-old is in an "I do it!" stage, insisting that he do everything himself. And her four-year-old has just started to become very literal. When Emma asked him to watch their dog yesterday, he sat and watched the dog for two hours.

It starts to feel almost normal with them.

They sit on the edges of my bed, and for a second, I'm tempted to think that we're all back in my apartment, on my living room sofa. As Emma goes on about her two-year-old and his new love of oven mitts, I lock eyes with Gwen, who's listening in. She puts a hand on her belly, next to Logan. I know her well enough to know: She can't wait.

~

After the family visits, Gwen and I meet one at a time with the psychiatrist Dr. Betty Stevens. I'm up first, following a young nurse to the consultation room down the hall. I'm still strangely chatty, asking where she grew up—Lewiston, Maine—and when she started with the hospital—almost ten years ago. Soon, I face Dr. Stevens' desk from an armchair.

She says very gently that she's here to help with any psychological impacts of recent events. She asks how I'm feeling, if I've had any flashbacks or nightmares that I'd like to share, and then if I feel safe. It's the first question that makes me pause.

"I *know* I'm safe," I think out loud, "but . . ."

"But?"

"I mean, there's no doubt that I'm safe. My friends are safe. I don't have to worry about them anymore. But I'm still . . . ready." She asks for what. "For something to go wrong, change. For one last surprise." I pinch my shoulders up toward my ears. Dr. Stevens nods with calm understanding. "I didn't sleep last night—I might've gone in and out, but I didn't feel the need. No matter how dark it got, I didn't want to shut my eyes." Ever since we arrived, nurses have been visiting Gwen and me every four hours to take our vitals, another blood test, or check on the pain. They visited me twice overnight. I was awake both times.

Dr. Stevens explains that's normal. She says I'm still processing the fact that I'm no longer in danger. While I might *know* I'm safe, there will be a lag before I *feel* it. She asks if I've run into any triggers that remind me of the cabins. If I have any fears about going home. Then if I have any questions. I admit that I've been more talkative than usual, asking everyone I meet as much as they'll let me. The doctor nods without looking surprised.

"After being treated as less than human," she says, "there's a grace period when every conversation feels like a miracle."

~

Heading back to my room, the hallway's crowded with police.

Some officers wear green ties over tan polos. Others are in blue shirts, the Maine crest stitched on their arms. The rest are in business casual—FBI, I'd guess. They carry themselves with even more authority, leading a huddle of police in hushed conversation. A nurse did warn us there'd be debriefings after we'd been assessed by hospital staff.

I make it past the crowd.

Coming up to my room.

I keep peeking through patient windows, thinking about Cole. I haven't seen him since he was ushered into one of the ambulances. I ended up staying longer on the beach. When the responders arrived, I didn't want them to lose time making sense of what had happened. So I showed them to those who needed the most help, and even after that, I found it hard to leave. I kept filling in where I could—grabbing a blanket for Ella, then water, and then, at one point, holding Myra's hand. Making the night less hellish where I could. When I finally got in an ambulance, the crew kept looking at me. They said I was the very last to leave.

Of course Cole is okay.

He was okay in my arms—better. He looked at me with real presence of mind. And he kissed me back—harder than I'd expected, as if neither of us were in pain. Since then, he's been getting the care he needs. I'm not *worried* about him. But now I can't stop wondering which room he's in. If he's kept the curtain open, too, with a renewed desire to talk.

I approach the nurse at the front desk.

She's on the phone but covers the bottom to ask how she can help.

I check behind me: just the police, out of earshot. None of them could be Nomen . . . right? With Cole's news on every front page, the group has lost its mission. They've become a contradiction. Instead of erasing fame, it's been at their core all along, in that first mother cell. Besides, with Rex in custody, and so many Nomen arrested near the House, the group's all but fallen apart. I shake off the paranoia and ask which room Cole Harper is in.

"I'm afraid we can't give that information."

It's a gentle stonewall.

Just like . . . Rex.

The déjà vu is that strong, almost convincing me that he's here—that he's in her chair, holding her phone. He had a similar tone: eloquently devastating. He could demoralize us and make it sound polite. The nurse asks if I'm all right. She tells whoever's on the line to hold. But just as fast as it came, I'm out of it again. I assure her I'm okay, and it's the truth.

~

That night, Gwen falls asleep in the middle of dinner. She's only halfway through her roast beef when she says she's going to shut her eyes for a second. She falls asleep fast, with her chin tucked into her shoulder, her spoon in one hand. She sinks into a mound of pillows; I gave her half of the ones my friends had brought for me. I'm starting to feel tired too—maybe that's not the right word. I must've been tired for a while, but now I'm feeling settled enough to . . . think about sleep. To drift toward it. I finish my dinner, listening to Gwen snore.

My eyes feel heavier.

But there's something I need to do.

I creep out of bed, into the empty hallway.

The police must've finished their interviews for the day.

Mine was more straightforward than I expected. They asked for basic information about the conditions of captivity, what exactly I witnessed of Rex's involvement. I sensed them trying to build a case against him. They asked if I'd like to be in a witness protection program, or if I'd want any kind of ongoing surveillance. I declined. Maybe I'll change my mind. But other than a few stabs of suspicion, I haven't felt a real threat from the group.

I stride to the front desk, still in my gown.

Someone's already in line.

While I wait, I survey the wing.

Two visitors sit behind me, one streaming cable news on his phone. The news alert is faint: a whoosh like a plane landing, followed by a struck bell. I hear the anchor launch into a story on the recovered celebrities. I feel seen even though no one's looking at me. Tonight's special guests include a criminal psychologist and a former FBI agent. The agent claims that the Nomen's plan backfired: Their celebrities are now even more famous, even more widely loved. The anchor agrees that with every attack, the Nomen only subverted themselves.

Apparently, Rex confessed to a key role in abducting Myra Mane, Max Connors, and Lane Driver, as well as engineering the mass kidnapping. It appears he led a years-long effort to get his loyalists hired at Madison Square Garden. By the time Myra's concert began, there were close to one hundred Nomen in the arena—running the metal detectors, patrolling the stands, and manning the surveillance systems. Each ready for their part in his plan.

The anchor adds that while Rex's motives are still being vetted, he's been smiling ever since he was caught. It's an unnerving image: a permanent mask. The psychologist says that Rex might've fetishized attention. That under his hate for celebrities—under all that venom, all that rage—maybe there was a seed of envy. After all, he didn't attack his targets. Not at first. He kept them in a fishbowl, his own private collection of some of the world's most visible people. Now in every headline, maybe Rex is ecstatic to taste notoriety for himself. "If that's the case," the anchor quips, "his prosecution will be the show of his dreams."

I'm still on edge when it cuts to commercial.

As if they might say my name.

Even with the surfeit of news, a few outlets ran stories about *me*—about me staying late to help on the beach. Gwen showed me the articles this morning, on an iPad borrowed from the hospital. The stories gave me a nickname: the Last Celebrity. But I don't want to hear about that now. It feels like an embarrassing misuse of attention, especially when none of the responders—the people doing most of the work—were called out by name.

I'm next in line.

There's a fresh face at the counter.

"Sorry, but do you know which room Cole Harper's in?" I squint hopefully at the woman with cat-eye glasses. "I'm not family, but . . . I just want to make sure he's okay. I'm sure he is, but . . ." The woman smiles, then gives me a look that's kindly conspiratorial. She types a few short strings on her keyboard before leaning closer to her screen.

"Three-twelve," she whispers.

I'm so relieved I laugh.

I thank her, my hands prayed together.

"And I shouldn't say this, either, but I love *The Redfins*," she whispers, glancing furtively from side to side. "You are the only writer in the world who's ever made me believe in magic—there, I said it." She raises her palms in surrender, shaking her head. The compliment's so unexpected I stand in place, at a loss for words. Eventually, I come to my senses and thank her. She gestures with warm authority down the hall, presumably toward Cole's room.

I thank her again and move toward it.

When I reach 312, the door is shut. The blue privacy curtain hides whatever's happening inside. I take a second to debate whether I'm really going to do this. It's intrusive, isn't it? But I'm already lifting my fist, knocking on the door.

I open it. "Cole?"

"Fiona?"

My skin reacts to his voice.

He pulls the curtain aside an inch.

Once he sees me, he smiles and yanks it all the way back. The rings slide hard across the rod. I can't help myself and walk up to his bed, reaching for his hand. There's good energy in his eyes, even with bags like purple thumbprints under them. I sense that he's running on the same fumes I am—our engines turned off, still skidding ahead.

I apologize for barging in.

"Never." It's earnest.

"I just wanted to see how you're doing." He looks handsome and somehow stronger than usual, even with the palpable exhaustion and the gauze taped on his arm. More peeks out from under the crew neck of his gown. Still, he seems content, with no signs of debilitating pain. "And I wanted to thank you for letting my friends know where I am. It really made all the difference." My eyes bob to his bed table, swung off to one side. His meal tray is there—plate clean, surrounded by toppled single-serving containers—next to a white bouquet.

"From my parents, believe it or not," he says, glancing at it. "They came from Chicago the minute they heard. I didn't think they would but . . . they showed up when it counted." He asks about Gwen, my friends. About my time with the police. I tell him everything, sitting on the bed by his knees. I tell him I'm still processing the fact that my people are safe, that we're no longer running for our lives. I tell him the shower in Gwen's and my room was euphoric, but I can still weirdly taste salt. And I really should get some sleep, but there's still too much adrenaline in my blood.

"I've tried to shut my eyes," I say, "but . . ."

"I know. Same."

I ask how he's been holding up, looking at the gauze.

Apparently, the doctors warned Cole that after the "improper wound care"—the way he kept pushing himself when he was hurt—he should expect scarring. Cole says this while ogling his nicked tattoo sleeve around the bandages. I reach toward him as he talks, my palm open and relaxed. He takes my hand, sliding his fingers between mine.

"Thanks for saving me on the lawn," I say.

"I don't know if I'd put it like that."

"How would you put it?"

"Well, I think we kept saving each other. I think we took turns saving each other's lives. I've never met anyone like you, Fiona." My cheeks flush, but I love how sincere he is, the way he's so direct with his compliments that it's almost indelicate. He's the only person I've ever met who makes pure conversation feel intimate and forbidden. "You give so much of yourself away, but . . . you also let me help you when you needed it. It takes a special person to do both." I tell him I don't deserve too much credit. "No, I think you do. Most strong people haven't figured out how to be weak too. They always have their guards up. They're in denial about their own limits. But there's an . . . emotional dexterity you have that's special."

I squeeze his hand. "I'm not that way with everyone." He asks what I mean. "There's something about you that . . . feels right." And whatever it is, maybe it's always been there. Because even when the dinner was raided, I never once thought Cole was involved. Even when he told me about *Rotator*—when he said he'd hand-delivered one to Rex . . . the feeling never stopped, not for a second. He was something I never had to question.

"I know what you mean."

He watches my hand in his.

"This might sound strange." He waits for permission. I nod, feeling like nothing can hurt us. "I know we ended up in one of my books," he goes on, "but since I met you, I've felt like I'm in one of yours." He looks at me with a palpable loss of control, as if I'm writing his every move. As if we're inside my fantasy genre, where anything is possible.

"What if we're both in someone else's?" I tease.

He considers the idea, amused. "Then I suppose they might get writer's block. We could be stuck in this room for days while they come up with what's next."

"There are worse places to be frozen."

He's laughing when his door opens.

A nurse steps into the room.

She stops short, as if she's intruding.

I stand quickly and head for the door. I tell Cole to get some sleep, that I'll see him soon. After the door shuts, I turn to take one last look through his window. Cole is still watching me, like he was hoping I'd turn around. My heart flickers up into my throat. I feel warmer, as if Cole is right here in the hallway—as close as he was on the beach.

~

The next day, I direct Nick through Greenwich Village.

We're coming up on Gwen and Logan's apartment. They're asleep in the row ahead of Cole and me, bobbing over the cobblestone road. We pass a British shop with pyramids of canned peas and salad cream in the window; then a cigar bar; and then an Alpine-themed fondue restaurant. Finally, we reach the line of brownstones on their block. The dashboard clock reads 4:12 p.m. when Nick pulls over at their front door. He announces that we're here.

Gwen and Logan stir awake. They blink hard, facing their windows. The neighborhood outside looks serene. There's no sign of the turbulence from this past week, not even a small crowd outside their front door. Gwen swivels toward me. We hug as close as we can with the back of her seat between us. I kiss one side of her head.

"I love you," she says.

"I love you too."

She reaches for Cole next.

She holds his hands in hers, tears forming.

Logan thanks us again for everything we did. He still looks shaken, even after having slept for most of the ride. His puffy eyelids are a raw shade of pink, his side part zigzagging over his crown. We haven't talked much today, but he alluded to a rough night at a motel, kept up by shock and relief.

He helps Gwen out of the car. She squeezes my fingers one last time—hard and quick—before stepping outside. Cole and I watch them climb up to their front door. They wave goodbye from the threshold, arm in arm. Their smiles are uneven, eyes dizzy. They both look like they'll need to sleep for the rest of the day, at least. I wave back even though she couldn't possibly see me through the tinted windows. I watch her until she's gone.

"Where to?" Nick asks.

I face Cole. I've spent the ride in his arms, wavering between heavy-lidded fatigue and full alertness. My gaze kept darting over to Gwen, checking on her. But now she's finally home. Nick is twisted in the driver's seat, ready to go anywhere we choose.

Cole waits for my decision. *"I'd want to see you when you have a million choices where to be, not just when you have one."* And right now, I do feel like I have a million choices. Nick is poised for an address, any address. He really would take me anywhere. I feel Cole's hand in mine, his wide palm, the edge of his thumb. I look in his eyes, smooth and deliberate. Gwen would be proud of me, because right now, I do feel like the weak one. I could stay here with him and unselfconsciously drift asleep. One day, maybe I will.

For now, I direct Nick to my apartment.

Ten people stand outside my building.

In small groups, they talk among themselves, glancing up at my place. My heart beats faster, but there's nothing on the fourth floor—no one in my apartment, lying in wait for me. They're just tourists, again, stopping for a photo of my window. Cole asks if there's anywhere else I want to go. I tell him I'm okay, that I just need a minute.

I keep holding his hand.

"Someone should write a book about you," he says. I laugh. "I'm serious," he insists, but I can't tell if he is. I'm still dazed. "You deserve credit for everything that you did. Ever since you jumped . . . you were the backbone of the whole rescue, until the last person was saved from the beach—even after that. Until you took Gwen all the way home."

"And who's going to write this book?"

"Maybe I will."

"You will," I repeat, drowsy.

"Or we could write it together."

"And what should it be called?"

He appears to think about it. He looks out the window, then back at me, more committed than I would've expected. "Let's call it *The Last Celebrity*."

ACKNOWLEDGMENTS

Thank you to my agent, Eve Attermann, for standing by me from the start, with your vision, clarity, heart, humor, and support. I count my lucky stars that we met. To Nicole Weinroth, in Literary Media: Thank you for pouring your expertise into advocating for my books. I feel very fortunate to work together. I am enormously grateful to the whole team at WME—including Rivka Bergman and Caitlin Mahony—who are second to none.

Thank you to my editor, Carmen Johnson, for being the turning point in this story, with the insights that grounded my imagination and gave Fiona her boldness. Thank you for your work with Faith Black Ross, asking the questions that took me deeper into the belly of the Nomen. To everyone at Amazon Publishing, for making this a reality.

Dan Brown, thank you for sharing your wisdom during a key juncture in the writing process, which, as always, lit the way forward. I can't overstate my gratitude for your honest advice.

Zibby Owens, thank you for including me in the Zibby-verse. You have lifted so many voices, introduced me to so many remarkable writers and readers, sparked new vitality in the publishing industry, and done it all with such authenticity and empathy. Thank you for your generosity.

Thank you to the authors and friends who have been particularly supportive of my work, including Jennifer Bardsley, Lisa Barr, Blake Crouch, Fiona Davis, Carrie Feron, Rea Frey, Tracey Garvis Graves,

Alison Gaylin, Emily Giffin, Kristy Woodson Harvey, Jean Kwok, Annabel Monaghan, Liz Moore, Colleen Oakley, Carl Radke, Pamela Redmond, Jill Santopolo, Wendy Walker, and Ashley Winstead. Thank you to the bookstores that have been standout supporters, including BookHampton and Booksy Galore in Pound Ridge.

The creative process can be winding. On the way here, a different novel was explored and set aside. I would be remiss not to acknowledge the individuals who, despite their packed schedules, kindly lent their time during my research. Markus Glocker, chef and restaurateur in New York City, thank you for sitting with me in Bâtard before service began and answering my novice questions. Will Cesark, executive sous-chef at Gabriel Kreuther, thank you for casting light on life as a chef. Kate Jetto, former pastry cook at the NoMad Hotel, and Abby Reisner, technical product manager at *NYT Cooking* and cookbook author, thank you for your expert contributions.

Thank you to my mom and dad, Parker and Michael, Emil and Cara, and Jim and Julie. Mom, thank you for making this possible in so many ways. To this day, I often ask you for your favorite among five to ten sentences, with just one word changed each time. And most of all, thank you to my husband, David, and our magical family.

ABOUT THE AUTHOR

Photo © 2021 Lea Cartier

Madeleine Henry is the author of five novels, including *Name Not Taken* and *My Favorite Terrible Thing*. Her work has been featured in the *New York Times*, *The Washington Post*, the *New York Post*, and *Entertainment Weekly*. Previously, she worked at Goldman Sachs after graduating from Yale. She lives with her husband in New York, where she is at work on her next book. For more information, visit www.itsmadeleinehenry.com.